Anne O'Brien was born and has lived for most of her life in Yorkshire. There she taught history, before deciding to fulfil a lifetime ambition to write romantic historical fiction. She won a number of short story competitions until published for the first time by Mills & Boon®. As well as writing, she finds time to enjoy gardening, cooking and watercolour painting. She now lives with her husband in an eighteenth-century cottage in the depths of the Welsh Marches.

You can find out about Anne's books and more at her website: www.anneobrien.co.uk

Recent novels by the same author:

THE DISGRACED MARCHIONESS*
THE OUTRAGEOUS DEBUTANTE*
THE ENIGMATIC RAKE*
CONQUERING KNIGHT, CAPTIVE LADY
CHOSEN FOR THE MARRIAGE BED

The Faringdon Scandals

To George, again,
who knows all about romance

Chapter One

The English Channel—July 1813.

'Hurry! Sky's clearing. Time we were gone.'

A sleek little English cutter lay off the French coast, hardly more than a shadow on the swell of a sullen sea and aptly named *Lydyard's Ghost*, dark sails furled. The Captain who had issued the warning stood at the helm, one hand steady on the tiller, eyes ever alert, from shore to sky to the stowing of the bales and casks. A compact young man from what could be seen, clad as the rest of his crew in heavy boots, smock and wide trousers, a thick coat pulled over all and a stocking cap well down on his brow, he watched with innate authority. A half-dozen rowing boats headed smartly back to the French shore, to Port St Martin, only one remaining to complete the unloading—a fine brandy—of its illicit cargo.

The Captain acknowledged a sense of satisfaction. It had all gone according to plan so far.

'That's it, Cap'n Harry. All stowed aboard.' An elderly, stout individual named George Gadie pushed himself away from the gunwale with a raised salute.

'Excellent! Get the sails up, George.' The Captain strode the length of the cutter with a leather purse in his hand, leaning to address the French smugglers in the rowing boat. '*Au revoir*, Monsieur Marcel. A lucrative cargo for us and a purse of guineas for you, as agreed. *A bientôt, mon ami.*'

'A minute, Captain Harry, if you will.' To the Captain's surprise, Monsieur Marcel swung up into the cutter. 'Another piece of cargo for you. Will you take it?'

The Captain frowned. 'Is it worth my while?'

'No.' Marcel guffawed. 'But *we* don't want it, do we, lads? Hoist it up, Pierre.' He gestured down to the sailors in the rowing boat who stood around a dark shape. Next moment it was lifted and pushed and finally tumbled over the side to fall aboard the cutter.

The Captain crouched to inspect. 'What's this?'

'Pierre found him on the quay. A brawl—and he came off worst.' Monsieur Marcel lifted his shoulders in deliberate contempt. 'English, and not dead yet, that's all I know. Pockets empty—robbed, I expect.' Marcel was already climbing back over the cutter's side. 'All I know is he's in with a disreputable crowd led by a slimy ruffian named Jean-Jacques Noir whose got his fingers in all sorts of foul pies. Noir'd sell his sister—damn! He'd sell his *mother* if it lined his pockets. And he'd use a knife against any man who stood in his way.'

The Captain stared down at the inert body at his feet. 'What do I do with him?'

'Take him back to England. Or drop him overboard if you wish.' Still seated astride, Marcel grunted with fierce amusement. 'He's up to no good here. Most like a English spy, passing on information or guineas, if he's in league with Jean-Jacques Noir. He obviously failed to meet Noir's demands. A falling out of rogues, I expect…' Marcel dropped back down into the rowing boat.

'Tide's turning, Cap'n Harry,' George Gadie at the cutter's bow warned.

'Right.' Looking across at the run of the waves, the Captain decided. 'We must go, so he must come with us.' A quick shake of hands, leaning down to Monsieur Marcel, and the heavy leather bag was tossed down to the French smuggler. 'Here's the gold as agreed.'

'Enjoy the contraband. The brandy's the best. And the silk.'

The Captain's smile glinted in a shaft of moonlight as the clouds shifted to bathe the dark-painted cutter in silver. Sails, fore and aft, were set with impressive speed and the cutter put out to sea with its unexpected cargo.

Safely underway, the Captain beckoned to George Gadie, who promptly turned the body over with rough hands and a careless shove of his boot.

'Let's see what we've got here, George. Less value to us than a bolt of silk cloth…'

The words dried at the sight. Blood and sea water disfigured the shoulder, breast and sleeve of a well-cut coat. A man of means then, Captain Harry recognised, although the garment was now ruined beyond repair. The Captain pulled open the lapels to show where the white shirt beneath, of finest linen beneath his fingers, was also dark with blood. Spying, then, was a lucrative business, if a dangerous one, he decided without compassion, for the dark hair was slick and matted from a ragged cut above the hairline. He was soaked to the skin, the wound still bleeding, his face and lips starkly colourless, pale as death. Deep lines of pain were engraved between well-marked brows, also bracketing his mouth. A knife wound, not dangerous but sluggishly oozing blood, angled down his cheek. He was deeply unconscious but, crouching, the Captain could feel the steady heartbeat beneath the heel of his hand.

George grunted. 'A spy, d'you think, Cap'n? Don't

look too dangerous now, does 'ee? The knife scar'll mar his pretty looks. Let's get him out of the way. Gabriel…!' Summoning his son, taking hold of shoulders and booted feet between them, they began to heave the dead weight against the boat's side planking.

'Wait.' The Captain put out a hand, grasping Gabriel's arm and crouched again. A weak groan came from the ashen lips. The man's eyes, heavy with pain and confusion, opened.

'Where am I?' A hoarse croak of a whisper.

'On your way back to England,' Captain Harry informed.

'No…I can't. I can't leave yet….'

'No choice. You'll do as I say.' The Captain's clipped reply was brutal.

A hand was lifted to curl weakly into the cloth of the Captain's sleeve. The pain-racked eyes tried to focus. 'Take me back. I'll pay you…'

'What with? You've no money in your pockets, my friend.'

'I don't remember…' The eyes blurred with incomprehension, closed and then snapped open as if searching for a memory. 'Jean-Jacques Noir…he broke his word….'

'I expect he did. You were robbed, it seems.' The Captain's lips curled in derision, a thorough distaste for what this man represented. Smuggling was one thing. Was he himself not a skilled proponent of the trade, the name of Captain Harry well known along the coast of Suffolk? Nor was he ashamed of it. But spying for the enemy was quite another matter. The Gentlemen of the Free Trade had a code of honour to live by, whereas spying, handing over delicate information to England's enemies, was despicable by anyone's standards. 'You were in a common brawl— perhaps you fell out with your French contacts.'

'What?' The eyes struggled again, without success, to focus. The line between the brows dug deeper. 'I don't remember…'

'What motivates a spy to harm his own country?' There was hard cynicism in the Captain's reply, at odds with his youthful features. 'I suppose you pass information to the enemy for the money. And sometimes it all goes wrong and greed wins. Whatever information you gave to Monsieur Noir, you were not paid for it. A wasted trip all in all.'

'Not a spy…' The voice slurred. 'Not a traitor…' As the cutter lurched against a freshening wind, the man's head came into contact with the side of the little vessel and he slid into unconsciousness again.

The Captain gave a short laugh and pushed himself to his feet. 'They all say that when the truth's out. And how would you know if you're a spy or not—if you can't remember?'

'Do we deliver him to the authorities, Cap'n?' George Gadie asked.

'Not sure.' The Captain's stern contemplation of the body was transformed into a grin of pure mischief. 'A prize for the Preventive men to compensate for their failure to capture our fine brandy and silks? Serve him right if we did. But I don't know... We'll see what he has to say for himself when we get back.'

'We could just tip him overboard, Cap'n Harry, as Monsieur Marcel suggested. Save us a deal of trouble.' The old fisherman, sometime smuggler, pursed his lips as if savouring the fast remedy.

'No. I'll not have his blood, distasteful as it is, on my hands. Enough of him, George. Let's get this cargo home and safely delivered.'

And as Captain Harry straightened to his full height against the gunwale, he tugged at the stocking cap and pulled it off as the little vessel kicked and picked up speed. To release a luxuriant ripple of dark hair into the lively wind. Wild and untamed, it curled and drifted around a classically oval face, drawing attention to sparkling grey eyes, as sultry as the sea in the heat of mid-summer, or as coolly silver as the flash of pale sun on water at daybreak. It left no doubt in the mind of any who might have been mistaken of what they were seeing.

Despite the seaman's garb, Captain Harry—Miss Harriette Lydyard—was a very attractive, very feminine woman.

Before she turned her mind and hands to the ropes and sails, she took the time to looked down at the still figure at her feet. He was pretty as George had so mockingly observed. Hair? Impossible to tell with the blood and the water, but not fair. Eyes—well, too dark from shock and pain to tell. She crouched again to lift one of his hands from where it lay lax and inert. Filthy as it was, yet it was elegant and fine-boned with well-pared nails. She ran her own fingers over his palm, the smooth fingers. No calluses here, so not the hands of a working man. Clearly a man of wealth, as confirmed by his ruined clothes. They were made by a London tailor if she knew anything about it. Which she didn't—but enough to recognise the skill was beyond anything produced in Brighton or Lewes. Gently enough she replaced the hand on the man's chest, although her sense of loyalty and justice damned him for his treacherous calling. Many would call smuggling a disgraceful operation, putting gold into the hands of the French enemy, but compared with spying—well, it did not compare, did it?

It was a striking face, a haunting face, without doubt. Unable to resist, Harriette Lydyard ran her knuckles down the unblemished cheek, along the firm jawline, and felt her heart thud in her chest. Now here was a face that would take any woman's eye. A faint ripple of awareness of this man who was in her power shivered over her skin. If things were different…

Harriette hitched a shoulder as a fitful cloud covered the moon and hid the traitor from her gaze. There was nothing she could do for him. For now he would have to take his chances, but with practical roughness she unwound his crumpled cravat—once impeccably starched and superbly folded—then wadded and stuffed the pad of cloth within the shoulder of his coat to staunch any further bleeding. If fate intended him to survive, then he would.

Head tilted, her appraisal moved back, of its own volition, to his face, the straight nose, the well-sculpted cheekbones, to be thwarted once again when the moon slid behind a bank of clouds.

Harriette Lydyard rose to her feet with a huff of breath. A shame that a man so attractive should be so reprehensible as to be a trader in English secrets. Still, she found the time and inclination to throw a heavy rug over the prone body and push a small packet of priceless lace beneath his head.

Some hours later Harriette breathed out steadily, a long sigh of relief. The excitement of a run was heady, the success of it heated her blood, but the dangerous tension of the landing was always acute. There was always the chance that it would end in disaster, their cargo taken into custody by trium-phant Excise men and the crew of *Lydyard's Ghost* hauled before the magistrate. As all Gentlemen of the Free Trade knew, the penalty for smuggling could be the noose.

Tonight, as smooth as the bolts of silk they carried, all went without a hitch. A silent cove. No sneaky Revenue lugger lying in wait for them, no squad of Excise men with a lookout on the cliffs. Would that all landings were as sweet. Captain Rodmell, the keen-eyed Preventive Riding Officer, and his company of dragoons were no doubt all asleep in their beds in the Guard House at Lewes, dreaming of apprehending a priceless consignment of liquor and tea, lace and silk, unaware of what was unfolding on the shingle beach at Old Wincomlee.

Standing on the beach at last, Harriette rubbed her hands down the sides of her breeches in satis-faction at a job well done. It was the perfect location for such an enterprise where a natural dip in the land and the cliffs created an inlet with a gently sloping beach, a smugglers' paradise. Harriette's own, much-loved, house, Lydyard's Pride, stood high above them on the cliffs that enclosed and protected. From there, an unshuttered lantern lit in the Tower Room above the east wing had sent its beams out to sea, assuring them that all was well for a landing. Now it was done. Barrels and bales had been speedily dispatched to the wel-coming hands of lords and labourers alike, by pony or brawny shoulders. The cutter, her own pride and joy, the *Lydyard's Ghost*, was beached and drawn up on the shingle within the bay as any fishing smack might be.

The beach emptied apart from George Gadie and his son, Gabriel, fishermen whose family had lived in Old Wincomlee for generations, smuggling in their blood. And in Harriette's, too, as a Lydyard through and through. All Lydyards had sailed between England and France for at least two centuries to bring back illicit luxuries that were taxed beyond belief. All except for Harriette's brother, Sir Wallace Lydyard, knight, Justice of the Peace and proud owner of Whitescar Hall. Her *half*-brother, not a true Lydyard, which probably explained the man's mealy-mouthed disapproval of the Free Trade. So it was on Harriette's shoulders to carry on the tradition and the responsibility of the runs, for the benefit of the whole fishing community of Old Wincomlee.

But now Harriette must deal with her unexpected cargo. He lay on the shingle where he had been dropped by two burly landsmen, more interested in disposing of barrels of liquor than in the comfort of the unknown and bloody traveller.

'Well, Cap'n Harry? What's it to be?' George asked.

Well, what was it to be? Harriette looked down at the broken figure at her feet. Leave him to die on the beach, and good riddance to a traitor? Hand him over to Captain Rodmell and the Preventive men?

Or…or what? He might even be dead for all she knew. His face was turned away from her, but one hand was flung out on the ground, fingers curled, as if beseeching mercy.

Against all her better judgement, that helpless gesture wrung her heart.

She looked up, tensing, eyes wide and instantly alert as she caught the scrunch of pebbles beneath booted feet. A figure strode across the beach towards them. Harriette promptly relaxed and raised a hand in greeting.

'It went well, Harry.' Her cousin, Alexander Ellerdine, his face full of wild energy, joined them. 'A good run, in a quick time.'

'Zan! Excellent.' A brief clasp of hands. 'And an equally good landing, all due to you. Monsieur Marcel is willing for another run within the month.'

'We can do that.' Alexander's confidence was as bright as the lantern in the Tower Room window. 'I'll pass the word.' He turned to go. 'Who's this?' he asked, appraising the body.

Harriette's lips parted to tell him. Then, uncertain as to why, she changed her mind. She wasn't used to keeping secrets from Alexander, but she would keep her knowledge of this man with the haunting face and wicked crime tucked away. Just until she know more of him—and had made up her mind what to do with him.

'An Englishman who fell on bad times,' she announced. 'We don't know anything more, other than that his clothes suggest he's got deep pockets. Marcel delivered him with the barrels and we brought him home.' She ignored George Gadie's angled glance, even as she felt quick colour rise in her face. Lies did not come easily to her.

'Shall I take him?' Zan offered with barely a glance and less interest. 'I'll hand him over to Sam Babbercombe at the Silver Boat.'

'No.' It came out sharper than she had intended. 'I'll take him.'

'Why would you want to do that?'

'No reason.' She tightened her lips as she considered the helpless figure. Hand him over to the rough care of the innkeeper in Old Wincomlee, who would kill him with neglect before he put himself out for a penniless, injured man? Never. And besides... Harriette felt an uncomfortable response touch her spine as the man groaned, little more than a sigh, and turned his head. The wound was stark and ugly on his cheek. For some inexplicable reason she did not want to abandon him into Alexander's care. 'He's half-dead already. It's closer to take him to Lydyard's Pride than the inn.' When she saw Zan's brows rise, she hurried on. 'He might have information of use to us.' Harriette cast about for logical reasons. 'It might be in our interests to restore him to health.' She chuckled to hide her discomfort. 'We can always extort money from him for saving his life! Sam at the Silver Boat won't care whether he lives or dies.'

'I don't see how he can know anything to our advantage...' Harriette watched, all the tension returning to her tired muscles as Alexander knelt to turn the man's face, to make what he could of the features. Harriette thought his frown deepened and caught his sharp, rather sly, glance. 'Going to save his life, Harriette? Play the guardian angel to soothe his brow?'

'Nothing of the sort. How foolish you are!' She did not like the smooth teasing, nor the hint of malice, but summoned a smile. 'We can't stand here arguing the case, Zan,' she responded lightly enough. 'Have all the goods gone?'

Alexander stood, his face alight. 'Yes. I kept some particularly fine lace for the fashionable ladies of Brighton. They'll pay handsomely.' To her inexplicable relief his interest in the man had died. 'Do you need help?' He wound a warm arm around her waist and pressed a quick kiss to her temple.

Momentarily Harriette leaned her head against her cousin's shoulder in gratitude, then straightened. 'No. George and Gabriel will take care of him. You can do one thing for me, Zan. Best if my brother doesn't get wind of this, or my whereabouts tonight.

You can head Wallace off if he wants to know where I am. Tell him I'll stay the night at the Pride and return to Whitescar Hall tomorrow. It might save my skin from a rare tongue lashing. And then send Meggie to me, would you? She'll know what to bring. And tell her—bring some linen and one of Wallace's dressing gowns. I think we'll need it.'

'I'll do that.' Alexander again searched her face with a quizzical gleam and ran his hand down Harriette's arm, an intimate little gesture that surprised her and impelled her to take a step away. Alexander had never treated her with anything but cousinly affection, not even a casual flirtation, certainly no attempt to engage her interest. Then the moment was gone, so fast that she thought she must have been mistaken. 'Don't waste too much energy on your bloody catch,' he now added, nudging the man's foot with the toe of his boot. 'Probably not worth anything. I'd throw it back in the sea and have done with it.'

A salute to her cheek, and Alexander strode off to where his horse waited on the shingle. The bloody catch, as he had put it with singular lack of compassion, was pushed ignominiously by Gabriel Gadie across the back of a pony, before George set off to lead the animal up the steep but well-worn track between the beach and Lydyard's Pride, the house on the cliff where the lantern still beamed its welcome. And Harriette, walking at the side of the inert figure, resisted a temptation to smooth her fingers over the dark hair.

Chapter Two

At Lydyard's Pride, the Gadies manhandled the man, with some rich cursing to accompany their efforts, into one of the many uninhabited bedchambers. Dusty, cold as a room in an unused house must be, at least it was furnished with a bed, chair and nightstand. Kindling was laid ready in the grate.

Harriette followed in their wake, wrapped around as she always was by a sense of belonging when she set foot in this house. Empty, shut up for the most part it might be, but Lydyard's Pride was hers and the walls closed around her like the embrace of a lover. She felt her breathing slow, her pulse level. She was safe in this vast mausoleum, left to her by her Aunt Dorcas, because Lydyard's Pride had always been passed from generation to generation of Lydyards through the female line. Harriette would have lived here if Wallace would only permit it, but Wallace thundered about her lack of years, her unmarried state, her need for a chaperone, whenever she raised the subject, insisting that she live under his authority at Whitescar Hall. How could she consider living alone and unprotected in this vast pile of a house that had had no money spent on its upkeep at any time in the past century. It would fall down around her ears and then where would she be? And since Harriette lacked the financial independence to defy her brother, Lydyard's Pride was shut up and gathered dust under the eye of an elderly Lydyard retainer and two girls from the village. Its only use was to signal to the Free Traders from the lofty vantage point of the Tower Room.

But this was no time for wallowing in self-pity. Harriette turned her mind to the uninvited guest as the two men deposited their burden on the bed.

'Gabriel—light the fire, then go below and send Wiggins up with hot water and cloths. Linen for bandages. And a bottle of brandy. Not a word of this, mind, outside this house.' She rubbed her palms down her sides and approached the bed. 'Let's get him out of these sodden clothes, George.' She turned back the collar of the ruined coat and began to ease it from the injured shoulder.

'I'll do it, Cap'n. It's not seemly, Miss Harriette,' George reprimanded.

Harriette smiled through her impatience. Despite her smuggler's garb, she had suddenly in George

Gadie's mind been transformed from Captain to lady of the house. 'Not seemly? He's probably dying, and will surely do so if we leave him as he is.'

'It's not seemly for you to strip a man to his skin, Miss Harriette!'

'I know the form of a man.' Harriette continued to struggle to pull off the garment, noting in passing the fine cloth, its superb cut. 'I've seen *your* spindle shanks often enough when you've been soaked to the skin and stripped off on the beach.'

Which raised a guffaw from Gabriel as he left the room.

'Dare say. Not the same. This'n's young and comely!' Nevertheless George began to pull off the man's boots. 'Don't blame me, Miss, when your brother hears and kicks up a fuss.'

'I won't. And with luck, Sir Wallace won't hear.'

Whilst George attended to the boots, Harriette struggled to ease the tight-fitting coat from her guest's shoulders. Best to do it as fast as possible whilst he was still unconscious. Exasperated, she pulled a knife from her belt and began to use it against the seams—it was ruined anyway. The shirt, of the finest linen as she had suspected despite the muck and blood that soiled it, gave her no trouble. She had already used his once-elegant cravat as an impromptu padding. Her lips curved in contempt as they had on board *Lydyard's Ghost*. Payment for state secrets must be high.

'Miss Harriette, I think you should leave.'

'Just do it, George.'

With a click of tongue against teeth, George stripped off the man's breeches, undergarments and hose.

Well, now! Harriette was not ignorant of a degree of male nakedness. On board the cutter, when sailors stripped off their shirts to haul and pull on rope and sails, she had watched without embarrassment the play of smooth, well-defined muscle as arms and backs took the strain, when thighs had braced, sinews taut, against the drag of wind and wave. As a member of the crew, it was an occurrence that no longer disturbed her. A man was a creature of blood and bone and muscle, much like a horse, superbly crafted to carry out a task against the elements.

She had seen a half-naked man before. But nothing like this man, fully naked. Harriette found herself locked in a moment of splendid appreciation.

His fine skin was smooth, unweathered, his physique magnificent, lean and rangy. Broad shoulders, superbly muscled under the skin, informed her unequivocally that the condition of his body mattered to him. Perhaps he fenced, she thought. Or sparred at Gentleman Jackson's saloon. Arms sleekly powerful, from using the reins if he was wealthy enough to own his own curricle or phaeton. She could imagine him looping the leathers, controlling and steadying the power of a pair of blood horses. He might be rich, but he was not idle, sinking beneath rolls of fat as did some of her brother's associates, who spent their lives doing little but eating, drinking and hunting.

Harriette's eyes lingered, moved on to the flat planes of hard flesh as his chest narrowed to a slim waist, a light smattering of silky dark hair arrowing towards a firm belly. Narrow hips, strong thighs, his powerful masculinity obvious, strong and impressively formed even though unaroused. She felt heat rise in her cheeks and her mouth dry, shocked by her very physical reaction to this man, whom she ought to despise—until George flung a sheet over the man's lower limbs with a frown, a curse and a muttered comment on what was right and not right for well-brought-up young women to see.

Still Harriette stood and simply looked, drawn by a force beyond her control. If she ever visualised the sort of man she would wish to marry, this man would take centre stage in her dreams. And here he was under her hands, within her power. Unfortunately unconscious. Perhaps just as well, she decided, blinking and ordering her wayward thoughts back into line as Wiggins delivered the requested items. She was hardly at her society best in fisherman's smock, boots and breeches, to capture a wealthy and handsome man as a husband. To capture any husband. So far in her twenty-three years she had proved a dismal failure.

Not that she would want this one, of course, with dubious morals and treacherous intent.

Consigning George to wash the mud and sand from his abused body, Harriette applied herself to his injuries. Any remaining bleeding was sluggish, and on cursory examination, the wounds looked far worse then they actually were. A hard blow to the head had broken the skin, hard enough to cause the confusion and the lack of consciousness, but she did not think there would be permanent damage. A crust of dried blood had already formed. Bruising spread over one shoulder, dark and ugly, as if he had been beaten with a club. A thin blade had split his cheek, not deep, not dangerous, and would heal well enough—although it might leave a scar. Most worrying was a bullet wound in his upper left arm— thank God, not his shoulder or chest—but the bullet had passed through the flesh, so no need to cause more damage by digging it out, which George would have had to do with more enthusiasm than skill since there was no doctor in Old Wincomlee. With luck, it too would heal well if cleaned and bound up.

Harriette set to work with water and cloth and gentle hands to cleanse and bind, wrapping his arm tight, applying a compress to his shoulder. Only when she was satisfied that she had done all she could did she allow herself to perch on the side of the bed and investigate his face.

He was handsome, a face that could lodge in a woman's mind, in her private longings. A striking male beauty. Blessed with a fine straight nose, straight brows, a lean face to match his body with fine planes and sharply elegant cheekbones. His lips, now soft and relaxed, were masterfully carved. Harriette could imagine them curving in a smile, or firm with temper. Softly she drew her fingertip across and along, a mere breath of touch. They were cold and unresponsive.

What would it be like to press her own lips to his? To warm them into life, to feel them heat and respond…? She had no idea.

Harriette Lydyard had never been kissed.

As if aware of her regard, and causing Harriette to snatch her hand away, his eyelids fluttered, then slitted open, a shine of green, yet blurred as they had been in the cutter. A murmur, a slur of words.

'Where is she? You promised… Had an agreement…'

Harriette leaned forwards to listen, smoothing her palm over his forehead, down his uninjured cheek.

'…you must let her go…let her come with me…'

So he had lost someone, a woman it seemed. Harriette allowed herself another soft caress as a keen regret settled in her heart. Searching for her was important enough to cause him anxiety. What would it be like to have this man search for her, raging at her loss? Her cheeks flushed, her heart fluttered a little. What would it be like to be prized enough by so desirable a man that he must seek you out, even to the point of wounding, even near death. What would it be like to feel those arms close around her and hold her body against his…?

How foolish! How shocking! What would Wallace say if he could read her entirely unseemly thoughts? Harriette snatched her hands away and pushed herself to her feet. A silly girl's dreaming. She would end up wed to one of Wallace's drinking, hunting, entirely unattractive cronies if he had his way. No future in wishing and sighing over a handsome man as if she were a child barely out of the schoolroom. And where would she possibly meet such a one as he? She was hardly likely to persuade Wallace to give her a Season in London. Or even Brighton.

'Where is she? You promised… I can't leave her!'

Against her will, lured by the undoubted anguish, Harriette was drawn back again to push the tangled hair from his face.

'Hush now. I'll care for you.' So racked and troubled. But who wouldn't be with a dent in his skull and a bullet through his arm? Yet a strange tenderness was stirred.

'I'm afraid for her….'

'There's no need to fear.' Empty words, but she must reassure him.

'Help me…' With a deep sigh, almost a groan, he lapsed into silence again, dark lashes heavy against his pale skin.

'I will. Sleep now…' She closed her hand around his and felt an instant response, weak, in truth, but a curl of his fingers around her own as if in ownership, as if an unbreakable bond existed between them.

Harriette's heart bounded heavily within her chest. Her breathing shuddered. In that one moment all she could desire was to stay beside him and comfort him, soothe his pain.

You love him! The words whispered in her ears, lodging in her mind. *You have fallen in love with him!*

'No, I have not! Of course I have not!' she remarked aloud, thrusting her hands behind her back like a small child caught out in some misdemeanour. As if she might reach out to touch him again because every instinct insisted that she do so, flesh against flesh. 'How could I possibly have done anything so ridiculous!' But her breath was short, as if she had just climbed the path to Lydyard's Pride, her skin heated, the blood singing through her veins to make her aware of every inch of her body.

'What's that, Miss Harriette? Regret bringing him

back here already?' George Gadie came to stand at her side. 'He'll live, I reckon.'

'And that's the best we can do for now,' Harriette remarked, furious with herself, but working hard to keep her voice calm, unconcerned. She drew her tongue over dry lips and prayed for a cold dose of common sense to cool her blood. 'We'll leave him to see if he recovers. One of the maids—Jenny— can sit by him.'

'Then I'll be back tomorrow, Cap'n, if you don't want me now.'

'You've done more than enough for me today.' She touched his arm in thanks. 'Go and let your wife know you're safe. It was a good night's run.'

'Aye, it was. Hope *he* doesn't cause you more trouble than he's worth. Should've passed him over to the Silver Boat, as Mr Alexander said.'

Harriette angled a glance. 'Would you have left Gabriel there under Sam Babbercombe's care, if he was wounded?' A grunt was all the reply she got as George opened the door for the maid, but she sensed his agreement. 'Come for me if he wakes, or takes a turn for the worse,' Harriette instructed Jenny, who settled herself on the only chair with a basket of stitching to keep watch. 'I expect he'll sleep through the rest of the night and much of the day.'

As Harriette walked slowly down the staircase,

her thoughts remaining fixed on the man who astonishingly had the power to light a flame in her blood, she came upon Meggie climbing ponderously towards her, a deep wicker basket on each arm.

'Well, Miss Harriette. Now what?' She puffed out a breath, cheeks red with exertion.

Harriette beckoned. 'Come with me and I'll tell you.' Retracing her steps to the first floor, she opened the door of the bedchamber she used when she could escape from Wallace and his overbearing wife, Augusta, and spend a night there. For furnishings and cleanliness it was little better than the one she had just left, but familiar with its lack of comfort she paid that no heed, walking immediately across the room to one of the windows, for the windows of the chamber looked out across the bay, offering a spectacular sweep of coastline.

Meggie, broad and stout, no nonsense snapping in her bright eyes, ignored the view as she deposited her burdens on the bed. Companion and servant to Miss Harriette Lydyard for more years than she cared to add up, and well used to her mistress's eccentric lifestyle if not totally accepting of it, she did not mince her words. 'What're you doing this time, miss? Mr Alexander did not say.'

Harriette's lips twitched wryly, knowing that her trust in Meggie could be absolute. 'I think I'm bringing a spy back from the dead.'

'A spy, is it? Do you think you should?' Meggie did not appear altogether shocked.

'No, but I can't leave him to die, can I?' The gleam of rich colour catching her eye, Harriette left the window and the view to dig into one of the baskets. 'His clothes are ruined. He'll need this until we can make other arrangements.' She unfolded a dressing gown in stunning red-and-gold satin, dragons chasing their tails, with heavy gold frogging on breast and cuffs.

'And he'll have to be at death's door to agree to wear it!'

Harriette chuckled. 'Sir Wallace sees himself as the epitome of high fashion.' She swirled the gown around her own shoulders and struck a stance remarkably similar to that of her pompous brother. 'As for the occupant of my one furnished bedchamber, he'll have no choice, however tasteless it might be.' She looked up, eyes pinning her maid. 'What did my brother say? Or did you manage to leave without his knowledge?'

'More like what her ladyship said. Sir Wallace was gone on business to Lewes.' Meggie stood, frowning, with her hands on her broad hips. 'Lady Augusta had a fist-full of dissatisfaction, as you can imagine.'

Harriette grimaced, a little pain in her heart as she imagined the downward turn of Gussie's mouth. Harriette had learned, almost, to live with the constant displeasure. 'I'd hoped Zan would be more discreet. Does Lady Augusta know I was on a run?'

'Of course she does. Can't keep it a secret, can you, when every man in the Old Wincomlee knows the identity of Captain Harry? At least they all have the good sense and loyalty to keep their mouths shut so the Preventives'll never hear the truth from them. And Sir Wallace'll never help the Preventives, even if he is a JP. He knows where his next barrel of fine brandy comes from! But as soon as he returns, he'll be up here before you know it, demanding to know what you're about. And why you've not returned to Whitescar Hall, to don a pretty dress and play the genteel young lady of taste and refinement.'

'Because I would die of the tedium of it all if I did! If Wallace's taken himself off to Lewes, let's pray God he stays there overnight, and I'll be undisturbed here for a while longer.' Harriette's eyes lit with mischief as she refused to let her spirits sink into her boots. 'Even better, I'll send a message that I've caught a chill—or a fever from France. That'll keep them away. Wallace fears ill health like the plague, and Augusta won't come here without him.' She stretched her arms above her head, loosening tight muscles, then ran her fingers through her windblown and knotted hair. 'I might even manage a week's freedom. Wallace won't come to see how I am if he thinks I'll spread some noxious disease in his path—and foreign at that! An enemy disease!'

Meggie snorted a laugh, then quickly became serious. 'But Lady Augusta's not far from the truth, Miss Harriette. You should be wed. Not that I can think of any of your acquaintance worthy of you.' She rapidly changed the subject with skill born of long practice as Harriette rounded on her, the light of battle in her eyes, in her face. 'I've brought you some clothes, so that when Sir Wallace *does* arrive to blister your ears, he won't be able to take exception to your appearance.' She scowled at the salt-and-sand-encrusted smugglers' garb, the scuffed boots. 'What he would say at this moment, the Devil only knows….'

A tap came at the door. Jenny entered, curtsied and ignored her mistress's unconventional attire. 'The gentleman's awake, Miss Harriette. I thought you would wish to know.'

'Is he now? A stronger constitution than I thought. Then I'll come.'

'Not like that you won't, Miss Harriette.' Meggie grasped her wrist without ceremony as she would have followed the maid. 'What would he think?'

'I don't care what he thinks.' Or perhaps she did. She might have little care for her appearance in general, and none when engaged on a run, but would she really want this unknown gentleman to see and judge her in her present dishevelled and scruffy state? Would she want him to look at her, eyes widening in disgust of her unseemly attire? Sir Wallace's disapproval meant nothing to her. But her captive spy… Shame tinted her cheeks a glorious pink at the thought that he would see and condemn her as being unredeemably *outré*. Still, if she were clad as a smuggler… 'Besides,' she spoke her thoughts aloud, testing the idea, 'our guest might speak more openly if…'

'If what?'

'Well, he won't confess his devious crimes to a woman, will he? On the other hand, to a man…' Twisting it up with a careless hand, she stuffed her hair back under her cap, pulled it well down. 'He might speak to a smuggler, mightn't he? Two reprobates together. The smuggler and the spy, Meggie. Now there's an unholy alliance, wouldn't you say? Not much to choose between us, many would think. Behold, Harry Lydyard.' She struck a pose again, the lawless smuggler in boots and breeches.

'One day, all that will get you into trouble, my girl!'

'But think how exciting it makes life, Meggie!' Perhaps she was unaware of it, but a shadow crossed her face. A little melancholy, a little regretful. 'Why would I want to be wife to one of Sir Wallace's sad associates when I can sail *Lydyard's Ghost* on a lively sea?'

* * *

Lucius Hallaston became aware first of a grinding headache, as if a band of iron were being tightened around his skull. And if that were not bad enough, his shoulder throbbed, as when he had once taken a heavy fall from his horse sufficient to crack his collarbone. At the same time his left arm screamed with a fierce burning pain. Was there any place in his body that did not hurt?

He struggled, trying to sit up, abandoning the attempt as his wits scattered. It was almost too much trouble to chase after them and reassemble them into some sort of order as the pain beat with the insistency of a military drum behind his eyes. Memory came back in patches, with disconcertingly looming gaps. Lucius shook his head as if to shake them into a recognisable pattern and wished he had not.

He opened his eyes cautiously. A gloomy room, dusty bed hangings, few meagre furnishings. The linen sheets that covered him were worn and smelt of must and mildew, although were clean enough. Where in heaven's name was he? It was no inn that he recognised. A young girl, a servant from her clothing, sat beside the bed, head bent over a needle. Mending more sheets, he thought inconsequentially.

'Where am I?' he managed to croak through a throat as dry as a desert.

'You're awake, sir.' The girl looked up, rose to her feet.

'Yes.' His voice sounded rusty to his ears. 'Will you tell me…?'

But then she left him, so that he almost wondered if he had imagined her, and the darkness claimed him once more. When awareness returned, it was to a different voice. Feminine yet cool and calm, instructing him to open his mouth and drink. An arm was behind his head, lifting him, and the rim of a cup pressed against his lips. It was cold and refreshing, a sharp tang of lemons, balm to his dry throat. And from somewhere came the soothing drift of lavender. He tried to thank the girl, the maid, for surely it was she—or was it? The voice was different—but it was all too difficult to work out truth from imagination.

He gave up and slept again.

Gradually, when consciousness returned, so did his memories. He remembered being in a boat. Remembered being set upon in the little French port. Port St Martin, that was it. Remembered failing in his task, outwitted and outmanoeuvred by that villain Jean-Jacques Noir. He felt anger rise within him, and shame that he should have been so tricked, but he had not expected such underhand treachery. Obviously he had been too naïve. He thought he might have been shot. Certainly he remembered pain, then blackness….

He did not know who had rescued him. One moment, he was being attacked and beaten on the quay, the next he was in the bottom of a small boat with water lapping against his cheek and a queasy swell. He remembered demanding to be taken back to France, and then nothing.

So where was he now?

A movement by the door as it opened. He risked moving his head and could barely repress a groan at the leaping pain. A young man approached in the sea-faring gear of boots and wide breeches, a heavy tunic, all worn and salt-stained. He took the seat vacated by the maid and leaned forward, arms on thighs.

Lucius found himself being appraised by a pair of cool eyes, as pale grey as to be almost silver.

'You are awake.'

'Yes. Where am I?' He would try again.

'Old Wincomlee, a fishing village in Sussex. You'll not know it but it's a mere handful of miles from Brighton. This is my home. Lydyard's Pride.' Stern, unsmiling but with a surprisingly educated accent and turn of phrase, the young man had at least given him some information, if his pounding brain could retain it.

'Who are you?' he managed, frowning furiously.

'My name is Harry Lydyard.'

'You brought me back. From France.'

'Yes. You were hurt.'

'So I owe you my life.'

'Perhaps you do. You bled all over my boat.' A tight smile curled the lips but then he grew solemn again, his voice taking on a hard edge. 'What were you doing in Port St Martin? Why were you set on?'

'I…' He sought for words in explanation—did he not owe his rescuer some sort of reasonable explanation?—but realising that he could not find the right words to say. Those that rushed into his mind, he must not say! Something deep and unpleasant in his gut prompted him towards fear and suspicion. Who to trust? It was becoming more and more difficult to know who to trust as time passed.

'You were delirious when we brought you back here. From what you said you were looking for someone. A woman, I think…'

He shook his head, winced, groaned.

'I see you're reluctant to tell me the truth, so I must draw my own conclusions.' Even sterner, the pale eyes piercing, pinning him to the bed in icy contempt. The tone of voice was a condemnation in itself.

'A matter of business, let us say.' The best he could do.

'A business that left you half-dead with a bullet in your arm, a crack on the head and your pockets empty?' Heavy cynicism lay strangely on the young face that swam before him.

'So it seems.' From the mists, he suddenly recalled

the barrels and casks in the boat, the bales. 'Were you engaged in the Free Trade? Are you a smuggler?'

The tone remained biting. 'Yes. I am.'

'You're very young to be a smuggler,' he commented, though why that should seem important to him he could not say.

'But not too young to do it well. I am an excellent smuggler.' The young man stood and advanced to the bed, leaned over to examine the wounds, fingers firm and searching, yet gentle enough, against his hair, his arm, but Lucius got the distinct impression that there was not much compassion in the solicitude, rather a hard practicality. 'You'll live.' The blunt statement confirmed it. 'The bullet went through your arm. A bang on the head—hence the headache. You were lucky. You've lost blood, but you're strong enough. Another day and you'll be on your feet again.'

Except that Lucius felt as weak as a kitten, and found himself sliding into sleep, unable to pull back, unable to keep his eyelids from closing. Not that he wouldn't be sorry to block out the disparaging stare of the self-confessed smuggler. 'I'm sorry. My mind seems to disobey my demands. Sorry to be a trouble to you…' He fretted at his unaccustomed weakness, sensing some urgency that he could not grasp, his fingers pulling at the sheet. 'I must get up now. I'll be missed if I don't…'

'You can't.'

'I can't stay here…'

'You must for a little while. Sleep now. You'll be stronger when you wake.'

And because he really had no choice, Lucius Hallaston did as the smuggler ordered.

Harriette continued to sit beside him. Her reactions to this man confused her. He wouldn't answer her questions and she did not think it was because he could not recall *anything* of the previous night. Some mystery surrounded him. No doubt he was a spy after all and she should condemn him for it, yet she had seen fear in his face—but perhaps that was just the fear of any man who was set upon, his life threatened by a pistol shot. And there had definitely been that deep anxiety, for a woman. He had not denied it, had he? She leaned back, arms crossed, scowling at the sleeping figure, unable to disentangle her emotions. Was he not hurt and in trouble, his wits still scattered? Did he not demand her compassion, her understanding?

On the other hand, what did it matter that she knew not whether to damn him or care for him? What did it matter that he might sell his soul, or at least England's security, for thirty pieces of silver? His treachery was entirely irrelevant because once he was recovered he would be on his way to whatever nefarious practice demanded his attention, and she would never see him again.

Yet still, accepting that, Harriette allowed herself a little time of sheer self-indulgence, of self-deception, for that was surely what it was, and allowed her deepest instincts to surface again. His voice, deep and smooth as honey, was as pleasant on the ear as his features were to her eye. For a little while at least she could pretend that he was hers and this was their home where the world could not encroach. Where she could live as she chose. She would walk on the cliffs, this man holding her hand, telling her how beautiful she was, how his heart beat for her, whilst she could tell him that her heart had fallen into his hands, as softly as a ripe plum. At night he would hold her in his arms, unfolding for her all the delights that could exist between a man and a woman. Rousing her with hands and mouth, with the slide of his naked flesh against hers... No harm in imagining the possessive touch of his fingers as they linked with hers, as they curled into her hair, holding her captive so that his mouth could take hers. No harm in considering the breathless, heated pleasure of that body, stripped and powerful, pinning her to the sheets, taking her, making her his.

Enough! Harriette's smile became contemptuous.

It was all an illusion, a figment of her sad imagination. He would approve of her being a smuggler quite as little as she would accept that he was a spy! Yet for a moment, still clutching at her ridiculous dreams, Harriette leaned over him and touched the sculpted sinews and tendons of his unbound arm, encircling his wrist where his pulse beat against her fingers, turning his hand, shivering when once again his fingers instinctively curled around hers and held on. Whatever he was, whoever he was, she was glad he was safe.

'Sleep now,' she whispered. 'I will care for you. No need to fear.'

She still did not even know his name.

It was a long night. The man slept but restlessly. When his breathing became ragged, Harriette dosed him with some nameless and evil-tasting concoction of Meggie's, thinking it at least as good as anything Sam Babbercombe would do. Then, since she hadn't the heart to summon Jenny back, she took it upon herself to sit and watch over him through the dark hours. So she sat and let the hours pass. Stood, stretched, looked out of the window at the changing shape of clouds over the waxing moon. Tried to read by the flickering light of the two candles and gave it up. Simply sat and watched the pain and confusion shift over his face, praying more fervently than she had for years that this was simply a fever that would pass.

At some point after midnight, his restlessness became more intense, hands clawing to grip the sheet as he fell under the control of some dream, head thrashing from side to side. Perspiration beaded his brow, the expanse of his chest. Although his eyes opened, the bright gaze was blurred and unseeing.

'Softly.' She stood to make use of a damp cloth soaked in lavender, afraid his restlessness would start the bleeding again. 'You're safe. You're in no danger.'

As if responding to her voice, he grasped her wrist urgently. Surprising her with its power. His voice was harsh, his question stark with fear.

'Marie-Claude. Are you Marie-Claude?'

'No. I am not.'

'Marie-Claude… Where is she?'

'She's safe.' It was an obvious answer in the face of his despair.

'I can't find her…' His grip tightened.

'You will. Rest now. She'll come to you….'

He lay quietly. Harriette thought for a moment that he had accepted her assurance, but then his movements became edgy as if still caught up in a web of anxieties.

'But she's lost,' he whispered, eyes opening blindly. 'I don't know where she is and I can't find her.'

Harriette was moved by a desire to give him some

respite from whatever tracked and haunted him in his dark mind as she enclosed his hand between both of hers. If she could anchor him to the present, it might stave off the monsters in his dreams. 'Hush. You need to sleep. I'll keep the nightmares at bay.'

It seemed that he focused on her in the end. But to no great satisfaction.

'No one can do that for me. No one can stop them.' Then he slid down the slope into unconsciousness again. His hand fell away.

Disturbed, Harriette bathed his face in cool water, his chest where sweat had pooled in the dip of his collarbones. Who was Marie-Claude? His wife? She did not think so since he did not seem to know her. Not, therefore, his lover, either? French, from her name. Had she some connection with his presence in France at Port St Martin?

There were no answers, only questions.

He seemed calmer, his sleep deeper. Harriette contemplated leaving him, but dared not, so she was committed to spending the night. The upright chair proving far too uncomfortable for sleep, she leaned her arms and head on the folded quilts at the foot of the bed and dozed, confident she would wake if he did. No one need know that she stayed the night with him. Her lips twisted wryly. Certainly not her imaginary lover who knew nothing of her dreams and who now was dead to the world.

* * *

When Lucius awoke it was daybreak, when she
had doused the candles and was watching the sun,
the faintest sliver of red-gold on the horizon.
Harriette found herself held by a direct stare, keen
and searching, and of a striking grey-green. The
earlier confusion was gone and now the eyes that
held hers were awake, aware. In their supreme confidence Harriette detected the recovery of a formidable will. Here was a man used to authority, to
having no one question his wishes, wearing the
habit of command like a glove, despite his unortho-
dox lack of clothing. She could not look away from
his regard, but forced herself to keep her expression
carefully controlled in defiance of the unfortunate
tremor in her heart. At least she had had the presence
of mind to stuff her long-suffering hair back under
her stocking-cap with the coming of the day. She
really could not face an explanation of her sex and
unchaperoned presence in his bedchamber.

'Good morning.' She broke the little tension.

'I feel better,' he replied.

'Does your head ache still?'

'Not so much. My shoulder hurts like the Devil.'

'It's badly bruised. Are you hungry?'

'Yes.' He sounded surprised.

'I'll send Jenny with some soup.'

He rubbed a hand slowly over his chin, grimacing

at the roughness, casting a glance down at his torso that the sheet did not cover. 'Will you arrange for some clothes for me?'

'Yes. You won't like them. Not much *haut ton* to be found in Old Wincomlee, and your own garments were too badly damaged, I think, to be of further use to you.'

'I'm relieved to be alive to wear them at all.'

A surprising note of dry humour. Harriette steadied her gaze. So far their exchange had been ridiculously innocuous, as if meeting in a polite withdrawing room. If she did not take the matter in hand, if she succumbed to cowardice, she would bid him good day and wave him from her door, as if he were not in possession of a bullet wound and an unsavoury reputation. She took a breath and stirred the mud in the bottom of the pool. 'Are you a spy?'

The humour was quickly gone. 'No. I am not a spy.' There was no hesitation, but then he would be unlikely to tell the truth, even if he was. 'Why did you think I was?'

'Marcel—the French smuggler who brought you to my cutter—said you were associated with an individual called Jean-Jacques Noir.'

A quick frown between his brows, a thinning of lips. She saw immediately that he recognised the name. 'I know him. But I am no spy.'

'Marcel says he is a man of vicious character.'

'Yes. I believe he is.'

She was getting nowhere. 'Who is Marie-Claude?'

He certainly recognised that name. His eyes snapped to hers. 'I don't know.'

A lie. He had looked dangerously uneasy, but nothing to be gained in pressing him if he would not say. It was, after all, none of her concern. 'Very well. I don't believe you, but can't force you to tell, except by torture!' She walked to the door, then paused, looking back. 'Will you tell me this, then— what is your name?'

'Lucius Hallaston.'

It meant nothing to her. She gave a brief nod and would have left him, aware of nothing but a deep disappointment that the man who seemed for some inexplicable reason to have such a claim on her was entirely disreputable. This man who had awoken her inexperienced heart and her emotions, who had reminded her painfully of what was lacking in her loveless life, had feet of clay. The disillusion settled like a heavy stone below her heart.

On her way to the door she stopped beside him, to press her fingers against the hard flesh of his shoulder. Yes, it was cool, the fever gone. But not in her own blood. Even so slight a touch sent heat racing through her blood. This is simply physical desire! Harriette felt her face flush with shame.

'Do you have family who will miss you?' she demanded, curtly, to cover her embarrassment.

'A brother in London. I won't be missed for a little time. You, I think I remember, are Harry Lydyard.'

'Yes.' She repressed a little laugh of wry mirth. 'I am Harry Lydyard.'

He still thought of her as a man. It didn't matter. He was devious, deceitful and well on the road to recovery. She would send George to deal with his needs and there was no need for her to see him again. Within twenty-four hours he would be gone from her life.

And good riddance! But her heart trembled as if at a great loss.

Chapter Three

Lucius Hallaston spent the slow passage of time whilst his strength returned alone, considering his situation. It was not an operation that encouraged optimism, although he tried. His body was sore as if trampled by a team of his blood horses, his head hammered, a sharp pulse of pain just behind his eyes, but he was not incapacitated. It could have been much worse, he supposed. He could be dead. True, lifting his left arm and shoulder was an excruciating movement, but if someone could find him some clothes, he could take control of his life once more. Or could he? The desperate failure of the enterprise in France was hardly evidence of his controlling the events of his life!

He pushed aside that bitter memory because to worry at it would achieve nothing but make his head pound more. All that would be required of him in the near future was to wait for further communication from Jean-Jacques Noir—and there would be one for sure—and explain away to his brother a bullet in his arm and a hole in his head with as much plausibility as he could dredge from the debacle.

His brows settled into a solid bar. It shouldn't be too difficult to smooth over the immediate problems. But as for Monsieur Noir... It was a damnable situation! Lucius bared his teeth in what was not a smile and fell to contemplating the array of cobwebs that festooned the curtains and the scurrying antics of a spider, trying not to allow the disdain he had read in the eyes of Captain Harry Lydyard to disturb him.

But it did. The young man's stare had been contemptuous, scornful of his obvious sliding round the truth. By what right did a common smuggler pass judgement on him, Lucius Hallaston?

By the same right you pass judgement on yourself. You deserve it for allowing yourself to get into this mess! his conscience sneered in his ear.

He must have dozed. When the door to his bedchamber opened again later in the morning, disturbing a quantity of dust, a sturdy individual, more appropriately clad for a day's work in a fishing smack than a period of duty as a gentleman's valet, entered. A bundle of clothes in his arms, he was followed by an equally robust woman with a determined air and lines of profound censure on her broad features. She carried a tray with a bowl, a ewer of hot water and a dish of something steaming that smelled—well, good.

'Morning, y'r honour.' The fisherman lost no time, depositing the bundle on the bed. 'I've been sent by Cap'n Harry to take care o' you.'

'My thanks.' Lucius pushed himself up on the pillows.

'Some rare bruises, I'd imagine.' Without hesitation, the fisherman thrust an arm around Lucius's shoulders and heaved. 'You've a tighter hold on life this morning, y'r honour, I'll say that. Thought you was a gonner—all the blood an' all. George Gadie, y'r honour. Fisherman.'

'And smuggler?' Lucius's memory was vague at best, but some aspects of his rescue were clear enough.

'Aye, sir…' Wariness flitted across the man's face but there was a glint in his eye. 'And you, y'r honour?'

'Lucius Hallaston.'

'Well, Mr Hallaston, the Cap'n says you're to drink this.' A mug of ale changed hands.

The woman who had been bustling round the room nudged George aside with bowl, spoon and napkin. 'I'll say one thing, though some would say it's none of my business. The sooner you leave here, the better for all our sakes, sir. Especially for—'

'Take yourself off, Meggie,' George broke in. 'Let the man drink and get his breath.'

'All I was saying was…'

'Least said, soonest mended,' George growled.

With a smile of thanks to Meggie that was ignored as she stomped to the door, Lucius gripped the bowl as best he could with his injured left arm, dipped the spoon and drank. It was good, deliciously aromatic to enhance the flavour of chicken. He realised how long it was since he had had anything to eat.

Meanwhile George sat down beside the bed, leaning forwards with arms on stalwart thighs as if anticipating a conversation. Much as Harry Lydyard had done. Lucius cocked his head, continued to spoon up the broth and waited.

'Are you a spy, then, y'r honour?'

Lucius abandoned the spoon and wiped his mouth with the napkin as he struggled against impatience. 'Why does everyone presume that I am? No, I am not a spy.' He read the patent disbelief in the smuggler's seamed face, but said no more. What proof had he but mere denial—but no point in dwelling on what could not be changed. 'Can I get to Brighton?' he asked, the uppermost thought in his mind.

'Expect so. When you can get to your feet.'

'I can do that. I don't want to impose on you more than I have already. The maid—Jenny, was it?—I must thank her. I think she sat with me during the night, when I was restless.'

'No. Not Jenny. It would be the Cap'n.'

Was there the slightest hesitation. Did he detect some disfavour in the gruff announcement? Impossible to tell. And why would the fisherman have any opinion on it? The beat of pain in his head made it not worth considering. 'Then I must thank the Captain. Lydyard, I think he said. A local family?'

'Aye, sir. The Capn's brother—he's the local land-owner. Sir Wallace.'

'Then I must thank Captain Harry for his hospitality before I go.' Lucius carefully placed the bowl on the nightstand.

'Don't think he's around.' There was that scowl again, the brusque reply. 'Shall I shave you, y'r honour?'

'No need. You hold the bowl and towel, but hand me the razor. I can use my right arm well enough, although the left's pretty useless. Have you a mirror?'

'Aye, sir.' George wiped the square on his thigh and held the smeared glass. He chuckled. 'You mightn't like what you see, though.'

It was a shock.

'By God! That's a mess.' Lucius looked at the reflection in the mirror. Ran his fingers over the growth of beard and then, gently, down the livid scar on his cheek, flinching at the soreness. If vanity was an issue, if his looks mattered as much to him as it did to his younger brother who was in the throes of incipient dandyism, he would be cast into despair. Together with the purple bruising on his temple and jaw, and the matted hair stuck to his head with God knew what, he looked a criminal fit for Newgate. 'It'll heal, I expect.' He winced as he once again pressed his fingers against the knife wound.

'So Cap'n Harry said. He cleaned it up as well as he could.'

'Hmm. Then let's see if we can put the rest to rights.'

Within the next half-hour Lucius had to admit to looking relatively more respectable. Shaving complete, he struggled into boots and breeches—fortunately his own, if hopelessly stained—and a linen shirt that was not his, but of good quality.

'Best we could do.' George gave him a helping hand to pull on the boots. 'Meggie's trying to find you a coat. Yours isn't in a fit state. Until we do—what do you think of this, y'r honour?' He held up the dressing gown with a rough flourish, unable to repress a guffaw.

'Hell and the Devil! Now that's an eyeful.' Lucius grinned as he shrugged his right arm carefully into the vibrant glory of rampant dragons. The other he couldn't manage so allowed the magnificent beasts on the left to simply hang.

'Sir Wallace's.' George smirked. 'We borrowed it. Like the shirt. He's an eye to fashion.'

'Has he now?' Looping the belt, Lucius was willing to tolerate it for the sake of respectability. 'My thanks. Now, if you can find me a coat and a horse, I'll be out of your hair. If I can get to Brighton…'

George shook his head. 'Don't think you should ride, y'r honour. Not with the blood you lost. I can arrange a pony and trap easy enough from the Silver Boat to get you to Brighton. If you had money,' he added slyly.

'And there's the rub. But we'll work something out.' Lucius rubbed his hand over his newly shaven cheek. 'I had a gold hunter with me when I went to France.'

'Not any longer, sir. Gone the way o' the rest o' y'r possessions.'

A peremptory knock on the door.

It heralded the entrance of a man driven by righteous anger and blunt discourtesy. His accusation followed without introduction.

'So the tales in the village were right enough.' The visitor slammed the door behind him, eyes narrowed into a glare. 'What's this? A nameless ruffian dragged from the high seas, and wearing my dressing gown?'

Lucius resisted the inclination to raise his brows at the intrusion, struggling to keep a civil tongue in his head. Nothing to be gained by taking the offensive. The man—a gentleman despite his lack of good manners—was perhaps thirty-four or -five, around Lucius's age, clad in a fashionable greatcoat of indeterminate drabness reaching to his ankles, with innumerable shoulder capes, the whole magnifying his rotund appearance and short stature. His face was broad, his complexion florid, telling of a close association with Free Trade liquor. Lucius heard George clear his throat uncomfortably. So this was Sir Wallace Lydyard, owner of the dubious taste in garments. But Lucius did not appreciate the overt hostility, the sheer lack of good manners or breeding.

'My apologies, sir,' Lucius replied as he rose slowly to his feet. A cool chill, the curtest inclination of the head, a deliberate lack of recognition. He would not be reduced to such discourtesy but, by God, he would not ignore such rank ill manners. 'The rumours you were so quick to take at face value are incorrect. I was an innocent traveller in France, injured and robbed through no fault of my own. Fortunately I was rescued by some gentlemen of the Free Trade.' Now, deliberately, he allowed his brows to lift infinitesimally. 'I was not aware that *that* entitled me to be painted as a ruffian of the high seas.'

'No?' Sir Wallace was not to be discouraged. 'What is any law-abiding Englishman doing in a French port if not to England's danger, when the

French are our sworn enemies, even at this moment engaged in battle with our brave forces in the Peninsula?'

'Urgent business of a family nature that can be of no possible interest to you, sir.' The raised brows were superb in their arrogance. Lucius had had enough of slurs on his character. 'If I am making use of your splendid garment, then I must offer you my thanks. My own coat is ruined or I should not have taken such a liberty. Perhaps you would be so good as to advise me of your name, sir?'

'Lydyard. Sir Wallace Lydyard.'

Again Lucius managed the slightest inclination of his head, icily polite, a barbed and poisonous weapon to depress pretension and boorishness. 'Lydyard. Let me make myself known, to clear any misunderstanding between us. I am Lucius Hallaston. Earl of Venmore.'

'Venmore!'

'That is so.'

Sir Wallace was flustered. 'My lord…' For once Lucius enjoyed the effect of his consequence with not a little malice. 'Perhaps I was hasty.' An unattractive flush mantled Lydyard's features. 'You'll understand—the circumstances, your presence here at the Pride…'

'I was unconscious when I was brought ashore. A bullet wound.'

Lydyard's eyes suddenly acquired an unpleasant reptilian gleam, and his glance snapped to George Gadie. 'Did you spend the night here, Gadie, to care for his lordship?'

George shuffled. 'No, Sir Wallace. I did not.'

'You were not here at the Pride?'

'No, Sir Wallace. The Cap'n sent me home.'

'So I heard correctly.' Sir Wallace's voice was soft, a slyness sliding across his features. 'My sister stayed here last night, then.'

'Aye, Sir Wallace.'

Lucius remained silent, unable to follow this line of exchange, even more when Lydyard's speculative appraisal was turned on him.

'You look much restored this morning, my lord.'

'Well enough to take my leave,' he replied curtly, yet with restraint. There were suddenly undercurrents in the room that made no sense to him, but his patience was at an end. No man addressed a Hallaston of Venmore in such an impertinent manner!

'Knowing my sister, I suppose she spent the night at your side, in this room.'

A warning flitted across his skin, like a draught from an ill-fitting window. 'Your sister, sir? I have no knowledge of your sister.'

With a grunt, Sir Wallace promptly turned on his heel and marched to the door. Opened it. 'Jenny?'

he bellowed, followed by a distant reply of assent. 'Tell my sister I wish to see her here immediately.'

Then he continued to stand beside the door, arms folded.

Lucius rummaged unsuccessfully through his incomplete recollections. He recalled Jenny, the dark-haired maid. But Lydyard's sister? 'As I said, as far as I have any memory of last night, I am not acquainted with your sister, sir.'

But Sir Wallace's lips curled in marvellous disbelief. 'Do you presume that your birth and title will allow you to compromise my sister? She spends a night here with you, in this very bedchamber, and her honour is *besmirched*.' He lingered on the word. 'However well bred she might be, however excellent her connections, she is unwed and, apart from myself, defenceless. What will her reputation be now? I had a marriage in line for her, but the bridegroom will surely cry off when he gets wind of this, my lord.'

'As far as I am aware, my care was undertaken by the Captain of the smug—the sailing vessel that rescued me. Harry Lydyard, your brother.'

'Ha! Such pretence does not become you, my lord!'

Light footsteps echoed on the stairs. Sir Wallace flung the door back.

'Come in. Come in. There's scandal in the air, with you at the centre of it, my dear sister. I should have known!' His tone, Lucius noted, despite his expressed concern, was not that of a compassionate brother, but rather that of a hanging judge. 'Once again you have put the Lydyard reputation in jeopardy, leaving me to smooth over the unpleasantness.'

A young woman stepped into the room.

So this was the Lydyard sister. Lucius cast a briefly appraising eye over her. Nothing like her brother in looks, thank God, but nothing more than a country girl with no hint of town bronze. Tall for a girl, her hair was dark, unfashionably long, tied carelessly with a ribbon to cascade in a thick mass of curls to her shoulders and beyond. A neat figure, fine boned and well proportioned. Pleasing enough features in an oval face with well-marked dark brows and a straight uncompromising nose. Her lips as this moment were tense and unsmiling. He would never have guessed at the relationship between the two, except that she did not refute her brother's harsh welcome. Her dress was unfashionably full-skirted and high-collared, drab and plain in an unflattering shade of green. As Lucius was forced to admit, he would not have given the young woman, who looked nothing more than a lowly governess, a second look in a crowded salon in Mayfair. Yet she bore herself with a confidence and an elegant simplicity at odds with her garments. Perhaps because she was no schoolroom miss, but a lady of more than twenty years. She stood just inside the door, calmly waiting for whatever would happen next, her eyes firmly on her brother.

'Miss Lydyard. It is an honour to meet you.' Lucius bowed as gracefully as he could manage despite the torn muscles. He smiled bleakly. 'As I have informed Sir Wallace, we have no prior acquaintance. Any accusations on his part are misinformed. Your honour is without blemish.'

Sir Wallace waved the apology away, his attention on his sister. 'Your guest at the Pride is Lucius Hallaston, Earl of Venmore,' he announced with relish. 'Were you aware of that?'

Entirely composed, Miss Lydyard ignored her brother and curtsied, eyes now lowered. 'My lord. I see you are much recovered.'

It was the voice that did it for Lucius. Cool, low tones, carefully controlled, calmly confident. Astonishing in the circumstances. And then the eyes confirmed it as they rose to meet his across the room. Oh, yes, he could not mistake those eyes. As cool as her voice, grey, almost silver in the morning light, like the flash of sunlight on water at daybreak. And her hands, now clasped firmly before her, her knuckles white, if he were not mistaken. So perhaps she was not as composed as he had thought. Long-fingered, capable hands, able to pull on a rope or manoeuvre a barrel on a moving deck. Or bathe a man's forehead with cool water and bind a wound…

The suspicion transformed itself into a certainty. This was Captain Harry. The knowledge, the memory of the Captain's intimate ministrations, lurched uncomfortably in Lucius's belly.

'So Harry Lydyard tended to you, did he, my lord? I fail to see how you could be unaware.' The words burst from Sir Wallace. 'A foolish notion that no man of sense would believe. This is my sister, Miss Harriette Lydyard. Whom you, my lord, have dishonoured!'

Seeing a chasm opening up before his feet, Lucius viewed the occupants of his borrowed bedchamber with distaste. Miss Lydyard continued to make no response to her brother's recriminations, a matter that earned his reluctant respect, except for the little line that had dug itself between her brows and a tinge of colour to her cheeks. She was not afraid of her brother, nor of the situation, even though her brother was accusing her of immodesty and him of some form of lascivious seduction, remarkable given the condition he had been in! As for the brother… Had he imagined it or had Lydyard's interest grown as soon as he knew his title? Lucius's head might ache, but there was nothing wrong with his wits. Here was a situation that had the makings of a trap set to catch a man of wealth and conse-quence and some degree of honour. How to snap up a prize for a spinster sister who was not in the first flush of youth or blessed with obvious beauty. And he, the Earl of Venmore, was to be the prize. Lydyard had said he already had a marriage arranged for his sister. Like Hell, he had! Lydyard had an eye to the main chance and had leapt to secure it.

Well, he would not be caught in that trap. Lucius's nostrils flared at the audacity of the man. And at the same time caught the eyes of the lady. Grave and solemn, they touched his and held there, and if he were not mistaken there was a plea in their silver intensity. But for what? Perhaps that he should not make it worse for her than it already was. He set himself to do his best. He owed her that much.

'As I recall, Lydyard, not that I recall much of it, I was unconscious for most of the night. I could have spent the night with an entire gang of smugglers in the room, together with their contraband and an invading force of Preventive officers, and been unaware of it.'

But Lydyard's smile widened to show an array of unpleasantly discoloured teeth. 'And would the gossip-mongers of London society believe that? That Earl Venmore spent the entire night with my sister in his room, in an empty house, with her honour still intact at daybreak? Hardly, my lord. My sister will be disgraced. Nor, I hazard, will it do much for your own reputation, robbing an innocent girl of her good name. We may be distant from

London, but news and gossip travels. One of the biggest catches in the marriage market as you are, if I am not mistaken, reduced to seducing and abandoning innocent girls. Will the gossips believe the innocence of all concerned? And your presumed unconsciousness throughout?'

The chasm not of Lucius's making yawned wider. 'No, probably not.'

'For certain they will not! You have rendered my sister unmarriageable, sir!'

And Lucius saw Harriette Lydyard grow pale, as she had never done when she had his blood on her hands. He saw horror dawn and spread over her face in a tightening of the skin along her cheekbones. Still she made no reply. On her behalf as much as his own, anger bubbled up, enough to make him light-headed in his weakened state. He had been neatly trapped, had he not, one disaster following upon the next, but if he read the girl's reaction right, she was as much a victim as he.

So he would take control of this situation. He had had quite enough in recent weeks—more than any man could tolerate—of being outmanoeuvred and manipulated, outwitted and outgunned. Jean-Jacques Noir might have got the better of him in France, but he was damned if he would allow Sir Wallace Lydyard to do so in—where was this God-forsaken place?—Old Wincomlee! Nor would he allow the man to take such a bullying tone of voice with his innocent sister. A vulnerable, gently reared girl did not deserve that.

Hell and the devil! Did he not have enough to plague him without this? But those grey eyes were suddenly dark like a winter sea, wide and anxious.

Harriette continued to stand where she had stood since the beginning of this appalling scene, a mere step into the room, wishing with all her heart that she could remain Captain Harry for just a little while longer. Or that the rotten floorboards of the chamber would collapse beneath her feet and swallow her down into a black hole. Her heart sank to the depth of her scuffed satin shoes. She had hoped to make her escape back to Whitescar Hall with no one being the wiser, certainly without any further conversation between herself and her wounded spy. And here she was, summoned by her brother as if she were a servant. She had managed, if nothing else, to dispose of her breeches, which would have added kindling to the flames, but Wallace, damn him, had come hotfoot. Wallace was furious. She slanted a look towards his unappealing features and her attention was caught. Perhaps Wallace was not so furious as he might wish to appear. Manipulative was more the order of the day. Her half-brother had seen an opportunity and was intent on making the most of it. Harriette did not know whether to descend into hysterical laughter or weep from the sheer incongruity of the whole situation

An earl! Her spy was an earl! Ridiculous. And was, furthermore, accused of dishonouring her. As if her private dreams had blossomed into reality. What arrant nonsense was that?

No point in her arguing the case with Wallace. When he was in this mood, he would listen to neither excuse nor reason, so she might as well keep her silence until he ran out of foolish accusations and the exquisite Earl had made his inevitable rapid escape from Lydyard's Pride.

She risked another glance at the Earl.

The ripple of laughter almost won despite the horrors. Because the Earl of Venmore was a Corinthian. All that Wallace wanted to be, tried so in-effectually to ape, here was his heart's desire in the flesh. Wallace had the ambition to be a sportsman, proficient and lauded for his abilities in the saddle, with pistol and rapier. To be admired for his splendid physique, his handsome looks. To be recognised as a leader of fashion. He never could. And here standing before him was the epitome of all his dreams.

And hers.

Washed, shaved, his hair settling into shining, elegant dishevelment, the Earl cut a splendid figure.

He was taller than she had thought, more than six feet, his shoulders impressively broad beneath the lurid monstrosity, and did she not know at first hand how the muscles ran sleek and smooth, as water over a rock, beneath his skin, the athletic moulding of his strong thighs and firm belly? Did she not know the smooth satin of his skin beneath her palms when she had washed and bound his wounds? And Harriette felt her face and her blood heat at the memory.

How degrading that he should look at her with such arrogance printed on his features, as if she were of no consequence to him. But then why should she be? If he were a man of intellect, the Earl of Venmore would have quickly detected Wallace's disgraceful plotting to catch a husband for her.

Her concentration was dragged back as her brother's anger filled the room.

'You have dishonoured my sister, Venmore. I demand retribution.'

'No...! There was no dishonour,' Harriette gasped, a knot of ice forming in her belly.

'Be silent!' Wallace rounded on her. 'This is not for you. Although many would say you brought it on yourself, cavorting as you do with the Free Traders. *I* will settle this. What hopes for a suitable match if this gets out—as it surely will?'

'Then there is only one remedy, is there not?' A cold interjection in the heat.

The Earl walked across the room towards her, slowly but steadily enough. His eyes were on her face, and Harriette saw banked fire there and recognised a lethal fury at her brother's wily methods. Even so, he bowed before her with inestimable grace.

'Miss Lydyard. There is one solution to restore your good name in the eyes of the world. Would you do me the honour of accepting my hand in marriage?'

Marriage! To become the wife of this man? The knot of ice melted in a rush of heat. If she could choose her heart's desire, would it not be this gift that was being offered to her, as in a childhood fairytale? A precious jewel on a silk cushion? She might have damned him as a traitor, but now she must acknowledge the depth of honour that he should come to her rescue, much as a knight of old would ride to slay the dragon—Wallace—and carry off the damsel in distress.

Would not this miraculous offer make her heady dreams come true?

But Harriette heard herself reply, her voice as distressingly matter of fact as his. 'No, my lord. There is no need. As we both know, my brother was ill informed. I am grateful and will never forget your kindness in making so great a sacrifice, but I must refuse your generous offer.'

She saw him react. That was not what he had expected. The muscles along his jaw tightened.

'Perhaps you do not quite understand the situation, Miss Lydyard.'

'I am not a fool, my lord.' A flash of impatience, which she strove to temper, but without much success. 'I understand *the situation* perfectly. As I see it, there is no *situation* between us.' And gasped as her brother grasped her wrist with painfully hot fingers.

'Show some sense, girl—'

'Sir Wallace,' the Earl interrupted icily, raising a peremptory hand as Harriette tugged ineffectually for her release, 'I need a moment's private conversation with your sister. Alone, if you will. Is there a library or drawing room in this establishment that we can use?'

Sir Wallace drew himself up to his most pompous. 'I'll not allow it. It's not appropriate that you—'

'Sir,' the Earl interrupted bitingly, without finesse, 'if I spent the night with Miss Lydyard behind locked doors as you imply, luring her into my bed and proceeding to destroy her reputation by the physical demands of my body on hers, five minutes in a library in the full light of morning will not make matters any the worse.'

Harriette froze at the brutal description of what had *not* occurred. And for the length of a heartbeat wished that it had.

'Five minutes, then.' Sir Wallace allowed Harriette to pull her wrist away. 'Take his lordship to the library, miss, and try to keep some sense in your stubborn head.'

They descended the stairs, Harriette leading the way into a library as dusty and disused as the rest of the house, what furniture there was shrouded in Holland covers. The leather spines of the few books on the shelves were dull, clearly unread. Immediately the door was closed behind them, a swathed form of a sofa strategically positioned between them, Harriette swung round to face the Earl. Her eyes were clear and bright and very determined. She might have been proud of her earlier reticence, but she could remain silent no longer, even if it meant rejecting the heart-stopping image painted in her mind by the Earl's savage words.

'There's no need for this, my lord. I know what my brother is about. I'll lay odds he didn't suggest marriage until he heard you were an earl!' She saw her sharp cynicism cause a slash of high colour along the Earl's magnificent cheekbones—whether from anger at her brother's presumption or disapproval of her lack of discretion she could not tell— but she would not simper and prevaricate.

'I wouldn't take your odds, Miss Lydyard. Sir Wallace certainly saw the opportunity.'

'I'll wager the *Lydyard's Ghost* he did! To get me off his hands, and to gain a connection with a man of wealth and consequence.' Harriette made no attempt to bury the bitterness. 'My brother is nothing if not ambitious. And I should tell you, I won't do it, just to further Wallace's ambitions. Not even if you were the Prince Regent himself!'

'Fortunately for both of us, I am not!' the Earl responded, taken aback. What was the impression he had gained not ten minutes ago? Here was no innocent, vulnerable, gently reared girl, bullied by her brother. Here was a highly opinionated young woman actually refusing his offer of marriage. And with a forthrightness that, quite frankly, he resented. His lips thinned. 'Would marriage to me be such an anathema, Miss Lydyard?'

'That's not the issue here. What possible advantage could there be for you in such a *mésalliance*? I think you must be all about in your head to even consider it, my lord!'

'The blow from a club might have rattled my senses as a temporary measure,' he snapped back, 'but I think I am sane enough.' *What possible advantage…?* The kernel of an idea began to form in his mind. That such a marriage might just bring him a glimmer of light, an unforeseen advantage….

'We know nothing about each other. How would I fit into your elevated social circle in London? I have no notion how to go on there. I have never been to London, not even further than Brighton. Why would you possibly wish to marry me? A beautiful debutante? No. A wife skilled in the social mores of London? Not that. A rich wife with powerful connections? Not that, either. So why? I am no fit wife for you.' Harriette kept her voice unemotional, ignoring the weight of regret that lay on her heart. He would never know how difficult it was to reject him. 'I am twenty-three years old, my lord!'

'And I am thirty-four, if that is of any interest to anyone but myself.'

She saw the flash of proud temper as she resisted him, but would not retreat. 'I agree your age is irrelevant. Mine is not. I did not think you obtuse, my lord.'

'Obtuse?' His eyes hardened, unused to being challenged.

'I am firmly on the shelf, with nothing to recommend me as a wife, fit for nothing but to be governess to my brother's children.' She stated the uncompromising truth without a quiver, her chin raised.

His face remained stern. 'I commend your shining honesty, Miss Lydyard, but marriage can be the answer—if you are not determined to be so stubborn.'

'What will your family say with a plain nobody like me for a bride, trailing behind you on your expensive doorstep, somewhere I expect, in Mayfair?'

'I have no idea, nor do I care,' he replied, struck by the sad little image. 'It seems to me, Miss Lydyard, that you sell yourself short. You are hardly a nobody. Your family is perfectly respectable.'

But Miss Lydyard did not retreat. 'Respectable! How damning a word is that? Compared with the Hallaston family, the Earls of Venmore, we are *parvenus* indeed. It takes no intelligence to guess the *on dit* of the Season. A common smuggler as the Countess of Venmore! As bad as Lady Lade. I can't wed you, my lord.'

At which he smiled, for the first time with some level of genuine humour. It lit his face, softening his mouth, rendering her instantly breathless. '*Not* as bad as Letty Lade. She, as I recall, before she was elevated to society, was a servant in a brothel and mistress of Sixteen-String Jack, who ended on the gallows. I doubt you, Miss Lydyard, have any such claim to fame.'

His face was alight with laughter, atrociously handsome despite the disfiguring bruises and the vicious path of the knife on his cheek. Harriette was forced to look away, forced to take a steadying breath as her dreams shattered before her eyes. He was not for her. To know that he had offered for her under duress, driven into an honourable gesture by her despicable brother, was entirely shaming for her. Without Wallace's spiked accusations, the Earl of Venmore would never have noticed her, much less invited her to share his life and his bed. She took another breath against the sharp dejection and wished with all her heart it could be otherwise, but she could not, would not, let him be a sacrifice for her brother's greed. It would humiliate her—and him. Marriage on such terms, when all he had shown her was kindness, would be beyond tolerance for both of them.

'Why did you do it?' His soft question surprised her.

'What?'

'Take on the appearance and identity of Captain Harry?'

'A family obligation.' She walked away to look out towards the cliffs where seabirds wheeled and dived in a joyous freedom, finding it easier not to face him.

'It's a hard burden for a family to ask of a young girl.' To her dismay he followed her to stand at her shoulder, a solid physical presence so that she was immediately aware of the heat of his skin against hers, the sheer dominance of his tall figure. But she would not allow herself to feel vulnerable.

'It's not just an obligation.' She felt an inexplicable need to defend herself to him. 'It's the excitement, too. *Lydyard's Ghost* is my own. So is Lydyard's Pride, this house that I love but can't afford to keep and where my brother refuses to let me live.' Unaware, animation coloured her words and her face. 'The smuggling runs have become part of my life. Without them, what do I have before me? I am unwed and unlikely to be so, whatever my brother might say. So I must die of boredom—a never-ending round of embroidery, painting, sedate walks under my sister-in-law's caustic eye. When Zan first took me on a run…' She flushed, regretting having laid herself open to his interest. 'It's in my blood, I suppose.'

'Zan?' he asked.

'Alexander Ellerdine. My cousin. My friend. He showed me the…the satisfaction of it. And since Wallace would not, I took on the family connection. The sea is in my blood, too. Lydyards have always had an interest in the Free Traders.'

The idea that had crept into Luke's mind blossomed into a fully fledged possibility. To rescue Miss Lydyard from dishonour—a matter of duty in itself—and at the same time…the cutter, *Lydyard's Ghost*! He turned to lean, careful of his shoulder, against the window shutter so that he might look directly at her, obliging her to raise her eyes to his.

'Since you don't appear to value my offer of marriage overmuch…' his mouth curled in a touch of self-contempt '…allow me to suggest a contract that might appeal to you Miss Lydyard. A business deal, if you will.'

'A business deal?' That she had not expected.

His eyes narrowed as if he contemplated some distant plotting. 'I find I might have the need for a fast cutter to give me easy access to the French coast. You own such a cutter.'

'Well—yes. But if you need one, would it not be simpler to just *buy* one?' Harriette's brows rose in blatant disbelief. 'Why saddle yourself with a wife?'

He thought fast of the advantages that he might just make use of. 'I need a trustworthy crew and an experienced captain with knowledge of tides. A captain with knowledge of the French coast and a connection there. And speed would be important—might be crucial in my planning. You could offer me all of that.'

Harriette folded her arms. 'I could. Why?'

'A matter of family business. It need not concern you.' And Harriette watched as a grimness settled about the Earl's mouth. It was like a shutter closing, she thought, masking any emotion.

'So you get use of the *Ghost.*' She pursed her lips. 'What do I get?'

'Simple enough.' He lifted a hand, palm spread. 'My title and consequence. My purse strings. I can give you comfort, luxury if that is what you would enjoy, social standing, independence. There will be no compulsion on you to paint or embroider from me! You will no longer be under the eye of either your sister-in-law or your brother. Is that not at least tempting? I own a number of houses that you might like. You might find that you enjoy a London Season.'

'Ha! With nothing to think of but what I wear and what I say, and if I can manage the steps of a country dance at Almack's without tripping over my feet? You should know that I have never been taught to dance, either!' She let the ideal filter through her mind. 'You think that money would matter to me?'

'As a smuggler, I imagine profit is an important consideration for you.'

'You would think that,' she replied enigmatically. If that is what he thought of her... But how should he not since he did not *know* her? 'Why would I choose to escape from my brother into your controlling, my lord?'

'You would not find me too rigorous a husband. Will you do it?'

Harriette studied the unsmiling, masterful features and was not sure, not sure at all. The Earl of Venmore did not seem to have the makings of an easy, tolerant husband. There was suddenly no similarity between this man and the helpless figure who had been tumbled broken and bleeding at her feet. This man who insisted on her striking this remarkable bargain with him.

'I don't know,' she admitted.

'Why not? Consider what a profitable catch I turned out to be.'

There was no mistaking the edge of a sneer in his voice. What a low opinion he appeared to have of her. Well, she would reply in similar vein. 'So there's something in this for both of us. You would be as self-interested as I in finding an advantage in this match.'

'Yes. Why not?'

Harriette dragged in a breath. Here was honesty between them at least. And it was tempting; she felt herself weakening. The Earl of Venmore was clearly a devious man, knowing that independence would be a priceless gift to her. What would it be like to share his life, to share his bed? She shivered at the thought of the Earl's physical ownership of her. It was an image that would destroy her resolution, she admitted in her heart, if she allowed it.

'You said you could not afford the upkeep of this house.' His words brought her back to the present. 'It obviously means much to you. If you wish to spend money to put this place back in order…'

Harriette stared at him.

'…then I could enable you to do it.'

Was he actually offering to pay to resurrect Lydyard's Pride from dilapidation to its former glory? Why would he put himself out to be so persuasive? There was no debt for him to pay. Harriette could find no words to reply between what her heart desired and what her mind informed her was only right and proper. Her mind, of course, had the victory.

'You don't have to, my lord. We both know my honour was not compromised.'

'I know it, as do you. But unfortunately the polite

world is not kind to even the veriest whisper of scandal. It can be cruel and malicious. If you have any ambition to attract a husband, you must be aware of the dangers for you if gossip wags its spiteful tongue.'

He watched her as she thought over his words with utmost seriousness. She frowned a little as she replied, as if her words were painful to her, as they were. 'It seems to me, my lord, that there are far more advantages for *me* in this arrangement. All *you* get is an unsuitable wife and the *Ghost*.'

'And it's important to me.' Surprising her, and perhaps himself, the Earl took her hand in his good right one and Harriette felt an arresting sparkle of light ripple through her blood. His clasp was firm around her fingers, strong with more than a hint of possession. Never in her life had she felt so dominated by a man. She was intensely aware of his forceful presence and their seclusion, of the strength of his will when he had set his mind to a course of action. His words confirmed it. 'Let us have plain speaking between us, Miss Lydyard. Is there someone whom you love, to whom you are promised?'

Harriette shook her head.

'Then we are both without entanglements and of an age to enter into this agreement of our own free will.'

'But that isn't so. I think there is a lady close to your heart.'

His brows twitched together. 'I don't…'

'A lady named Marie-Claude.'

His eyes flashed a warning. 'No. Whatever I said in delirium, you misunderstood, Miss Lydyard. She is nothing to me.' His response held a hard bite. 'I promise to be an attentive and tolerant husband. I will defend your name and your honour with all the power I have. I will not make more demands on you than you are willing to give—and in return you will allow me use of the *Ghost*. Miss Harriette Lydyard, will you do me the honour of accepting my hand in marriage?' His proposal held none of the warm emotion that might be expected in a bridegroom towards the woman who would put her future into his hands, but he kissed Harriette's fingers, lips cool on her skin, that stirred a hot little flame in her heart. 'It would please me, restore us both to the good graces of polite society and solve all manner of problems for you.'

A proposal of marriage. Harriette floundered in a morass of indecision. How remote, how austere he was, as if it meant nothing to him. And perhaps it didn't. She could not do it. It would bring her more sorrow than happiness.

Then the Earl smiled at her. What an impossibly charming smile he had, making him too danger-ously attractive. And suddenly Harriette found herself tottering on the edge of forgetting all her clear reasoning as to why she should not take this step. It was so very appealing. Her gaze was caught by his so that she felt as if she were pulled along as by waves in a strong tide. If she were not careful, she would be dragged inexorably below the surface and then she would be lost…

'Miss Lydyard? My future hangs on your reply.'

'Really?' She looked askance.

'Really, Miss Lydyard!' His mouth firmed into an impatient line.

She must give him an answer of course. And did so with dry appreciation. 'Your tongue is as smooth as French silk, my lord. The only thing I regret is that, if I do agree, it will please my brother.'

'He is no longer of any concern to you. For you, Miss Lydyard, if you will accept my offer, you now belong to me.'

It was outrageously proprietary. Intensely possessive. Very male and very confident. Harriette's heart leaped within the confines of her outmoded bodice. And again, a harder beat, when his clasp tightened and he pulled her slowly towards him. Was he intending to kiss her? Fear struck.

'I should tell you, my lord, that not only can I not dance, but I have never been kissed, either.'

'Then it will be my pleasure to show you how it is done, to consolidate our agreement.'

As a kiss it surprised her. It was very gentle, the softest of meetings of lips, hardly more than a sharing of breath between them. Harriette felt he had made an effort not to frighten her, but now fear was not in her mind. She sighed, taking a step closer, and, sensing it, the Earl slid his good arm around her waist and drew her closer still, firm against his chest, his thighs, whilst his lips warmed and teased. Enveloped by his arms, it was as if all her senses became startlingly alive so that his scent, his touch stroked her, to fill her with a delight that she could never have imagined. Gentle as it was, it reduced her to a shimmer of liquid pleasure. Until he released her, tilted his head as if struck by a thought, before placing a final caress between her brows.

'So we are agreed? It would not be appropriate for me to kiss a lady who was other than my betrothed.'

And Harriette, hopelessly entranced, gasped at his slide into light humour. How could she possibly tell him that he had stolen both her breath and her heart in that one simple undemanding gesture? 'Then I must accept, mustn't I, for I am not in the habit of allowing any gentleman to kiss me. But one thing I would ask.' She lowered her eyes so he would not see the anxiety that began to build in her chest again.

'Since you saved my life, I think I am duty bound to grant whatever you request, Miss Lydyard.'

'I don't want a society wedding. Not at some fashionable church in London under the eyes of the *ton*. Not in the midst of your Corinthian set.'

'Very well. Then where?'

'Here. With a special licence.'

'Then it shall be so.'

Relief swept through her, and astonishment that he would agree so readily. He had not even asked her to explain, something she did not wish to do. 'If I am to escape, then let it be quick. Do you know a bishop, my lord?'

'I think I can lay claim to it.' Then, 'My name is Lucius,' he prompted.

'Lucius.' She tried it on her tongue. Heavy. Classical. Aristocratic. She must have frowned.

His mouth was a touch sardonic. 'If you don't care for it, try Luke.'

'Is that what your family call you?'

'My brother, Adam, does.'

Harriette tried it in her mind. *Luke!* She liked it. It suited his dark good looks. 'Then I will.'

'So we are decided. As long as I don't have to wed you in this garment.'

'I doubt your own coat will be redeemable— although I'm sure you have any number of such fashionable garments. I should tell you I took a knife to the seams. I thought you were bleeding to death.'

'Then I must thank God you did. Although Weston might not be too happy at the destruction of his masterpiece.'

'Whoever Weston might be, he did not have to

deal with an emergency! I promise I won't wed you in boots and breeches.'

'I can ask for nothing more, Captain Harry.'

'I am very grateful.'

Reaching out, he startled Harriette by running a finger along the edge of her jaw, lifting her chin so that she must look up at him. Then with a swift movement belying his bruising, Luke swooped and kissed her again, hard and sure.

His demeanour might be cool, but his mouth held the heat of a searing flame. His previous kiss had warmed her with pleasure. This was a brand that scorched her, fire consuming every inch of her body. It stirred a hunger in her of which she had no experience. It turned her limbs to water. Harriette pressed her hands against his chest, not to make a distance between them but simply to savour the warmth of his body, the solid beat of his heart under her palm.

Then, as quickly as he had taken her, he released her.

'I don't need your gratitude, only your acceptance, Miss Lydyard.'

He took her hand to lead her back to break the news to Sir Wallace, the only sensible thought in Harriette's mind—*What have I done, offering to wed a man whose way of life might be totally immoral?* followed quickly by—*Why would the Earl of Venmore need the use of a fast cutter to get him to France?* A question that lodged, hard and heavy as a stone, in Harriette's chest. For if the Earl intended to use the *Ghost* in some nefarious practice with the enemy—and did all the evidence not point to that?—how could she be attracted to a man who might very well be a spy?

A smuggler. A smuggler as Countess of Venmore? By God! What had he done?

Whilst George Gadie set to work to negotiate the hire of a horse and gig from the tight-fisted landlord of the Silver Boat, Luke was left to juggle a range of unpalatable thoughts, all centring on Harriette Lydyard. For most of them he had no answer. Such as, why had he fought so hard to get her? And what had happened to his legendary charm, his ability to conduct an elegant flirtation, that he had made so ham-fisted an attempt, stricken into damning silence when she had listed her faults and accused him of not wanting a bride such as she? He had simply stood there like an ill-educated and mannerless boor, all his presence of mind buried beneath a cold dose of honesty, skewered by the lady's forthright stare. The fact that all her observations were a fairly accurate reading of the situation was by the by. What had she said? Unfashionable, no fortune, no looks to speak of, past the age of a débutante with no inclination to come out into society.

Dispassionately, the Earl reconsidered his bride.

Miss Lydyard had sold herself short. Blinding honesty was certainly one of her attributes. That's what he would get. An honest, outspoken wife, a capable woman who did not faint at the sight of blood with the courage not to retreat before her brother's bullying and intimidation. His wealth, his title, his entrée into society held no apparent attraction for her. He smiled sardonically at her reaction to his prestigious tailor. Unfortunate Weston! She did not even know who he was.

And, no, she was not unattractive. There was an elusive charm about her, of which he thought even she was unaware. When she had explained about this ruin of a house, full of vital energy, her features had lit, her eyes—and what remarkably beautiful eyes they were—had glowed. No, she was not unattractive at all. When she had smiled, she had been transformed. He thought that he had not seen her laugh, and wished he had. Instead there had been that sudden shadow of fear when she had asked for a discreet wedding. What had that been about? What woman of his acquaintance would resist the chance of a society wedding, to be the envy of the *haut ton* when she became the Countess of Venmore? He was not so naïve that he did not appreciate his own worth as a bridegroom. But there had been a lingering sadness there.

Who would have thought any woman would have

tried so hard *not* to marry him? A harsh laugh escaped him. A wise man, he decided, would make a fast escape and thank the gods for it—but an honorourable man would not. Luke had no intention of allowing Harriette to suffer through the strange workings of fate that had tumbled him into her boat. Nor of his name being coupled with her dishonour. His family name deserved better than that, as did her own.

Would he regret this further complication in his life? He shrugged the thought away abruptly, until his bruised shoulder caused him to hiss through his teeth at the pain. Probably he would. Did he not have enough troubles at the moment with discovering the present whereabouts of Mademoiselle Marie-Claude? He frowned, not seeing a way forward there, and contact with Jean-Jacques Noir was becoming hazardous. Should he tell Harriette about that? No. Not yet, at least. Better to keep his mouth tightly shut and his fears to himself—as he had been warned that he must.

For now he had the prospect of a wife, the last thing he wanted at this point in his life when he was living a lie and burdened with guilt, but in all honour, he could not abandon her. A strange alliance. A smuggler and a…what? Spy? Traitor? Some would undoubtedly say the latter. An unscrupulous pairing, but Miss Lydyard had the *Ghost*, too good a chance to miss it if it allowed him to save an innocent young woman from harm.

And whatever happened, he would make sure Miss Harriette Lydyard did not suffer for her compliance.

Would Harriette Lydyard enjoy being a countess? Somehow he doubted it. He would wager she would rather face a gale-force wind in the *Lydyard's Ghost* than a dress ball. But she wanted freedom from family restrictions; he saw the value of a fast ship to France. Both had an eye to a main chance, as she had observed in those cool tones of disdain, pure self-interest for both of them.

And what did he think of a girl who wore breeches and boots, evaded the law and ran the gauntlet of the Revenue men without any hint of fear? He ought to be outraged. Luke smiled wryly. Somehow he could not summon that emotion in his dealings with Miss Harriette Lydyard. He ought to be thoroughly outraged, condemning her morals and her sense of propriety. Even now, their final exchange in the library remained to echo uncomfortably in his mind.

As he was about to open the door, Harriette had stopped him. 'If I am to wed you, does this mean that you would prefer me to give up smuggling?'

'Yes,' he had replied in some surprise, without hesitation. 'How could I wish my wife to be involved in criminal activities? Ah!—that's to say…'

'I suppose you think it's a vicious, damnable trade.' She must have seen him searching for a tactful response. 'Most people do, you know, even though it puts food into the mouths of poor women and children in fishing villages, who might otherwise starve.' She raised her hand when he might have replied. 'I understand—you don't have to hide your condemnation of it, or me. I will just say this, my lord. I will consider retiring from the Trade, because it is your preference.'

And that was as much as she would promise. Now he must live with the consequences. Was it possible to build a future on a fleeting and wholly inexplicable admiration for Miss Lydyard, simply because she had rescued him and saved his life? An admiration because she had faced him and flung his offer of wealth and consequence at his feet as so much dross?

One memory remained with him. That, smuggler or no, she had been eminently kissable. He had tasted her lips and found them as soft and sweet as any he might dream of. Lucius had been astonished at the response of his body, even in its weakened state. Lured into kissing her a second time, a surge of desire had taken him aback; his loins had tightened in powerful arousal when her lips parted beneath the pressure of his mouth. Her slender, competent hands pressed against his chest had lit a curl of heat in his belly at the same time as a purely masculine urge to protect her from the dangerous life she was living. He wanted her! Even now, at the memory of her slender form held in his arms, he experienced the same physical urgency to do exactly what her despicable brother had accused him of doing.

It's only a strong dose of lust, he informed himself sternly. A woman and a smuggler—a scandalous situation that has piqued your imagination—nothing more.

Luke frowned at his logical assessment. Perhaps. And yet—those pretty lips might speak sharp words, but they could lure a man's soul from his body if he did not take care. And being a man of sense, with other demands on his time and his emotions, he would do just that.

Chapter Four

'A countess, indeed!'

'Unless I imagined it all.' Sitting in her bedchamber in Whitescar Hall, Sir Wallace's stuffily respectable home, it seemed far beyond Harriette's comprehension.

'There'll be no speaking to you with such consequence!' Meggie's eyes twinkled, then grew flat, anxious. 'Do you suppose he means it?'

'I think he would rather not!' Harriette replied with disconcerting candour. 'He only did so at Wallace's insistence that my reputation would be compromised beyond redemption if he did not. Which just goes to show you can't trust Wallace. For years he's been lecturing me that, because of my hard-headedness in *consorting* with the Gentlemen of the Free Trade, I have no reputation to speak of.'

'Of course you have. You should have been married years ago, and would have if your brother would put himself out for you and spend a little money on you. But her ladyship has you in mind as unpaid governess of her spoilt brats as soon as they leave the nursery, you mark my words.'

Which Harriette knew very well. She imagined, dismally, the prospect of teaching her two nephews to mind her and their manners, when their doting mother did nothing but give in to their imperious demands. Unless she snatched at this opportunity with both hands. She looked down at her hands, turning them over, then over again, as if she could still see the imprint of his fingers where they had held her. As if she could still feel his sheer strength of will as he had worn down her resolve not to allow him to be a martyr to her brother's vile machinations. And he had kissed her—twice—so it could not have been an unpleasant experience for him. For a moment it was as if the Earl stood beside her, a bold, commanding figure, so that her heart jolted and the nerves in her belly skittered like mice behind the skirting boards. Until, aware of Meggie asking a question, she looked up.

'Forgive me, Meggie. I was daydreaming…'

'I asked what you would wear for your wedding.'

'I have no idea.' She shrugged, pretending indifference. 'I have nothing that was made any time within the last decade.'

'No, you haven't. And you're not likely to get

anything new from her ladyship. Is that why you wouldn't go to London for the ceremony?'

'Of course not!' But, uncomfortable under Meggie's cynicism, Harriette sighed. 'Then, yes. Do you blame me?' To present herself in St George's in Hanover Square, to be gawped at and gossiped over, every inch of her open to ridicule and disparagement—she would die of embarrassment. But there was another reason, as well. After all his kindness, how could she open the Earl to that same sharp-edged contempt? If she was to be his wife, she would not make the burden even more heavy. She owned it to him not to create more scandal than would inevitably occur with such a hasty and unworthy match.

So a wedding at Old Wincomlee with no one but the rector and the necessary witnesses would serve them very well. 'And I will wear nothing of Augusta's choosing,' she declared. 'She has no taste and would have me clad in puce or green, both of which I detest. And feathers!' Harriette managed the smallest smile as she caught Meggie's scowl. 'Enough of this, Meggie. It's foolish talk. Shall I be honest between the two of us? I doubt I'll see the Earl of Venmore ever again. If he has any sense, he'll bolt for London and not come near Old Wincomlee. What man of sense would tie himself into a relationship with Wallace and Augusta? And without doubt, I am no catch!'

'Miss Harriette! Have I taught you to be so untrusting of the male sex?'

'No, but Wallace doesn't inspire me to trust, and you can hardly blame the Earl, can you, if he banishes me from his thoughts?'

'I suppose you pointed out to his lordship all the unappealing consequences of a marriage to you.'

Harriette held Meggie's fierce expression. 'Of course I did. I could hardly accept his offer when the choice was not his.'

'You're too honest for your own good, miss. Anyone would think you didn't want him.' Meggie stood foursquare, hands on hips. 'Now listen to me, miss. It seems to me the Earl's a man with his own mind of how to go on. He'll not be pushed and bullied against his will by such as Sir Wallace. If he says he wants to wed you, then wed you he will. Don't you want him?'

'Do I want him?'

If Harriette closed her eyes, she could bring Lucius Hallaston's face to mind without difficulty. She could hear his voice, supremely confident, and his specific words as if they were engraved on her heart. He had commended her *shining honesty*. That was better than nothing, wasn't it? His formal kiss on her fingers. It probably meant nothing to him other than good manners, but to her it was a revelation. And then his mouth on hers, first light and unthreatening, but entirely masculine, and then boldly demanding. The sensation of his body pressed dominantly against hers. She knew every inch of that body, did she not? Sleek-muscled, smooth-skinned, impressively male. Harriette could not repress a shiver along the skin of her arms. Did she want him? Yes. Oh, yes, she did, even if he did not want her, even if he found the *Ghost* of higher value than her own person.

What had he said? *You belong to me now.* Harriette shivered again.

'Yes, Meggie,' she admitted, 'I do.'

'Then that's settled. And if he asked you to wed him, then I swear, it'll happen. Otherwise he would've told Sir Wallace to go to the Devil and good riddance, reputation or no reputation. He'll be back here before you know it.'

'He might.' A wry twist of her lips. 'It depends on how much he wants the *Ghost*. And what he wants to use it for.'

'What possible use would he have for a smuggling cutter?'

'I don't know.' It hurt to think about it. 'I suspect that was the attraction rather than my hand in marriage!'

Meggie clicked her tongue. 'Never mind that. Come with me.'

Harriette followed Meggie up a mean, ill-lit rear staircase to the top floor of Whitescar Hall that housed the servants and the nursery where Harriette was intended to live out her days as unpaid governess. She marched past that closed door to the end of the corridor where Meggie entered a room that was unused. An iron bedstead, a chair, a nightstand with bowl and ewer, all draped in Holland covers.

'Help me, miss.' Flicking aside an old velvet curtain that served as a dustsheet, they began to manoeuvre one of two large chests from beside the wall. Snapping open the hasps, Meggie lifted the lid.

'Goodness. What's this?'

The pungent scent of lavender rose from the interior to make Harriette sneeze. Inside were layers of linen wrappings, with glimpses of delicate materials.

'Your mother's clothes. What I could get my hands on, anyway.'

'My mother's?' Astonishment stilled Harriette's hands on the edge of the chest. 'I thought my father had rid himself of all her things… And that Wallace finished off what my father had missed.'

'Well, I kept these,' stated Meggie grimly. 'It was wrong to rob you of all your memories of her, to destroy her name as if she'd never existed, just because she was a French lady and we took to war against the bloody revolutionaries. Doesn't seem sense to me. A kinder, more gentle lady… So I locked these away from prying fingers. For you,

Miss Harriette, if you should ever need them. Though sadly old fashioned they are now…'

Harriette's astonishment grew. Meggie, one of the least sentimental of women, yet here she had kept her mother's memory alive.

'They would have been destroyed, or Lady Augusta would have taken them,' Meggie continued with thinned lips. 'Can't have that, can we?'

'I have nothing of hers.' Dismayed to feel the burn of tears, Harriette swallowed hard, staring down into the chest as if she could conjure her mother's image from the contents.

'Well, now you do. Not fashionable, but better than anything *you* own. They'll fit you, too. The colours are still good.'

With little more than a vague recollection of her mother, Harriette had been brought up on Meggie's tales of a romantic but sad figure. Chantelle Marie-Louise D'Aspre. Even her name was romantic. Wooed by her father on a visit to Paris in the days of the old King, he had swept her off her feet, married her and brought her back to Whitescar Hall. Had Chantelle felt as hemmed in as her daughter? Perhaps she had not lived here long enough, dying from some unexplained fever before her baby daughter was six years old.

'All very stylish when she was a young girl,' Meggie reminisced. 'Nigh on thirty years ago now, of course, when she came to Whitescar Hall. So lovely and full of life, she was. She deserved better than your father, God rest him!'

Together, they lifted out the layers, exclaiming at the sumptuous magnificence of their discoveries. French fashions with fitted bodices and full skirts, hand embroidered, quantities of silver lace, the glorious materials sliding and drifting through their fingers. Nothing like the prevailing mode for high waists and narrow skirts, but the quality was of the best and, even if said with deliberate waspishness by Meggie, it was not difficult to find something better than anything Harriette owned.

'There, Miss Harriette.' Meggie lifted a quantity of silk, soft cream, embroidered with tiny flowers, from the bottom. 'If I'm not mistaken, you have your wedding gown here.'

Harriette flushed with pleasure. If the Earl did return—not that she had any great hope, of course—what would he think if he saw her clad in this glory of silk and lace?

Luke's journey to Brighton was uncomfortable, excruciatingly painful when the gig discovered every hole and rut in the road, but surprisingly illuminating on the subject of his reluctant betrothed. Sam Babbercombe of the Silver Boat sent a young lad with him to drive the gig and return it to its rightful owner. From this enterprising youth who saw himself as a budding whip, Luke learnt a lot about Captain Harry. Clearly the lad admired him— her—his pronouns tended to be mixed—and he was pleased to be voluble, passing on a range of opinion and fact. Nothing that would recommend the lady as a suitable countess, but it said much of her life in Old Wincomlee.

Luke listened, gaining a sense of his bride's loneliness and isolation, and of her improper lifestyle. The Captain was a good sailor. Never seasick and always pulled his—her—weight. Brave as a lion, she was. Could use a pistol, too. She once fired at a Revenue man who was threatening to club Gabriel Gadie on the head, not to kill him, but winged him pretty well so he dropped the club.

She made a rare Captain, not like that brother of hers who was a disgrace to the name Lydyard. Sir Wallace—he'd never set foot in a boat, much less led a midnight run to the French coast. Enjoyed the brandy well enough, but the Lydyard blood had run thin with that one. Now Mr Alexander Ellerdine— Miss Harriette's cousin—he was a good man. But Captain Harry? She didn't turn a hair when faced with injury or blood. Good hands she had, with man or beast, as his lordship would know. Had she not patched his wounds…?

Luke let the boy ramble on, taken by the notion that

if Captain Harry had doctored his wounds, as she clearly had, then she had seen him stripped and naked. Had touched him, bathed and cared for him. He had no recollection of it, except perhaps for a hazy memory of waking in pain, with cool water on his face and chest, cool hands on his skin. He could imagine those grey eyes taking in every inch of his exposed body. His muscles tightened, an uncomfortable jolt of primitive desire through his belly, at the fleeting memory of her most intimate attentions. But Captain Harry—or Miss Lydyard—had taken on the task without comment, with no sign of embarrassment.

He turned back to his loquacious coachman. Captain Harry sailed the cutter whilst Mr Alexander was happy to take the organisation on the land from Captain Harry's shoulders. Good friends, they were, too. Brought up together. Wouldn't be a surprise to anyone if a match wasn't made between the pair of them. Captain Harry could do much worse and Mr Alexander had a warm spot for his cousin….

Luke's ears pricked up. A cousin and a good friend. Had Miss Lydyard not admitted the same? But a match between them—she had said nothing of that, not even when he had asked her if she had affection for another man. Any other emotion was immediately dispelled from his mind by a bolt of intense jealousy. Unwarrantable, illogical jealousy, clawing at his skin, as remorseless as the ache from the bullet wound in his arm. She was *his* bride. She would be *his* wife.

How can you be protective of her, when you have only just met her, when you have no claim on her affections? Cold realism raised its head to replace the heat of possession. *This is a marriage of pure necessity, not of love, made on the back of a cold, bloodless business agreement. A man can only experience jealousy over a woman who owns his heart. Miss Lydyard intrigues you, nothing more.*

Before he could consider his reaction to this uncomfortable advice, they were into the lanes and streets of Brighton and Luke directed the lad to the Castle Inn where he had left his curricle at the start of his escapade, which effectively directed his thoughts away from Harriette and back to Jean-Jacques Noir, the man with whom he had dealings in Port St Martin. A rogue who had robbed him and left him with a bullet wound as a brutal warning. Never again, Luke vowed. No Hallaston of Venmore would ever again be at the mercy of the French ruffian. He would not be set on and fleeced next time. *He* would set the terms. And if Noir wanted guineas from him, then he would have to dance to Luke's tune. Particularly since he now held a new card in his hand—a neat little cutter with a well-trained crew. How he might make use of this advantage was at the moment beyond his comprehension, but the chance might arise…

But as he ordered a tankard of ale and waited whilst his horses were harnessed, the looming problem of Jean-Jacques Noir, one that had ruled his whole life for the past two months, was once again thrust from his mind. A challenging figure in water-stained boots and breeches, wind-tangled hair curling onto her shoulders, silver eyes glinting, Harriette Lydyard stole his attention.

And what thoughts would be running through Harriette Lydyard's mind at this moment, he wondered, lines of cynicism hard around his mouth? Probably entertaining as much doubt about the whole affair, he acknowledged, as his own.

Restless and moody, Harriette was forced to undergo a week of intense boredom. Under orders to remain at Whitescar Hall and not set foot within the doors of Lydyard's Pride or on the deck of *Lydyard's Ghost*, she was finally contemplating disobedience as she idly flicked though the pages of the *Lady's Gazette* in one of the parlours. If Venmore was gone for good, what was the purpose in her sitting here waiting for him? She might as well resume her old life and launch the *Ghost*. For the first time in her memory, it did not appeal—why was her life so unattractive, so lacking in colour and excitement, after Venmore's cataclysmic arrival in her cutter? She cast the magazine aside as a tap on the French windows from the terrace startled her. The window opened.

'Hush!' Alexander warned, closing it quickly behind him, shutting out the spaniel that would have followed on his heels. 'I've no wish to attract Augusta's attention.' He entered with flourish of fresh air and energy and mud on his boots that brought a smile to Harriette's lips.

'Zan.' Harriette stood and held out her hands in greeting. 'Come and talk to me. I'm paralysed by boredom. Let Toby in if you wish. He doesn't bother me.'

She could not remember her life without Alexander, a few years older than Harriette, at its centre. Son of her father's sister, her own strong-willed Aunt Dorcas, and James Ellerdine, a local and entirely ineffectual landowner, Alexander had been a wilful child and had grown into a man driven by a love of outwitting the authorities. A love of money, too, Harriette suspected. They had been friends for ever, from the days when they had run wild on the beach, Harriette escaping from her governess, Alexander from a father who would have turned him into a farmer and a dull lord of the manor. Mr James Ellerdine had no inkling that his son had taken up with the Free Traders and would have disapproved if he had. Nor did Harriette know of it until the day when Alexander took her on her first smuggling run, revealing for her the heady thrill of it all, a remedy against soul-crushing boredom, against the terrible drag on her spirits of seemly respectability, as imposed by Lady Augusta.

And when they were in danger of being discovered, it was Alexander who sprang to her aid, providing her with a ready defence against Wallace's disapproval. Harriette had thus spent many fictional nights at Ellerdine Manor when Aunt Dorcas was still alive, whereas in reality she had been perfecting her skills as a member of the brotherhood of Free Traders. Alexander had always been her true friend.

An attractive man with the dark hair and deep blue eyes of his father, a lithe and athletic build, no none could have blamed Harriette if she had set her cap at him. But she never had, had never felt the inclination. Why she did not respond to him as a grown woman to a handsome man she had no idea, but Alexander was her cousin, no more, no less than that.

Now he stood before her, his mouth stern. 'You can't do it, Harry.'

'I have to. Augusta says I must mend my ways, at least until the wedding…'

'I don't mean not leave the house!' His tone was sharper than usual. 'You can't marry him!'

'Oh, that.' She laughed softly. 'I can, you know. And I will. How did you know about it? I thought it was all to be secret until the fateful day and the knot tied! Just in case the Earl makes a run for it and we never see him again.'

'Servants' gossip,' he snapped. 'I thought *you* might have told me. How can you even consider it, Harriette? All that nonsense about your honour being compromised. Typical Wallace, of course. You shouldn't have let yourself get pushed into it. Listen to me, Harry! Tell Wallace you've changed your mind.'

'I can't.'

'Why can't you?'

'Wallace says I need a husband.'

'Then tell him that you'll wed me instead.'

Momentarily Harriette was lost for words. Perhaps her cousin was merely funning—although she could not think him guilty of such insensitivity—but obviously he did not mean it, or why had he never given any sign of a desire for marriage before? She replied in as light a mode as she could, 'I won't, dear Zan—because you haven't asked me. Nor do you have to. It's not necessary to rescue me, you know.' She squeezed his hands, grateful for his thoughtfulness. 'I'm quite resigned to it. I might even enjoy it and find a taste for fashionable life.'

'No. Never. I'm asking you now, Harriette.' Such urgency drove him that Harriette felt Alexander's fingers tighten uncomfortably around hers. 'Wed me. I can give you a good life, all the comfort you could wish for, even if not the luxury at Venmore's disposal. We'll live at Lydyard's Pride. Isn't that what you want?'

'But you don't love me.'

'Neither does he.' Alexander released her hands and took an impatient turn around the room, treading mud as he went. 'But at least I know you, and you know me. You know I'll never beat you or neglect you or give you cause for jealousy. Besides—how do you know I don't love you?'

'Because you've never mentioned it until now. I don't expect Venmore will do any of those things, either,' she replied, unsure whether to be startled or mildly amused at her cousin's venom. 'I can't marry you, Zan. I have agreed to wed the Earl. You should be grateful to me for refusing you. You will when you meet a girl who takes your heart.'

Completing another circuit, Alexander grasped her hands again, his eyes fierce. 'Do you want me to make lover-like assurances? I can do that. I have always had an affection for you, Harry. We'll deal well together. You can have the sort of life you want, away from Wallace and Whitescar Hall.'

'You are very kind, and I know you mean well, but—'

'Do you want his money, his consequence?' A scowl descended on Alexander's attractive features.

Harriette had never known him so impatient or unjust, except when a run was threatened through bad weather or a patrolling body of Preventive men. Yet here he was attacking her, accusing her of an arrogance she could not recognise in herself. 'I would not have believed it of you, that you would rather tie yourself to him than to me for the sake of a title.'

'But that's not true, and you know it,' she replied in brittle denial. 'I have no ambition to be a countess. How can you say that after all the years we have known each other?'

'It seems like that to me.'

'Then you have misunderstood me.' Now Harriette allowed a spurt of temper to break through her disbelief—an unexpected rift threatened, emerging from nowhere. Surely Zan knew her too well to attack her with such intolerance? 'Don't frown at me, Zan. There's enough unhappiness without us being at odds.'

But Alexander was not to be won over. 'He'll want you to stop smuggling.'

'Yes, he does.'

'And will you? Will you obey him—a dutiful little wife?'

She might wince at the jibe, but Harriette lifted her chin. 'He has not ordered me to do so. But it is what he wants. I owe him that, and it's not for you to discuss.'

'Venmore will demand you give up the Free Trade, see if he doesn't.'

'No, you are wrong. He has not *demanded* it. Don't let us quarrel over it, Zan.'

Alexander looked as if he might ignore her plea, then it seemed to Harriette that he took a step back from the brink. 'I thought we could live at Lydyard's Pride together,' he replied more mildly. 'Make it our home.'

'No, we can't. I know you love the house as much as I, and it was your own mother's legacy that she willed to me, but it's not possible.'

As if he could find no more words of persuasion, his eyes searched her face, fingers tight around her wrists, holding her hands palm to palm.

'Zan?' She pulled firmly away. 'You don't really want me as your wife, you know.'

And he relaxed, releasing her. Rubbed his hands over his face as he laughed lightly. 'Forgive me, Harriette. You must think me a bully—as bad as your brother.' He leaned forwards to kiss her cheek in cousinly affection. 'Very well. Have what you will and I'll not stand against you. I'll wish you all happiness for your future. And remember that I will always be your friend.'

There, it was gone. The shadow, the displeasure, the determination to get his own way. Harriette, too, relaxed with a wistful smile at her cousin. She had been mistaken. He only wanted to rescue her after all.

Alexander headed back towards the window where the spaniel waited patiently. The smile he cast her over his shoulder was as sharp as the wind that stirred the dried leaves in the beech hedging beside the terrace. 'All he can offer is a title and a bottomless purse.'

'Is he as wealthy as that?'

'Of course. Didn't you know? The Hallastons are as proud as the devil and could purchase Lydyard's Pride twenty times over with the change in their pockets and not notice the loss.'

'I didn't know. ·

'I wager Wallace did! Or why the urgency to snap Venmore up? Never mind, Harriette—' as she felt colour drain from her face '—I doubt Venmore will blame you for his predicament. Just don't lose your heart to him, will you?'

'Of course not! I wouldn't do anything so ill judged.'

But she feared—she knew—that somewhere between his landing in a bloody puddle in her boat and his unemotional statement that she now belonged to him, she had done just that. Even the thought of marriage to Lucius Hallaston, however unlikely it might be, of being kissed by him, owned by him, fluttered the nerves in her belly and drove bright colour to her cheeks.

Alexander smiled. 'Then all I can do is to wish you every happiness, cousin.'

Perhaps she had imagined the lack of enthusiasm in his reply. As for Alexander's rescuing her—why, in the core of her heart, she had no desire to be rescued at all.

Chapter Five

The Earl of Venmore waited outside the little church of St Mary the Virgin in Old Wincomlee, contemplating whether Miss Harriette Lydyard would put in an appearance for her marriage or whether, in his absence she had turned in revolt against her brother and had changed her mind. He consulted his watch—a new purchase. She was late. Above the stand of elms to the left of the church he could make out the wings and chimney stacks of Whitescar Hall, the Lydyard residence. Should he go and hammer on the door and ask for the lady?

Probably to be told that Captain Harry was somewhere in the Channel, escaping to France, battling against the waves in the *Lydyard's Ghost*!

She was late.

Frustration—or was it actually fear that she would leave him standing at the altar?—shortened his temper. Luke found himself at a loss. In truth, he had never met such resistance in a lady, and to his sardonic amusement, it did not sit well with him. Unaware, he placed his palm over his breast pocket, over the letter he had received to his surprise the previous week. An unusual letter from a bride to her prospective bridegroom.

> *My lord,*
> *I shall understand if you decide that marriage to me is not what you want and that you do not wish to be coerced into it. No one can pretend that I am suitable material for a countess. Nevertheless, I shall be at the church at the time and date specified. If I do not see you then, I would thank you for your attempts to deflect my brother's wrath from my shoulders.*
> *It would after all be an easy matter for you to buy a fast cutter to get you to France.*
> *I wish you well for the future and hope that you revise your need, whatever it might be, to work with Monsieur Noir.*
> *Harriette Lydyard*

Quaint. Merciless in its summing up of the situation. Appallingly direct. Perhaps it would be better all round if Miss Lydyard did decide to cry off, better for both of them. And since no one outside this village knew of the match, it would be no harm done.

And yet, Luke discovered, that was not what he wanted at all. Miss Lydyard was more of an attraction than her cutter. He was considering this strange whim when George Gadie rounded the west buttress, hove to beside him and saluted him with a grin.

'She's on her way, y'r honour. A slight disagreement, do y'see, about whether to get out the coach... Miss Lydyard wouldn't.'

And there she was, walking briskly towards him.

Luke felt an easing of the constriction in his chest.

She had got her own way and walked, approaching along the path from the side gardens of the Hall to the Church, Sir Wallace and Lady Augusta following at some distance. Miss Lydyard covered the ground swiftly, creating a charming picture to take his eye. Dappled summer sunshine illuminated her through the soft green of the elm leaves and the frisky breeze ruffled her skirts and ribbons as she strode towards him, as if conscious of her lateness, with fluid and vibrant elegance.

But this vision of Miss Lydyard was not what he had expected. Not at all. He had seen her in breeches and boots. He had seen her in a dowdy, unappealing gown that did not flatter and had seen better days. Now this lady...! Even if she did stride towards him as if she were about to board *Lydyard's Ghost*. The Earl of Venmore cast an experienced eye over his betrothed, soon-to-be bride.

French style and gloss, was his first thought, from the days before the Revolution, before fashions began to move in the direction of austerity. It was a dress of spring, of romance, cream silk embroidered with sprigs of flowers in softest palest green and yellow. Full skirts caught back with cream ribbons from a plain satin petticoat embroidered and rouched round the hem. Elbow-length sleeves allowed a fall of fine lace. A fitted bodice emphasised her waist, quite different from any garment a connoisseur of London fashions would have designed for the Countess of Venmore. A lace-edged scarf in finest linen crossed over the bosom to tie behind. Altogether remarkably pretty, both feminine and frivolous. And someone had tamed her hair to catch it up on the crown of her head in cream ribbons, to fall in luxuriant curls to her shoulder. The *débutantes* of the *haut ton* would *never* have worn such a gown, but Harriette Lydyard did so with style.

Which realisation struck Luke as solidly as a punch to his well-muscled stomach. So that was it—and he had never even given it a thought. An obvious reason for Miss Lydyard, if she had any pride, not to want a society wedding. She had nothing fashionable to wear and her brother, now that the groom was caught and at the altar, was not going to waste more money than he need on the bride.

He *should* have thought of it. The fact that he had not given it even the slightest consideration caused him a momentary brush of shame. Of late he had acquired an ingrained selfishness, not a desirable quality in a man of his breeding, he admitted with a grimace. He should have provided her with something suitable—an easy enough task to send a dress as a wedding gift. But there again, he thought, she might have too much pride to accept such a gift from him. For her it would have hammered home once again the vast distance between them as she had so coolly listed for him. The problem, he mused as Miss Lydyard came to a halt in front of him, was that he did not know her. All had to be achieved through guesswork and careful manoeuvring if he did not wish to ride roughshod over her sensibilities. And as yet he did not know what those sensibilities were.

But now she was here, standing before him, cheeks flushed becomingly from the speed of her approach, eyes sparkling, lips curved in a delicious smile. How could he have ever considered reneging on his promise to wed her? And, taken aback by this fragile vision in silk and lace, by a need to sweep her up and protect her from the cruel jibes of high society, the Earl of Venmore could do nothing but take his smuggler's hand in his and kiss the tips of her fingers. They fluttered in his hold.

'Miss Lydyard. I swear, a man never met so elegant a bride at the church door,' he said gallantly.

'Pretty words,' she replied with a tilt of her head. 'The bride is not as elegant as her bridegroom. I wasn't sure you'd come.'

'Am I not a man of my word?'

'I don't know,' she replied with devastating frankness. 'Perhaps it depends on how much you need the use of my cutter. You never did tell me what you were doing in France!'

'Miss Lydyard, you do me an injustice.' Luke felt the sting of irritation. No, he was not completely altruistic in his motives, and his forthright bride had unerringly homed in on it. Now was not the time to dwell on it. With solemn gallantry, he tucked her hand beneath his arm. 'Whatever doubts you may have, you may be certain that I need to fulfil my promise to you!'

Her smile lit her eyes, transforming her face with sudden beauty. 'Good. Then let us do it before we both change our minds! Then we can escape Wallace's prosing on the sad state of my reputation!'

'Well, my lady, the deed is done.'

'Yes.'

Harriette was astonished. Her marriage to the Earl of Venmore was completed, over and done within the time it took to launch *Lydyard's Ghost*, the gold ring with its circle of sapphires, a Hallaston heirloom, securely on her finger. Wallace had hidden his triumph. Augusta did not try. Alexander stood in dour but silent acceptance. Meggie looked apprehensive. As for the groom, he spoke the required words with solemn composure that soothed her nerves and allowed her breathing to settle. The only time she had felt any reaction from him was when her name was read by the Reverend Dance—Harriette Marie-Louise d'Aspre Lydyard. A sharp acknowledgment in the tautness of his arm beneath her fingers. He had not known of her French blood, of course, and she had not thought to tell him. Would he object? But then why should he? Though he might, of course, consider a smuggler with French blood too much for a man to accept in the present political climate.

Otherwise Harriette could not fault him, the epitome of fashion and elegance, as far from the dishevelled spy as she could imagine, his good looks enhanced by the understated quality of the striped silk waistcoat, deep blue coat, the impeccably ruffled shirt and the exact arrangement of his cravat. And to his credit the Earl had not decided to overawe them with a fashionable entourage, nor had he brought any members of his family with him. A relief, yet Harriette struggled with the conflict it set up within her own mind. Perhaps he was ashamed of her after all; perhaps he appreciated the value of a wedding far from critical eyes even more than she.

Would anything ever be straightforward again?

This was no good! Harriette had made her vows clearly, with no maidenly modesty, almost in a challenge. All she could do was to be herself. The Earl had agreed to wed her and must take her on trust. They must both make the best of a dubious bargain.

Yet for her it was not a bad bargain at all. At his side in the cool gloom of the little church, she had risked a glance. Sensing it, Luke had turned his head, held her gaze, and smiled. Within the shadows of the church his eyes were dark and fathomless, impossible to read. Dignity made her return the contact despite the flush it brought to her cheeks, but beneath the calm exterior, desire made her heart tremble. How splendid he was. He moved with far more ease now, as his torn muscles healed. The bruising on his temple had almost vanished, a mere shadow, whilst the scar on his cheek was healing fast. Perhaps it would not even leave a mark to mar his striking looks. For now it made him attractively rakish, and formidably handsome. During his absence she had forgotten a little and had managed to control her fluttering nerves, but now they reappeared, a cloud of butterflies, just when she needed all her confidence for what she must ask him as soon as they were wed.

'I didn't know of your French connections,' Luke commented as they stepped from the church porch out into the sunshine.

So he *had* reacted. Harriette's regard was firm, steady. 'My mother was French. Does it matter?'

'No. Just that you had never mentioned it.'

'Not everyone is so tolerant since we are at war. My father preferred to forget her when she died. My brother prefers to forget my connection with the enemy.'

'I'm sorry.' A little silence that Harriette could not interpret. Then, when it almost became uncomfortable, 'Do you need to return to Whitescar Hall?' Luke kept possession of her hand, neatly tucked through his arm so that she was acutely aware of the heat of his body, could feel the steady beat of his heart against her. Such warnings of future intimacy that she could not imagine. She swallowed. Her nerves were returning in force, shivering over her skin that felt sensitive to every movement of the silk of her gown.

'No,' she replied abruptly. 'I have all I need with me.' She indicated Meggie, who stood, two band-boxes at her feet, beside the Earl's smart curricle, gleaming dark blue, with a pair of glossy dark bays.

'Then shall we go? We can rest overnight on the way to London. Have you a warm coat with you?'

Harriette closed her fingers on the fine material of

his sleeve, steeling herself. 'One thing I would ask, my lord. I know you would not want this, but…'

His eyes gleamed quizzically. 'If I cannot grant my bride her heart's delight on the day of her wedding… And I will do so if you will call me Luke as we agreed.'

'Luke.' She took a breath. 'I want to stay at Lydyard's Pride tonight.'

'You do?' She could hear his surprise. Why would anyone want to stay in so run-down a house? Except that it had a place in her heart, and tonight, for the last time, before she put it all behind her, it was important that she did. For herself. For those who had depended on her for so long. But she would not tell him that. 'Then we shall.' He lifted her hand from where he had held it against his arm, but only to entwine his fingers with hers, so particular a symbol of unity between them. Lifting their interlaced hands, he kissed her knuckles lightly, perhaps an insignificant gesture, but one to set her heart to trip against her whalebone stays. Then, not insignificant at all to Harriette, he bent his head to touch his lips to her cheek.

Such a light kiss, entirely appropriate in public from a groom to his bride, but to Harriette with her heightened senses it seemed shockingly intimate. As the blood rushed to her cheeks, she felt an unaccustomed shyness descend. She would have to learn to deal with this man if she was to hide her emotions from him. What a burden it would be for him to know that a wife, taken for convenience, without either friendship or affection between them, threatened to melt into a puddle at his feet from a passing kiss to her cheek!

'I've had some of the rooms put to rights at the Pride,' she informed him as if that were the most important thing in the world, not the riotous surge of her blood at the touch of his mouth. 'A meal is arranged for us. It's just for tonight. We can leave tomorrow, as soon as you wish.'

'Then that is what we shall do.' If he was surprised he did not show it, but pulled her gently in his wake as he made his way to inform Sir Wallace that they would not, sadly, be staying at Whitescar Hall to take a glass of contraband brandy in celebration of their marriage. 'I expect it will give me better memories of the place.'

Harriette repressed a sigh of relief. 'Yes, Luke. I hope it will.'

Lydyard's Pride, despite Harriette's assurances, was not much different from the cobwebbed desolation Luke remembered from his enforced stay. He supposed there was a limit to what could be done in a short time with one elderly retainer and two maids. Perhaps there was less dust in the library, a less desolate air with the holland covers removed, but nothing could rob it of the all-pervading damp from the ill-fitting windows and the incessant wind from the sea.

Why did she care for it so much? He did not ask because Luke sensed a careful reticence in his bride on the matter, intriguing in a lady who could be astonishingly forthright in others. He doubted she would have given him a satisfactory answer.

No, it would not have been his choice to spend his wedding night here, where he would, he presumed, have to woo a nervous bride. But was Harriette nervous? He thought that she might be, a virgin anticipating her wedding night with a man who was still very much a stranger to her. When he had kissed her—a fleeting affair—he had felt her retreat from him. But watching her instruct the maids to deliver their luggage to the one habitable bedchamber, he was not sure. Uneasy she certainly was—there was a sharp tension about her that he did not recall from their previous acquaintance—but she was not nervous. What a strange mixture of competence and reticence she was, and he discovered a need to seduce her into revealing more of her thoughts to him, the emotions that drove her.

He would like to feel her relax and soften under his hands.

* * *

The evening fell into the twilight of a summer night.

'We shall eat early, sir,' she informed him. 'Luke!' she added with a glimmer of a smile. 'Forgive me. It will take me a little while to get used to you!' Which made him laugh. 'We don't keep town hours here, I'm afraid. Perhaps I can offer you a drink. The brandy is excellent. I can personally recommend it.'

They sat in the library, in the uncomfortably upright chairs, the upholstery frayed and mildewed, and made desultory small talk about his journey from London. She asked about his damaged muscles. Luke answered her questions, sipped the brandy, acknowledging its quality. She was waiting for something. But what? Was it something she expected from him? Perhaps he was misreading her and it was merely a case of wedding nerves.

But she looked up, turning her head, listening at every noise in the old house.

From the library they moved to the dining room, where they sat formally at opposite ends of the table, the vast expanse between them polished inadequately for their use and set with a strangely haphazard mix of tarnished cutlery and old china of exceptional taste, but liberally chipped. Only the glasses were fine and old. Luke found himself watching and waiting, every sense on the alert. There was no doubting it. Harriette glanced up, reacting to every sound. When the door opened to admit Wiggins with a bottle of claret, she fumbled, unusually clumsy, and dropped her napkin to the floor.

She must be afraid of him. He could think of no other reason for her fingers pressed so firmly, white-tipped, against the edge of the table. Such a thought—that she might view an intimacy between them with trepidation—lodged uncomfortably in his chest.

The claret poured, Wiggins departed and Luke could stand it no longer, unsure whether to be impressed or amused. What did she expect of him? That with the blessing of the law he would pounce before their supper was eaten, strip that very pretty gown from her body and ravish her with no thought but for his own pleasure? It was an arresting thought as the candlelight glimmered on the pale skin above the lace-edged neckline, drawing his eye to the swell of her breast and the lovely column of her neck. It would be no hardship for him to do just that, he acknowledged, as his heart picked up its beat at the thought of cupping one of those elegant little breasts in the palm of his hand, but hopefully with some finesse and an eye to the lady's comfort. So, when once again his bride lifted her head at the sound of a distant owl hoot from the elms, he knew he must tread delicately to put her mind at rest.

'Harriette.' He broke into her lengthy description of the quality of the hunting in the vicinity, folded his hands on the polished wood and fixed her with a straight but compassionate look. Waited until her eyes lifted from her glass, widening at his serious tone. A tension, a strange mutual recognition, snapped between them as their eyes met, startling him with its intensity. It was incredible. For a moment he forgot what he had intended to say.

'Yes?' she asked.

Luke cleared his throat. 'There's nothing to worry you, you know.'

'I'm not worried.' She blinked, breaking the connection.

He sighed softly, intent now on reassurance. 'I'm trying to put you at ease. There's no need for you to…to be so anxious. I shall treat you with every care, every consideration. Our betrothal might have come about in an unnatural fashion, but I shall honour and respect you as my wife. My demands on you will not overstep the bounds of propriety. I have wed you to restore your good name.' He almost winced at the formal words, but could think of no other way to put her mind at rest. 'I am experienced enough to know what will bring you pleasure. You need have no fears that my demands…' His words dried as he saw the colour rise from the lace at her neckline, her eyes widen.

Harriette looked startled, but replied readily enough, 'What need I not fear about your demands?'

'That you share my bed and the physical demands

of my body every night.' How to say it to a nervous virgin? 'You need not fear that I shall consummate our marriage without…ah, care for your sensibilities…' Could it get any worse?

'Oh, I understand.' She shook her head, an action that made the loose curls dance on her shoulders, and gave a breathless little laugh of, he thought, relief. 'It's very kind of you to reassure me.'

'Good.' No, it wasn't. He was still puzzled. So what was it that she thought he would demand from her? He did not think it was terror of his fulfilling his sexual gratification that had tinted her face so alluringly. 'I just thought I would say it.'

'Thank you. It was very kind of you. Ah…perhaps you would like another glass of claret?' Harriette returned to a description of the countryside and, obligingly, he followed her lead. He could not force her to say what clearly was filling her whole awareness.

At last Wiggins entered with arthritic footsteps and a vast silver tureen as tarnished as the cutlery. He shuffled towards Harriette, removing the domed lid.

'My lady.' He had barely dipped the ladle when hard on his heels came the maid that Luke remembered, Jenny. Without pause she addressed Harriette from across the room.

'Mr Alexander's boy's at the door, miss—my lady, that is. All's clear.'

'Good!' Harriette was on her feet in an instant,

already moving to the door with the briefest glance in Luke's direction. 'Stay, if you will, sir. I shall only be gone a minute.'

The tureen was already on its way back to some distant kitchen. Suspicions, clear and immediately well formed, leapt into Luke's mind. The tension of minutes ago had quite vanished, leaving Harriette all competence and confident action.

'Forgive me.' Harriette turned in the doorway with an apologetic smile. 'This is unavoidable. I would not have had it happen, tonight of all nights, but it's urgent business and I need to go to the Tower Room. I shall return immediately. If you wish, I'll send Wiggins back with the soup….'

But Luke had no intention of meekly drinking soup whilst his wife involved herself in this *urgent business*. He pushed himself slowly but purposely to his feet, driven by intrigue and a simmer of impatience, the impatience quickly gaining the upper hand. Was she not going to tell him what she was about? Did she think he would sit by and accept without comment, when he knew very well what demanded her attention? No, by God! He would not. There she stood, ridiculously garbed in silk and ribbons, astonishingly pretty with sparkling eyes and ruffled curls, about to involve herself in a nefarious and undoubtedly illegal venture, and all without telling him.

Would it be dangerous? He had no idea, but

breaking the law might have unpleasant consequences for her. His wife must not be allowed to put herself in any sort of danger!

In an instant, before he had even thought of what he was doing, he had covered the distance between them with long strides to clasp her wrist. Loosely enough, as she turned to go, but firm enough to hold her still.

'It's smuggling, isn't it? You said you would give it up.'

'If I recall correctly, I said I would consider it.' Suddenly her eyes losing their sparkle, were flat and cool on his. 'I won't be involved after tonight. But on this occasion, my final night here, my responsibilities are with the Free Traders.'

The words were spoken before he could think. 'What would you do if I forbade it?'

An ominous silence hung between them for the length of a heartbeat.

'Would you?' Harriette became very still, her eyes searching his face as Alexander's words echoed in her mind. *Venmore will demand you give up the Free Trade, see if he doesn't.* 'By what right would you forbid me? I agreed to consider your wishes, and I will. I was not aware that you would forbid me in that hectoring tone.'

'And I was not aware that I was *hectoring*! But as your husband, who has some concern for your well-being, I might consider it wise to be so.'

He could see that she chose her words with care. 'I see. So as soon as your ring is on my finger—' she spread her fingers where the sapphires glittered '—you would immediately govern my actions, dictate what I may and may not do. You don't even know what I *am* going to do.'

'No, but I have my forebodings.'

'Well, to answer your question, in the light of your *forebodings*, if you forbid me, *my lord*—then I would have to consider your demand carefully.'

He would not let the deliberate formality rankle. 'But would you ultimately obey, my lady?'

The sparkle returned in those grey eyes in a definite challenge. 'I don't know,' she stated honestly. 'What would you do if I refused?'

He could have pushed the confrontation, he supposed. Demanded her obedience as a conformable wife of not many hours' standing. Instead he found himself caught up in the limpid translucent gaze that held his. And truth be told, he experienced a tremor of laughter at her sheer audacity. What a fascinating woman the new Countess of Venmore was turning out to be.

'So? What is it to be, Luke?' A tilt of the chin. 'I think it is not in my mind to obey you. So do I do this thing with or without your blessing? Time is of the essence.'

And, relaxing his fingers around her wrist, Luke

capitulated because he knew he must. Without doubt she would defy him, seeing a duty to her fellow smugglers, and he did not want to put that burden on her tonight of all nights. His relationship with Harriette Lydyard was not going to be as smooth as he had anticipated. His mouth curved in wry appreciation of this new force in his life.

'I suppose you have a duty to fulfil tonight. No, I'll not give you my blessing, madam wife—but I think I'll come with you.'

Harriette stared in amazement, a smile softly curving her lips. This exact outcome had troubled her all evening—that Luke would disapprove and clash with her in sharp confrontation. Well, he did disapprove, but his reluctant acceptance soothed her heart. The light encircling of her wrist in his fingers drove a thrilling sparkle through her blood. Nor was it just the excitement of the run. The sparkle leaped into glittering flames when she saw Luke's face soften into a smile. He was so beautiful, and he would not stand against her.

'There's no need. It's a task of no more than five minutes and entails no danger.'

'As your husband I consider it *my* duty.' Smoothly, he slid his hand from her wrist to take her hand in a companionable clasp, conscious of a spike of satisfaction, deep and warm, when Harriette gave a little laugh and returned the pressure.

'Come then. It's not dangerous, but it's illegal. Don't say I didn't warn you.'

She led the way, carrying a branch of candles from the hall table, along abandoned corridors, then up a steep and narrow staircase that opened into a circular room in the Tower that rose up from the eastern wing of the house to overlook the cliff top. The view would have been magnificent, but the room was close shuttered. Harriette walked directly to the table in the window embrasure, pulled back the shutters and took up the tinder box that waited ready to hand. With skill of long usage she struck a flame and lit the large oil lamp. It glowed, sending out a strong and sure beam.

'I take it there's a run on tonight,' Luke remarked laconically when Harriette did not bother to explain.

'Yes.'

'And the message from Mr Alexander's boy?'

'That all's well for their return. It has to be now because of the tides. Too early, and there's not enough cloud cover for comfort.' She stood before the glass, a charming picture, he thought, spreading her fingers wide against it as she looked up at the racing clouds shimmering over the moon. The sapphires—his sapphires—glimmered balefully. 'But it's safe enough and no Preventive men on the cliff.'

'So you're signalling for them to come in.'

'Yes.' She slanted a look towards him. 'It's not legal, you know—to signal to a smuggling vessel.'

'I know. How would my consequence survive if I were taken in the midst of so disreputable a task?'

'You could claim all ignorance and put the blame on your wilful wife, who had wed you under false pretences.' He saw her smile in the light from the lamp, her eyes shining pure silver.

'Should I be amazed that you did not postpone the wedding so that you could sail with them?'

'This is the first run I have not led since—well, I don't recall.' Perhaps with a touch of regret, she looked out over the sea to where the little cutter would emerge from the darkness. 'But, no, they are quite capable of doing it without me. George will lead. I gave them the use of *Lydyard's Ghost*,' she replied, quite solemn, which made him smile.

'So our married life will not be interrupted by your need to sail the seas.'

She tilted her head as if considering it. For a long moment he wondered what she would reply. 'No. I won't be involved again. Or not unless there is great danger. I promise it, if that is what you want.'

'Harriette. What an enigma you are.' He lifted her hand from the glass and pressed his lips to her palm, cool from the cold surface, with sardonic amusement. '*This* was what had your nerves stretched to breaking, starting at every sound. And all the time

I thought it was the thought of spending a night in my bed. How vain of me to consider that *I* might be your priority.' He discovered within him an unpalatable rapier thrust of very male resentment that she should not put him first, and again the sharp spur of guilt. After all, why in God's name should she? 'I don't even figure in your plans, do I?'

'Not true. It's just that I worry until they are safely returned.' It was clear to him that she had no thought that he might begrudge her preoccupation. 'Death and injury are cheap in such a venture. How would their families survive if the Gentlemen are hurt or killed? Or arrested? I'm a Lydyard and so must care, must I not? The fishermen of Old Wincomlee are our people.'

Which put him entirely in his place. 'Of course. Are you finished here?'

'Yes.'

'Then may I suggest we return to eat the soup before it's too tepid?'

'I think you rate the talents of my borrowed cook too highly. I think it would be tepid on the first occasion and won't have improved for the delay. But the beef might be edible.'

Luke laughed. So did Harriette as they stood together in the shadows outside the pool of light from the lamp. And Luke was drawn to this appealing woman in the romantic gown who laughed softly, the glow of the lamp reflected in her eyes. He stepped closer, wanting to savour the moment of closeness, charmed when she did not resist, and took her into his arms. Her lips were as cool as her fingers had been as he began a gentle exploration, his tongue sliding over the satin smoothness of her bottom lip, searching the delicate corners. Her body was soft against his hardness, her arms light as she raised them to encircle his neck. Luke found his arms tightening, his mouth demanding more from hers. Her lips parted so sweetly against the demands of his tongue.

Harriette sighed against him.

Not here. Not yet. Luke dropped his hands, stepped back, surprised by the heat in his belly and the immediacy of his erection. In this elemental room enclosed by dark skies without, illuminated by the circle of lamplight within, it created a magical tug to his senses. To lower her to the floor, strip away the layers of silk and feast on her drove his control to snapping point.

Not here!

His new bride deserved more subtlety than he seemed capable of in that moment. 'I admire your concern for your fellow criminals,' he informed her carefully, relieved that his voice echoed none of the rampant upheaval in his body.

'Do you?'

'I'm not sure,' Luke found himself replying candidly. 'But without doubt I admire you.'

The meal was as dire as she had predicted, the dining room chilly enough for Harriette to resort to a Kashmir shawl that had seen better days, but the wine was good, of course. And she relaxed from the tension that had plagued her until she knew that all was safe, leaving her strangely light-headed. The lighting of the lamp had in some inexplicable way broken the ice between them. Would he have forbidden her? He was certainly capable of it, she decided. And, even more crucial, would she have obeyed him? It was an uncomfortable confrontation to face on the first day of their marriage. Uncertain, Harriette turned her mind from it. Now all she had to face was a night spent with this man who was able, with the briefest of touches, to turn her blood to fire and to rob her of all her confidence.

The heat of his kiss was still on her mouth, the sensation of his arms still round her shoulders holding her hard against him. Harriette glanced through her lashes and saw that Luke had abandoned his battle with the beef and was watching her, a touch of speculation, no humour in his face. She was unable to guess at the direction of his thoughts, but it crossed her mind again that he was already regretting his noble gesture. Well, it was no better for her than it was for him, and there was one issue that still stood between them. So she would step across the divide and ask him. He might not like it, but that couldn't be helped.

'I would like to know one thing,' she announced.

'Of course.'

'Why were you in France? Why were you set on and wounded and robbed—but not killed? Why did you bargain for the use of the *Ghost*?'

No, Luke was not pleased. Harriette doubted he had ever been questioned over his actions in his life. Her eyes fell to where his fingers had tightened around the stem of the wineglass. She prayed for its safety.

'When I asked you before,' she pursued, 'you wouldn't tell me. You said it was family business. But now I'm your wife.'

'I know.' The groove between his brows was deeply etched. 'I can't tell you.'

Can't or won't? 'Who was the woman you were looking for? Marie-Claude?'

'I can't tell you that, either.'

'I see.'

Harriette did not see at all. Dread settled in her chest, a weight of despair, as she watched her husband's handsome face settle into bleak lines. She had hoped he would explain, denying all wrongdoing. Some trivial matter of business that had gone wrong, even a debt that had become dangerous and brought revenge. Anything. But not silence, not an inability to met her eyes and fingers as white as bone on the old glass. For if he was silent… Had she indeed married a traitor who was working for Napoleon to enable a French victory over England? Was the man Jean-Jacques Noir some treacherous go-between for gold or information? It was not beyond belief. The Earl of Venmore would not be the first Englishman to sell his soul to the devil, bought by French gold, and Harriette did not know him well enough to cast aside such suspicions as unworthy. He might have been honorable enough to rescue her from scandal but was that only because the *Ghost* was a tempting acquisition? Dismay filled her.

As for the unknown Marie-Claude—did she hold a place in Luke's heart? If so…then her marriage to him was based on an empty façade. Worse than that, on the unpalatable base of lies and deceit. Against her will, against the promptings of all good sense, Harriette had fallen in love with him when he was helpless and at her mercy. How could she have been so wrong in her judgement, to allow emotion to swallow up cold logic? And since she did love him, why was it that love could bring with it such torment?

At last, Luke's eyes lifted to hers, clear and completely without shadow. His voice was low and even, expressing words that were obviously difficult for him, and she strained to hear the truth in them. 'Harriette—you will think the worst of me, as I know. Yet I would ask you to trust me, even without explanation. I'll tell you when I…when I am free to explain. But not yet. Forgive me, not yet.'

Luke's words were light and without inflection as she weighed them. Regret was there, a depth of it. Sincerity, too. A deep unhappiness at the very core. His eyes did not waver from hers, but held her, breath suspended, as if to impress the truth—however meagre it might be—on her mind.

'Can you accept my word? My silence is not of my own making.' Abandoning the remnants of the meal, Luke pushed back his chair and came round the table to her side. Taking her hands in his he lifted her to her feet. 'It's not spying. On my honour, it's not. Nor is it treason, if that's what worries you.'

'Yes, it does.'

'I know. But on my oath, Harriette, I will do nothing to put you in danger or destroy your good name. Have I not wed you to restore your reputation? I will do nothing to destroy it. Nor would I do anything to dishonour my own name or that of my family.' His expression was stern; the grip of his hands tightened around her fingers as if he were unaware of their power, only slackening when she winced. 'Do you believe me?'

'Yes. I think I do,' Harriette offered. But there was

a frown in her eyes and that dangerous wedge remained driven between them.

He could not tell her the truth. Her heart was sore that he did not trust her enough with his secrets.

'I will protect your honour and your name with my life. I swear it. All I can ask is that you will give me time.' Turning her hands within his, he pressed his mouth to the soft inner skin of her wrists and then her palms.

And Harriette was seduced by Luke's promise and the caress of his mouth against her skin. Time, yes. She could give him that. And his arms were strong, his shoulders broad, his words surely without deceit. Perhaps he would prove his innocence to her. Perhaps all her fears would be smoothed away, flat and calm as a summer sea with nothing to hurt or destroy. Perhaps everything would be put to rights with patience and time, and a solution to whatever it was that drove Luke to dangerous scheming.

'Will you put your trust in me, Harriette,' he asked again, his lips now light against her fingers, 'as you gave yourself into my care? You trusted me enough to wed me. I swear, I will never hurt you.'

He bent his head and took her mouth with his.

Voices, edged and insistent, broke the kiss. They both turned their heads, listening as the sounds grew louder, the slam of a door a sharp note. Running feet. Without warning or courtesy the door to the dining room was flung back to smack against the wall. Harriette recognised the intruder immediately. Tom, Alexander's messenger, lurched to a halt on the threshold, slight chest heaving. His frightened eyes moved from Harriette to Luke, then back again as he gasped.

'Excise, on the cliffs, Cap'n Harry. A party of dragoons. Headin' this way. And the cutter's lights're in the bay. The *Ghost*'s 'ere with 'er cargo— three blue flashes been seen in the bay.'

Preventive officers! Disaster!

Harriette's mind scrabbled to make decisions. The worst possible outcome on the worst possible night. What malicious turn of fate had sent the Revenue men hotfoot to Old Wincomlee on her wedding night? A decision was needed from her, as it was entirely possible for the noble Earl of Venmore and his bride to spend the night in the gaol at Lewes if the cargo was intercepted. She choked on a ripple of hysterical laughter. No time for that now. She found that her hands had tightened around Luke's as if for support. But would he give it? She had no idea.

'What do we do, Cap'n? Use the cellars?'

'Yes. Tell Mr Alexander to come here. I'll arrange it.'

Tom fled.

'What are you going to do?' Luke asked.

'Solve the problem of Captain Rodmell and the Revenue men,' Harriette replied without hesitation because she really had no choice. 'Will you help me?'

'Will we end up in gaol?'

'It's possible.'

'What better way to spend our wedding night?' The dry comment was not lost on her, but there was no fear in him, rather an unruffled acquiescence that impressed her. 'What do you want me to do?'

So he would help her. She would find time to thank him later. But for now... 'It would be best to fire a beacon on the cliff top, but we've no time. Go up to the Tower Room, Luke. Can you find your way? You must close the shutters to block the light six times. Count slowly to ten in between each. The spotsman on *Lydyard's Ghost* will see the warning. It should do the trick and he'll know what to do. If he sees the warning, you'll see six rapid flashes from a pistol in reply.'

'I can do that.' He was already on his way to the door. 'And then?'

'Can you find your way down to the kitchens? If I'm not there, Wiggins will tell you what's afoot.'

'And you?'

Her face was pale, her skin taut over her cheekbones. 'We've a cargo of contraband to hide and the Gentlemen to keep safe.'

She turned to go through the door before him.

'Wait.' His outstretched hand touched her arm and she immediately stilled. 'Is it dangerous for you?'

His eyes were dark and sombre. Harriette felt his concern like a warm cloak to wrap her safe from her fears. She managed a smile through her anxieties, placing her hand over his. 'No. I hope we can come about. I'll not consign you to a prison cell.'

'Have a care, Harriette. I don't choose to lose you just yet.'

The words hummed beneath her skin, through her veins as she sped towards the kitchens.

Luke carried out his instructions to the letter without bothering to consider what he had got himself into. Six slow gleams of light from the Tower Room. Followed, to his relief, by six brief flashes—presumably from the pan of an unloaded pistol—in reply. The warning given and received. By the time he found his way back down the stairs to the kitchens it was to join Wiggins, the two maids and his wife.

'They've been warned,' he murmured in Harriette's ear, standing behind her, lightly holding her shoulders.

A brief smile of thanks angled up and back, but Harriette's attention was elsewhere. 'Now we wait.'

So they did. He drew her back closely against him, responding to the fierce protective instinct in his blood with her hair curling over his hands. Desire, all sharp claws, took him by the throat, ridiculously inappropriate desire for a woman he barely knew and with a cargo of contraband to dispose of, the Revenue men at their door. But she was warm under his hands, against his body, the scent of lavender bringing back a distant hazy memory of when he had lain under her hands, wounded and incapable. As Harriette moved against him, brushing his body with her own, his loins stirred and he drew in a breath, appalled at his lack of control.

'Not long,' she spoke softly, a hand raised to his in warning pressure, bringing him back to the present.

There it was. The shuffle of muffled hooves on cobbles. Whispered commands. The kitchen door into the courtyard was pushed back and a procession of men carrying barrels and bales and small casks began to make their way through the kitchen, down the steps into the cellar below. Stepping from his hold, Harriette nodded, wasting no words, to George Gadie who led them in.

To Luke's inexperienced eye they worked silently, efficiently, professionally. Well drilled with an astonishing degree of discipline in the rapid disposal of the goods. They had done this before, many times, and Lydyard's Pride was the key to it. A valuable base as a place of storage for illicit goods, as well as a source of a signal to the approaching vessel. Which perhaps explained Harriette's inexplicable love for the old house, her determination to be here on this night of all nights. Luke stood and watched, having the sense to keep out of the way. Until the procession dwindled to a halt, ended, and George Gadie emerged from the cellar, a grin very evident.

'All done, Cap'n.'

'The ponies?'

'Mr Alexander took them away. Best not to wait. They'll be back with their owners by now and no one the wiser. Our luck's in. No sign of the Excise yet.' He wiped his sleeve across his face. 'I'll leave you, y'r honour, and your good lady—' A thundering knock interrupted, probably from the stock of a rifle, echoing from the region of the front door. 'That's 'em. Revenue men, damn 'em!'

Instantly Harriette began issuing orders, Captain Harry in satin and lace. 'Get yourself off home, George. It's Captain Rodmell, I expect. Wiggins, bring him up to the dining room. Announce him as if nothing has happened.'

'Of course, my lady.'

Luke had no idea what Harriette intended when faced with a troop of dragoons and their officer, but her masterful command sent an answering excitement surging through his limbs and spurred him into action. Hers might be the experience in this crisis, but he could see a way that might help the outcome.

'Jenny,' he addressed the maid. 'Fetch up a decanter of port and one of brandy to the dining room—and glasses.' He smiled briefly at Harriette. 'We can't have the upholders of the law going away without hospitality, can we?'

Harriette laughed. 'No, we can't do that.'

The Earl and Countess of Venmore were seated in magnificent isolation at opposite ends of the dining table, the Earl in the act of raising a glass of brandy to his lips in a toast to his new wife. The candles had deliberately been placed to bathe Harriette in golden light, and cast Luke into shadow. Wiggins ushered in the Customs' Riding Officer.

'Captain Rodmell, my lady.'

The Captain, tall and spare, features tight at being thwarted of his victorious capture of a valuable cargo, launched into his accusation without apology, eyes fixed on Harriette as if he would prize the information from her. 'Miss Lydyard. We have reason to suspect that a landing was made in this cove not two hours ago. The cargo has vanished, in the blink of an eye. I believe that these premises are being used for the storage of that contraband. I demand permission to search the house.'

Luke sipped the brandy, silent, watchful. So

Harriette was already a suspect because of her name. How would she respond? She looked a little startled, deliciously feminine and helpless. Would she carry it off? His pulse picked up its beat, his heart began to thud. He would allow her to dictate the order of events—for now.

'Contraband here? I can't believe it, sir,' she responded. She rose to her feet and advanced towards him, holding out one hand with impeccable grace.

'It would not be the first time, I wager.' Unable to resist without rank bad manners, the Captain took her hand and inclined his head curtly. 'The inhabitants of Old Wincomlee have a reputation for illicit trade.'

'As I am aware, Captain Rodmell.' Amazingly compliant, artfully feminine. 'Which fisherman does not eke out his livelihood with the odd barrel of brandy or bale of silk?'

'Which you, Miss Lydyard, apparently condone.'

'I may condone it, out of charity for their lack of means, but I know nothing of such goings-on, Captain. How should I?'

'And I suppose you know nothing of the activities or identity of a Captain Harry Lydyard, either?' The sneer was heavy. 'Nor it is a matter of the odd barrel, the odd bale. I am not talking of small-scale smuggling here, madam.'

Harriette raised a delicate lace-edged handkerchief to her lips as if in some distress. 'I know nothing of a landing here to help you in your search for these hardened criminals, Captain. It fills me with fear that such activities go on so near my own home. Nor, I regret, do I know the identity of this Captain Lydyard. He is no member of *my* family, I assure you. More like a local villain who has adopted our name to cover his tracks. I cannot imagine how he would dare. I advise you to speak with my brother, Sir Wallace, about it. He will help you in dragging him before justice. Sir Wallace is a Justice of the Peace, you understand.'

'Nor, I suppose,' Captain Rodmell continued, flushed but determined to the end, 'do you know of this house being used to escape the legal paying of taxation on certain imported goods?'

'Certainly not, Captain. The Pride is not engaged in such an outrageous trade. I refute any such suggestion.'

'A light is not shown from the Tower here on nights when a run is made?'

'I know nothing of that, either. If it is so, it is not by my orders. I would have no truck with such activities, sir! How could you think it?'

Luke was astounded, and absurdly impressed, to see the spangle of tears on Harriette's cheek.

'But this is your house, madam, is it not? Which could make you guilty by association.'

'Yes. It is mine. As for guilt...' She dabbed at the tears.

Luke watched in continuing admiration. She was holding her own well, but perhaps now was the time for a little decisive intervention. He could turn the direction of this scene quickly and bring an end to any threat from Captain Rodmell. Quietly, he put down his glass and stood, drawing the Captain's eye. This would now be guided to a satisfactory conclusion with his hands on the reins.

'There is a need to clarify the matter.' His voice held a nice bland of hauteur and irritation. 'The house is mine, Captain.'

The Captain cast him a jaundiced eye, lip curling. Luke felt the urge to laugh. Rarely had he been so summed up, cast aside, written off as a mindless dandy with no thought but for his clothing and the quality of the brandy in his glass. 'And you are, Sir? Not an inhabitant of Old Wincomlee, I presume.'

Luke drew on all his dignity and severe disap-proval. 'I am the Earl of Venmore. Today I married Miss Lydyard. Her property is therefore now mine. And you, Captain, are disturbing our wedding night with accusations for which, it seems to me, you have not one shred of evidence.'

The Captain looked discomfited, but not unduly so. 'My apologies, my lord. But still there are rumours... It is my duty to investigate and without doubt a cargo has vanished from under our noses this night.'

'I understand. You have my sympathy, Captain. But *I* have nothing to do with smuggling. Nor will I. Now if you would care to take your men and—'

But the Captain dug in his heels. 'I'm not satisfied, my lord.'

Harriette interrupted. Shockingly. Horrifyingly. Luke felt his muscles tense, his heart pick up its beat. 'Perhaps you would wish your men to search the cellars, Captain Rodmell. And the Tower Room. To put your mind at rest.'

'I don't think it will be necessary, my dear,' Luke managed. What was she thinking, to invite the Captain to snoop and discover? Too chancy by half. His quick glance in her direction told him that her eyes were bright, her self-control perfect. Did she think the Captain would refuse the ingenuous offer? Luke would stake his fortune on the Captain carrying out his duty to the final letter. Had Harriette cast them all into the mire?

But Harriette walked softly towards him, placed her hand on his sleeve, a melting plea in her face, pure mischief in her gaze. 'It will answer the question, my love, far more quickly than any of my protestations. Then the Captain can leave, honour satisfied. And we, at last, can be alone together.'

Her lips curved, her lashes swept low over softly

glowing eyes, her chin tilted provocatively. She was flirting with him, openly, outrageously. So be it. Reacting fast, Luke covered her hand with his, his eyes fixed on hers. 'My darling girl. That is what I would wish for, too. Nothing must keep me from your side, from your bed…' He raised her fingers to his lips.

'Ah, Luke…I can barely wait.' Whisper-soft, full of promise. Disgracefully expressive.

'My heart. When we are alone again…' Swallowing the laughter, Luke allowed his lips to linger on her fingers.

'My lord…my lady!' Captain Rodmell slapped his gloves against his thigh, supremely embarrassed.

'Captain Rodmell. Of course, forgive me.' Harriette dragged her eyes from Luke's face as if it were the most difficult task in the world. 'Perhaps you would direct your men… Wiggins will show you to the Tower Room…and the cellars.'

The dragoons were dispatched, Luke holding his breath at what would be found. Annoyance, yet deep intrigue, skittered along his nerves. Why had Harriette not followed his lead, to overawe the man with aristocratic consequence and send him on his way with a sharp reply? Not his usual response to those who upheld the King's law, but essential in these circumstances as far as he could see. Whilst Harriette had wilfully torn up his plan and cast it to the four winds. The gaol at Lewes seemed a distinct possibility.

'Perhaps I can offer you a glass of brandy, sir?' he offered Captain Rodmell.

'I doubt it's paid taxation, my lord,' the man replied caustically.

'I think it has, sir. I brought it from London today, to drink with my bride on my wedding night. Perhaps you would drink our health?' Luke was already pouring a glass.

'Thank you, my lord. Your health. My lord. My lady.'

He drank, tossing back the brandy as if it was distasteful to him. Captain Rodmell did not believe a word of their little charade, Luke considered, but could do nothing without proof. Which the dragoons would discover and report on any minute now. One of his men returned with a brief rap on the door. Luke found his muscles straining, until Harriette's hand tightened on his arm.

'Nothing here, sir,' the dragoon announced. 'Tower Room shut up under covers, shutters nailed tight. Looks unused to me, sir. Cellars empty. Nothing in the stables except a team of bang-up blood and bone. And a smart carriage.'

'My horses and curricle, Captain,' Luke explained, disbelieving. 'We leave for London tomorrow morning.'

'You searched the cellars thoroughly,' the Captain demanded. 'They'll be extensive in a house this size.'

'That we did, sir. Nothing to find, sir.'

Captain Rodmell swung to face the Earl and Countess. 'Then again I ask pardon. It seems that on this occasion I have been mistaken. Goodnight, my lord, my lady.' He bowed stiffly, then retreated. They heard his heavy tread echoing down the hall, full of disbelief and disapproval.

Luke and Harriette stood and looked at each other as the sounds died away. Luke saw the gleam in her eyes, the infectious curl of her lips. She was alight with the moment, full of vitality, glowing with triumph. It was infectious, reaching out to him, anchoring them together in a moment of dangerous idiocy in which they had both played an outrageous role. The exuberance of the moment had completely obliterated the strain of distrust between them. Luke saw it, recognized it for an unexpected blessing, and gave silent thanks.

'Harriette…! Hell and damnation!'

She laughed, low and soft. 'Did you not enjoy it?'

'Enjoy it? No, I did not!' But flames of energy, pure and bright, were leaping within him, racing along his veins. 'All I could see was our valiant Captain hauling us off to Lewes along with all the barrels and bales I last saw disappearing into the cellar. I didn't imagine that, did I?'

'No. You saw them. You should have trusted me.'

'How did you do it?'

'A double cellar, constructed well nigh a century ago with this in mind. A trapdoor leads from the cellar down into a secure lower chamber. It's impossible to see without knowledge of it and I'm sure George had the girls sweep sand across the floor to hide any footprints or sign of the joints where the slab meets the solid floor. It's well made, hard to detect.'

'And the Tower Room?'

'Wiggins put it to rights. He's not as ancient as he might appear.'

Luke seized a glass and tossed back the brandy, much as Captain Rodmell had done. 'God help me. Shall I have to do this often?'

Harriette tilted her head. 'I don't think there's a need in London.'

'I don't think my reputation can stand it.'

'Mine could. Until I rescued you and things went awry...' Her bright laughter died, and she looked away.

'Ah, Harriette. I didn't mean...' He had hit a nerve and regretted it. Regretted anything he might do to rob her of that magical vivacity that lit her with an inner beauty. How had he ever thought her to have few attractions, for her looks to be little out of the common way? How had he ever mistaken her for a man! Without thought he covered the space between them and framed her face with his fingers, his hands smoothing her tumbled curls away, inordinately pleased when the tension in her ebbed under his hands.

'You have skills I would never have imagined, Madam Countess.'

'Whilst you showed remarkable ability in duping his Majesty's Preventive officers, sir.'

She was delightful. 'I did, didn't I? And were you flirting with me in public?'

'Most definitely I was, my lord. Captain Rodmell, an honourable man, did not know where to look.'

'You were very adept.' He ran his knuckles along the silken skin of her jaw.

'I was very inexperienced.'

'Then let me show you…' He lowered his mouth to hers.

Blood ran hot for both of them. It astonished Luke how the demands of his body, the sheer primal desire of a man for a woman, could rule his mind. The only image was the one he had earlier denied, that of pouncing without thought to strip the layers of silk and lace from her body and ravish her with no concern but for his own fulfilment. The candle-light still glowed on the delicate skin above the lace-edged neckline, highlighting shoulders and the swell of her breasts as he forced his lips to follow its path with at least some degree of finesse. His body was suddenly suffused with heat, his loins painfully, urgently, demanding release.

This was no way to approach an inexperienced virgin.

Deliberately, for the second time that night, Luke stepped away, registering her look of confusion, regretting being the cause of it.

'Do you not want me?' she asked.

'Yes. You are my wife.'

She lifted her chin. 'That's no answer.'

'No. It isn't.' Even as he acknowledged the faint reprimand, he cursed himself silently for his insensitivity in handling this unpredictable girl. So he would remedy the slight, nor would it be far from the truth. 'You are lovely and desirable, and I want you. What man would not want you?' He closed the distance again, now aware that she was shivering—with nerves rather than the incessant draughts. 'But I don't know where our room is,' he murmured, his mouth against the white column of her throat as his hands loosed the ribbons that held her hair.

'Shall I take you there?'

'Unless you wish us to shock your servants further.' He struggled to keep the words light. It would be so easy to overwhelm her, to spring and devour.

Harriette linked her fingers with his and led him upstairs, wordless now, the wild thrill of the hour driving her. Then they were behind the closed door of her room, where his mouth raced over her face, lingering on eyelids, the soft hollow of her temple, the fine edge of her jaw, heated kisses. Knowing hands made short work of the French gown until she stood in her shift and trembled. Luke made to blow out the candle.

'No. Leave it.'

'Are you sure?'

'I want to see you.'

His eyes gleamed, a sardonic curl of his mouth. 'I thought you already had.'

'Yes. But not through your choice. Not like this. Do you need help with your boots?'

'No, I do not.'

Luke lifted her onto the bed, placing her softly against the pillows, bending to kiss her again because her lips held the sweetness of honey, impossible to resist, and was caught there, unable to look away. Her soft mouth was made for pleasure. Her eyes wide, luminously silver in the candlelight, were full of mystery.

Harriette longed to respond, to touch him, to push the fine shirt from his shoulders and savour the hard flesh she already knew, but faced with this reality she found her wild confidence waning. Her cheeks burned, her lips and throat dried.

'Should I touch you?'

Luke sat back, took her hands, placed them against his chest, holding them.

'What do you feel?'

Harriette smoothed her palms over the linen, over the firmness of his muscles, his skin warm through the fine material. In some strange way it settled her.

'Your heart is beating hard.' Turning her hand beneath his, she transferred his palm to her own breast, pressing it there. 'As does mine.'

For a brief moment he replaced his palm with his lips, then held her gaze, his words a promise. 'I'll make love to you with all the skill I have, Harriette. There is nothing for you to fear. Only to accept and enjoy. I'll do nothing that is beyond your bearing. Do you understand?'

'Yes.'

And as Luke released her to pull off his boots and strip off his own garments, Harriette caught her breath. How could she have forgotten how superb he was? Returned to health, the light gleamed on the smooth-carved skin, the scatter of dark hair over chest towards belly, tempting her to touch again. Long and supple, the muscles of hips and thighs were splendidly powerful. If she had any doubts of her own desirability, it was instantly dispelled. Aroused and magnificently erect, his need for her was evident.

Then she forgot everything under his touch as he

pushed the shift off her to expose her body to his gaze. Gentle. Persuasive. Everything he had promised her, but insistent, supremely confident in his ability to arouse and pleasure, allowing her no space for reticence nor yet for embarrassment.

'Let me touch you. Let me show you how good this can be.'

His voice was soft in her mind, his words encouraging when he felt her muscles tense. Every inch of her became immediately awake to the slide of his tongue, the delicate edge of teeth, the searing heat of lips. She shivered, hot desire shocking her, pooling in her belly, between her thighs.

Luke held his breath. She was lovely. Glossy elegance, firm muscles below the satiny skin. Breasts high and firm. He bent his head to her nipples, then the shallow dip between her breasts where the scent of lavender captured his senses. Flare of hips from her narrow waist enticed, the elegant length of her back from nape to swell of buttock seduced. His hands stroked and splayed in languorous movement, soothing her, beguiling her. Her scented hair enfolded him, her sweet breath warm against his cheek. Desire gripped him ruthlessly as she moved her legs to entangle them with his, a subtle movement that was almost his undoing, challenging his control when she pressed her mouth against the beat of the pulse in his throat, a murmur of pleasure that vibrated and spread from her to him.

Sliding her hand down over waist, hip, thigh, Harriette marvelled, gasped, winding her arms around his neck as he parted her thighs and settled there. She could feel the tension in him, the tight knots of muscle in his back as he controlled every movement as he made it easy for her. Instinctively, she lifted her hips—was this not what he wanted? It was what her body dictated as she felt his erection thrust hard against her, and she sighed as he pushed, slowly, deliberately, lingering when he felt resistance and her own intake of breath. With a cry she arched her body against him, and he thrust deeply into her, filling her. Harriette found herself holding her breath, afraid to move against this impossible invasion, until slowly, he began to rock, holding her so that she had no choice but to move with him, echoing the slide of skin against skin, thigh against thigh. Her own desire flared as the heat built, nerves consumed.

The fire became intense.

'Luke!' she gasped.

Immediately he stilled. 'Have I hurt you?'

'No.'

'Shall I stop?' Hoarse. On the very edge of control.

'No.'

'Then come with me. Stay with me.'

His lips on hers were amazingly soft, his fingers

gentle in her hair, even as his thighs were hard, demanding. Still with enough presence of mind to hold his weight from her, he drove on, unable to hold back.

His mouth took hers, his tongue possessive in that final plunging moment.

Harriette Lydyard. Now Harriette Hallaston. Luke savoured the thought in his mind. Something in her touched his emotions, his heart, certainly his physical desires. By no means the first woman to share his bed, yet she had taken him by surprise. He was not in the habit of taking his pleasure with virgins, preferring rather a worldly mistress who knew her place and her role in his life, who could intuitively give and receive pleasure. This had been outside his experience, all his expectations. Harriette could never be described as worldly, and by her own admission had no experience, yet she had proved to be a web of contradictions. A charming innocence, but certainly no shyness. A lack of knowledge, but a desire to learn and discover, a delicate reticence but one that was willingly overthrown as her confidence bloomed. An unwary man could be entrapped in such a web. What had he hoped for from this unusual union? Friendship, possibly a deep one. A caring, tolerant acceptance of each other if they were fortunate.

It had proved more than that, far more, but quite

what he did not know. Admiration and gratitude, he acknowledged. Was that all? What he did know was that the delicate web had wrapped itself around him and for that short time in her arms had enslaved him. Now her dark hair curled invitingly over her breasts. He allowed it to spiral around his fingers, and clenched them into a fist as he felt his body harden again.

'What is it?' she murmured, her face turned into his shoulder.

'You are beautiful,' he stated, moved by the discovery.

What could he do but lift himself over her again, finding her ready, hot and wet and eminently desirable, spread beneath him. What could he do but bury himself again within her, losing himself in the dark, satin depths.

His self-control was suddenly not good, not good at all.

Harriette's dream, admitted later to no one but her own innermost thoughts as she lay and studied Luke's sleeping face, had come true. He had wed her and told her she was beautiful. Not that she believed him for a second, but at least he had no distaste for her. Stretching her limbs, marvelling at how he had lured her into such heart-stopping awareness of him, she leaned and pressed her mouth to his, soft as a feather.

'I am yours now. For ever,' she whispered.

Beware! her mind advised her heart. It would be dangerous, painfully so to be drawn into foolish imaginings. Luke did not love her, but had merely been seduced by the flash of heat, of overwrought emotion caused by the exhilaration of the night's events.

Ah, but did she love him? Oh, yes, she feared she did. Sense told her it was not possible to fall in love with a man she did not know. It was merely the unfortunate result of her never having met a man so good to look at before in her life.

But she could fall in love. She had done so, a treacherous and sudden fall, as from the deck of a ship in a turbulent sea, with such ease that it frightened her. It made her tremble.

Luke woke her at dawn to make love to her in the full light of day, sunbeams filtering through the curtains to warm and soften, casting dappled patterns over their skin. Breathless sighs, long caresses, slow kisses. How slender she was, the muscles sleek and softly defined from her active life. Luke pressed kisses along the curve of her throat, the gentle slope of her shoulders. His tongue lapped at the seductive swell of her breasts, the pertly aroused nipples.

She shivered beneath the inexorable onslaught of his mouth and hands, shuddered, every nerve ending alive, alight. Lured into unthinkable intimacies of her own. With astonishing freedom Harriette traced his collarbone with the tip of her tongue. Pressed her lips to the healed wound in his arm, the skin where the bruising had faded to a mere shadow, sliding her palms over the hard muscle, flat nipples and down to the lean thighs, the heavy weight of his sex. Where she hesitated.

'Touch me,' he spoke harshly.

And she did, enclosing the firm length of him until he groaned his denial and anchored her wrists above her head, before beginning his own on-slaught. Harriette quivered as his mouth drifted over her ribs, belly, to the throb of her thighs. She dragged in a breath, tightening her grasp of his shoulders in consternation.

'Luke…'

Relentlessly, he continued with knowing fingers and tongue, teased, stroked, refused to allow her peace until, in a flood of sweetness, Harriette turned her face away and gasped at the outrageous build of desire within her. Until she shivered, Luke's mouth swallowing her cry as he took her beyond her control. Beyond everything but the sensation of Luke's body, above hers, his erection iron hard.

And then he was deep inside her.

'Look at me!' Luke ordered, wrapping her hair around his hands, his wrists, as if it was she who held him captive. She looked into his eyes dark with passion. And was captured, lost, drowning, her heart beating in time with his.

More powerfully now, he thrust home. Deep and long, driving with an urgency that overwhelmed him, as physical need took precedence over care for her inexperience. Luke felt her gasp again, her whole body tense around him, and control was no longer an option for him. He fell from the knife-edge, into the dark, helplessly, magnificently overcome by the slick heat of her, taking her with him.

'Well, Captain Harry?' he murmured when he could, looking down at her, framing her face with his hands.

'Well?' A little wary. Entirely satisfied.

'Was that as enjoyable as a fast run in a stormy sea?'

Head tilted, she kept him waiting as if in thought. Then smiled. 'Yes,' she replied simply.

'Madam Smuggler—you are as charming as you are beautiful.' Her mouth, reaching up, laughed against his in mute invitation. 'An insatiable woman...' How could he not comply?

And did so.

Chapter Six

Absurdly satisfied with the events of the previous day, Luke made his way to the stables at Lydyard's Pride to find someone who could be trusted to organise his curricle and pair for later that morning. A sleepy stable lad—whom he recognised as Tom, Alexander Ellerdine's messenger—showed willing but inept, so Luke stripped off his coat, led the horses into the yard and applied himself with a curry comb whilst the lad tackled the harness. It was a pleasurable enough task with thoughts of Harriette imprinted in his mind as he picked the hay-stalks from the manes and tails of the two bays. The result was not quite to his exacting standards, but it would have to do. He found himself, to his amusement, remarkably tolerant. His hand moved caressingly over the velvet coat of the bay. Much like the soft vibrancy of Harriette's hair when he had turned his face against the elegant length of her throat, the urgency of his desire momentarily eased...

'Venmore!'

He raised his head at the unexpected voice with its note of command. A man stood watching him from the entrance to the yard. Not quite aggressive, but nor, Luke thought, was he friendly. Luke straightened, at which the man walked forwards, now smiling, and offered his hand in greeting.

'I'm Alexander Ellerdine. Harriette's cousin.'

'Of course.' Luke shook hands. He should have known, and had obviously mistaken the antagonism. There was little family resemblance other than dark hair and slender build, but he recalled that the man had been at the church. So this was the cousin who, according to local gossip, might have made a match of it with Harriette. The man's handshake was firm, his expression open and welcoming. Luke decided that the gossip and his first impression was at fault.

'Congratulations on your marriage, my lord. I didn't get a chance to wish you well yesterday. And also many thanks.'

'For what?'

'The rescue operation last night. A dangerous moment—the whole cargo could have been lost.' The friendly smile gained a sardonic twist. 'You never know with the Revenue men and Rodmell is an efficient Riding Officer—the best we've had in this area for years, more's the pity. Someone lays the information and the dragoons appear where you least expect them. But Harriette has a cool head in emergencies.' Alexander slapped his hand against the neck of one of the bays. 'That's why I'm here now. To see Wiggins about moving the goods on tonight. A fine pair of animals, by the way. I don't think I've seen finer.'

'Yes. They are. Home bred. I've a useful stallion at Venmore.'

'A smart curricle, too.' Alexander ran a hand over the highly lacquered rail of the vehicle. 'An ambition of mine to own one, but not one I'll ever achieve. The lanes in this part of the world don't lend themselves to anything better than a gig.'

Luke smiled wryly. 'I know. I had the dubious pleasure of travelling in mine host of the Silver Boat's rattle trap to Brighton. It did nothing for my injured shoulder.'

And Alexander laughed. 'So you did.' He walked round the bays to appraise their good points. 'I have to say—I admire you, my lord.' He returned to lean against the animal's flank as Luke once again applied long slow strokes to the gleaming shoulder.

'Admire?' Luke squinted up.

'For taking Harriette on, all things considered.'

'What things should I consider?' Luke asked quietly, straightening, senses suddenly alert.

'Well, there's her background for one thing. You

must be aware. Not every man would be willing to introduce her into his family.' Alexander grinned. 'The Lydyards have not always been respectable, despite Wallace's stuffy consequence. And Harriette has no inheritance to speak of to entice a husband to ignore the…the difficulties.'

'Oh? Which background should I be aware of?' Luke kept his expression perfectly bland, as if discussing the finer points of his horses. Awareness roiled in his belly. His first impression, he decided, had not been wrong at all. There was something about Alexander Ellerdine. Luke acknowledged that he did not like the man at all.

'Well, the strong links with our enemy across the Channel—you know about Harriette's mother, I take it.'

'Yes, I do.'

Alexander shrugged. 'It's not to everyone's taste when they're killing our soldiers. And then there's the smuggling. Lydyards have always been smugglers, of course. Your family must be very tolerant, Venmore.'

Luke forced himself to reply laconically. 'Harriette will not be the first lady with French blood to make her mark in English society. And, since she's agreed to step back from the Trade, I don't see that we need to broadcast the smuggling connection.'

Alexander's eyes narrowed infinitesimally.

'Agreed, has she? I didn't know… But still, rumours tend to spread, do they not? Even as far as London.'

'Only if someone ill wishes us enough to sow the seeds.'

Alexander smiled ruefully, eyes gleaming. 'Not me, my lord, if that's what you suspect. I wish Harriette nothing but good fortune in her marriage. It's just that some would see smuggling as no better than treason, France being the enemy.'

'They do?' Luke felt the chill of ice spread through his veins. Where was this leading? Alexander Ellerdine was making an excellent argument to blacken the name of all smugglers, yet he appeared ingenuous in his manner. Was this deliberate provocation? Or an innocent exchange of opinion? Besides, he had known of Harriette's smuggling before he had wed her.

'I don't subscribe to that line of thought,' Alexander continued, running his fingers through the bay's mane. 'Life's hard for the fishermen, and without the income from the Trade it would be even harder. Legality is a fine line when your family is near starvation and the winter seas are too rough to put out. What does legality matter when the cooking pots are empty? Everyone in Old Wincomlee turns a blind eye to the signalling from the Tower Room.'

'Yes, they would,' Luke agreed, carefully feeling

his way. 'Signalling's essential, I should suppose, to get a boat home safely into the cove.'

'True. But what do you suppose we do when there's no cargo to be had? When times are hard in bad weather and the local folk go hungry with no income?'

'What do you do?'

'Think about it, my lord. Everyone knows of the Gentlemen. But who has not also heard tales of the fraternity of the Wreckers?'

Luke's voice remained even, all his willpower focused on showing a mere bland interest. 'Wreckers? What do you imply, Ellerdine?'

Alexander replied, equally cool, 'If you lived in these parts you would know what goes on. It's all part of the life on this coast and has been for generations of Lydyards. The signalling on a dark and stormy night is not always to bring in one of our own vessels. It's a bloody business, but common enough and highly lucrative.'

'Are you saying that Harriette is involved in this, Ellerdine?' Luke asked quietly, rising to his full height, fixing his informer with a cold, green stare. 'You will excuse me if I say that I don't believe you.'

'No? Ever heard of the *Lion d'Or*?'

'I don't think…' But there again, why should he?

'A vessel out of Dieppe with a cargo of silk. It came aground on the rocks out there, three years ago now.' Alexander indicated the rocks on the headland with an expansive sweep of his arm. 'The silk sold on to the London market for a tidy sum.'

'And the crew?'

'Lost.' Alexander shrugged. 'It happens. There was nothing we could do.'

'Who lit the light?' Luke heard himself demanding.

'Who do you think?' Luke found that he could not bear to watch the self-satisfied smile cross Alexander Ellerdine's face or the dramatic gesture of his hand. 'The lamp shone out from the Tower Room at the Pride, luring the brave *Lion d'Or* to her rocky grave.'

There was no time for Luke to question further. And had he not heard enough? Light footsteps in the distance informed him that Harriette was approaching across the stable yard. Then she had joined them. Ellerdine turned to her, bowing with ironic but graceful courtesy.

'We were just speaking of you, cousin. And how is the Countess of Venmore this morning?' And planted a kiss on her blushing cheek.

Alexander left them to find Wiggins and make arrangements for the disposal of the contraband. Harriette turned to Luke with a shy smile and a leap of joy in her heart, only to face the cold implacability of a marble façade. Luke regarded her with what could only be a deep brooding appraisal. It was as if she had thought to dip her foot in a warm summer pool, only to find a thin sheet of ice covering the surface. It chilled her blood. Nor were there any soft words of greeting for her as she had expected.

'It's time we left, Harriette. Are you ready?' Clipped, flat vowels.

'Yes. Of course.' She frowned. 'Is something wrong, Luke?'

'Why should there be?' She watched as he forced the taut muscles of his shoulders to relax, and his face softened into a brief smile—a smile that she sensed was entirely without warmth. 'Go and collect your travelling garments—the wind will be cool. The curricle will be harnessed by the time you return.'

'Have I done something you do not approve of?'

'Not a thing.' But his eyes remained coolly watchful. It was as if some impenetrable barrier had been erected between them. 'Any problems are of my own making,' he continued. 'You must forgive me if I seem preoccupied.'

What did that mean? What had she done, for surely some blame must rest on her shoulders? Did he regret the passion that he had lavished on her in their bed? The marriage? Did he regret everything? Harriette found, to her shame, that she had to battle against a threat of tears.

'Go and fetch what you need for the journey,' Luke repeated.

The distance that had so startlingly opened up between them seemed to yawn. Harriette turned to do as she was bid because she could think of nothing else to say. Was this the man who had held her in his arms, kissed her, possessed her? Was this cold formidable man the one who had introduced her with such skill to all the delights possible between a man and a woman, who had woken her again with hands and lips at first light to renew his amazing assault? Was it wrong for her to expect some degree of warmth from him now, even though he might not love her?

Harriette's world was suddenly turned on its head. What had occurred to cause this separation? She would wager it was not her smuggling activities. When they had worked to save the cargo, had there not been some overpowering, overwhelming link stretching between them? Had there not been a living connection, bright as cold steel, hot as fire? It had pulsed through their blood, driving them into each other's arms. Surely she had not misread that glittering bond?

Was this the man who had acted out of honour to repair her reputation, when no blame could be attached to him, when he could have turned his back and abandoned her to whatever filth society chose to cast on her shoulders?

Then perhaps her judgement was all wrong, all built on a fatal inexperience of fashionable behaviour. Perhaps that was the way of polite society, that tenderness in bed was just a lie, to be transmuted into bleak tolerance in the light of day. She must remember this lesson for it would be a dire mistake if she ever forgot it. She could think of nothing worse than allowing Luke to discover that her feelings for him were more than that same cool tolerance. How humiliating, how demeaning it would be. So Harriette marched back to the house with a determination to preserve the same unemotional façade as her husband had so expertly shown to her. *I will be as politely cold as he if that is what is demanded of me.* When the tears pricked behind her lids again she blotted them with her sleeve. She would not weep. She would not! It was her own fault. She would bear the consequences, allowing no one to see the scars such a betrayal left on her heart.

Harriette was given no time to dwell on her misery. Her cousin was waiting to waylay her in the hall, as if there were nothing amiss.

'Before you go, Harry—will you let me make use of the Pride in your absence?'

She struggled to focus on his words, when her thoughts were scattered spindrift in a gale and her heart seemed to be in pieces within her breast. 'The Pride?'

'Yes.' He grasped her forearm, shook her a little. 'Let me use the house.'

Did she want that? Lydyard's Pride was hers. She

might choose to make use of it when danger threatened, but did she want the smuggling fraternity
making free of it in her absence, even under
Alexander's control?

'I'd rather you didn't, Zan,' she said, unhappy and
distraught but determined. 'I don't want it known
as a haunt of smuggling with Rodmell and his men
descending on the house every time we draw breath.
Use the Tower Room, of course, by all means.
Wiggins will light the lamp for you.'

'I want to use the cellars here…' Alexander's grip
tightened to keep her attention.

'No. I don't want that except in a dire emergency.
Use the church if you have to. Reverend Dance will
let you in. You've done it before.'

Alexander drew a breath, as if he would argue his
case, then lifted his hands with a deprecating smile.
'I don't agree, but it's your decision.' She sensed his
displeasure, but he kissed her cheek, already making
for the door. 'Enjoy your new life, little cousin.'

Leaving Harriette to make her way back to her
bedchamber, the scene of such happiness, now
empty and desolate. All she could do was simply
stand and look at the disordered linen on the bed and
wondered if she had imagined it all.

'What's happened?' Meggie demanded, from
whom she apparently could not hide her hurt.

'Nothing.' She smiled bravely. 'We are about to

leave.' She tied the strings of her plain straw bonnet with no thought to their neatness.

'Never mind that. Has he hurt you? He has, hasn't he!'

'No, Meggie. I can have no complaints. How should I? Did I not enter into this marriage with my eyes open?'

I will make sure that he doesn't hurt me again, she vowed silently. But of course he already had.

Despite his denial, Luke could not get Ellerdine's words out of his mind. A ship lured on to the rocks, all crew lost, the cargo commandeered. And Harriette at the very centre of it.

Impossible! his instincts insisted.

For what reason would Ellerdine lie? his mind responded. *You already know full well she's a smuggler!*

There was one source he could tap. Why should he not make every effort to learn the truth? And easy enough to do, as he ran that source to ground in the kitchen, where he was taking a tankard of ale.

'Tell me about the *Lion d'Or*.' Luke took a seat opposite George Gadie, poured his own ale. 'Was it lured on to the rocks at the headland?'

'Couldn't say, y'r honour.' Gadie wiped his mouth with the back of his hand, squinted round the room as if to ensure no one would hear. 'Wrecked here for sure. Some years ago now.'

Luke leaned across the table, fixed him with a stare. 'Was my wife involved?'

'Well, y'r honour…' Gadie rubbed his nose. 'Cap'n Harry launched the cutter to rescue the crew—just a young lass she was then. Not that there was anyone left alive to rescue, mind. Them's vicious rocks at the headland. But we took up the bodies—buried in the churchyard, they are. And we saved what we could. Silk, it was. Mr Alexander dealt with it.'

'Was the lamp in the Tower lit?'

The sailor's eyes slid away. 'Couldn't say, y'r honour. Too busy to notice. It *shouldn't* have been— not on a night like that.'

Was the man being honest or was he protecting Harriette? Luke considered, frowning into the ale. He suspected that George Gadie would be loyal to Captain Harry, no matter what the crime. What an appalling picture, of his wife luring unsuspecting sailors to their deaths.

If he chose to believe it, of course. But the sliver of ice in his belly had become a frozen knot.

'Anything else, y'r honour?'

Luke could think of nothing. For what else might he learn to cause him grief?

Luke helped his new wife into the curricle and turned his horses' heads towards London, conscious throughout of the stiff figure seated beside him, who had not smiled once, nor offered any conversation, since she had taken her seat. It struck him that he had been in some manner a naïve fool. He should have made it his business to discover more about Harriette Lydyard and her disreputable ancestors before embarking on this match. Alexander Ellerdine's casual remarks continued to play through his consciousness. Luke controlled the power of his hands on the reins with less than his habitual skill, and his fingers tightened, causing the horses to jib and toss their heads until he cursed his heavy-handed lack of skill and forced himself to relax his hold.

Harriette a member of the Wreckers? He could tolerate smuggling—just—as long as she gave it up. But Wrecking? There could be no justification for such a despicable operation. Bloody murder, luring ships on to the rocks to rob and plunder, the sailors abandoned to their own fate with no thought to their rescue. There was no profit to be gained from rescuing sailors, plenty from saving the bales and barrels. Luke felt his blood run cold. George Gadie's confirmation—if that's what it was—had been no help at all in putting his mind at rest.

Was Harriette capable of such vileness? He slid a glance to the pale, expressionless face of his wife beside him.

What did he know about Ellerdine—apart from a tendency to dislike him on sight? Cousin. Friend. A possible suitor. Harriette clearly held in some affection. Luke grimaced silently at the man's slick friendliness that, to him, held the taint of malice. The easy offer of information that would wound, tear. Why should he believe a man he did not know and did not respect above Harriette? She had never been anything but honest with him. Well, almost. She had not told him of her French mother until after the wedding, had she? An unimportant point. Had she hidden other secrets from him, masking them with her feminine charm?

There was only one remedy. He must ask her outright. He needed to know—but what if she admitted it? How could he reconcile himself to such knowledge? But he could not retreat from the truth.

'Are there many smuggling gangs on the coast?' he asked Harriette, breaking the silence between them.

'Yes,' she replied coolly. 'Enough to keep the Riding Officers busy.'

'And Wreckers. Do they exist here also?'

'Of course. Why?' He felt her sharp unsmiling glance, but did not turn his head.

'Do you know of any?'

'Yes.'

'Tell me.' Now he looked directly at her, searching her face for any sign of guilt, dreading that he might see it there.

'The smuggling gang in Rottingdean has a reputation,' she replied, holding his gaze without difficulty. 'Captain Dunk is their leader, a butcher by day and many would say a butcher by night, too.'

'What about Old Wincomlee? Do your smugglers lure ships on to the rocks?'

'No. Why do you ask?'

The slightest hesitation. Then brutally. 'Would you do it, if the opportunity arose?' He found himself holding his breath.

'No. I would not.'

Again he turned his attention from his horses and held her eyes with a hard glitter of emerald. Harriette had denied it, and with some heat. Her gaze was clear and direct.

'Why would you think me guilty of something so reprehensible?' A little line deepened between her fine brows.

It went a long way to restoring his composure, and Luke attempted to shrug off his discomfort, relaxing his fingers around the leathers. He had no proof, after all, that Harriette was engaged in anything other than the shipment of contraband and the fooling of the Revenue men. He had known about that before he wed her, and accepted it, so why cavil now?

Hell and the devil!

He liked her, admired her, wanted her in the most basic way a man could want a woman. Enjoying the intimacy of her body, the slender elegance of it stretched against his, warm and supple in response to his demands, had been a revelation. The perfume of her hair, the taste of her skin—even now the memory of it could arouse his wayward flesh, he acknowledged in sharp discomfort. She had delighted him. She had stirred some possessive desire within him to rescue her and protect her, apart from the primitive need to bury himself deep within her and claim her for his own. In that one short night he had discovered an exhilarating awareness of her, an overwhelming response to her.

Could he allow it to disintegrate? Would he change his opinion of Harriette Lydyard on the word of a man who it was his instinct to dislike on sight?

Dispassionately Luke viewed the bleak future. The marriage was done and she was his wife, and it would be entirely wrong of him to accuse her of crimes of which he had no proof. The best he could do was to end her attachment to smuggling and make what he could of this ill-matched marriage. Moving to London, away from Lydyard's Pride, was the obvious way to achieve that.

Harriette had never lied to him, had she?

Yet the fate of the *Lion d'Or* continued to fill his head with the discordant clamour of church bells.

* * *

Grosvenor Square. Hallaston House, as ostentatious as its address, enough to impress and overawe Harriette with its tiled floor, glittering chandelier and sweeping staircase, and a somber-clad butler, Graves, who ushered Harriette into the library.

There are secrets in this house, was Harriette's first impression. *Just as Luke keeps secrets from me. Echoes of grief and loss. They hang in the air like cobwebs. There is no happiness here.*

'The Countess of Venmore.' The astonishment in Graves's voice was superbly under control as he announced her. 'My lady—Lord Adam Hallaston.'

Harriette, exhausted by the strains of the day, stiffened her spine and prepared to meet her new family.

A pair of Hallaston eyes focused on her in a mixture of shock and disbelief. Adam Hallaston, younger than herself in age, rose slowly to his feet from where he had been lounging in a deep, silk-upholstered chair. The resemblance to Luke was striking, although Adam was fairer, and still growing into the tall Hallaston frame. He sketched a hasty bow, momentarily stuck dumb, yet with the presence to take her hand and bow over it. His greeting was startling.

'So he did it at last!'

Harriette looked enquiringly. 'What exactly?'

'Married!'

'Did you not expect him to do so?'

'Of course,' Lord Adam replied matter of factly. 'Eventually. But there've been a shoal of débutantes casting lures, and he didn't take the bait, not once.'

Amused, Harriette decided to speak the truth. 'I am not a débutante. I am a smuggler.'

'Ah…' He struggled for a reply.

'Nor did I trap your brother with bait.'

'No… I did not mean to imply…' Lord Adam's face flushed in embarrassed fascination. 'It's just that we don't wed young in the Hallaston family.' An ingenuous explanation. 'Marcus wasn't married, either.'

'Who is Marcus?' Harriette enquired.

A silence that could be touched, stark and edgy, settled on the opulent book-lined room. A heavy grief stirred Harriette's senses. But Adam recovered promptly enough.

'Marcus was our brother. He died, almost a year ago now.'

'Forgive me. I didn't know…' Harriette found herself at a loss. All the inexplicable tensions of the day to tear at her nerves, and now this. Why had Luke not told her of this?

'Are you really a smuggler?'

'Yes. I am.'

'Why did—?' Adam stopped short of inexcusable rudeness, although his eyes, greyer, darker than Luke's, sparkled with interest.

'Why did the Earl wed me?' Harriette supplied softly.

'Well…' Vivid colour again rushed into his cheeks.

'You mean, someone so far from the fashionable ladies of the *haut ton*?'

'Ah…'

Harriette found explanations deserting her. She would not offer trite explanations that there had been a long-standing attraction, or a sudden irresistible passion. What could she possibly say after the frigid, hurtful silence between them over the past hours? Let Luke perjure himself if he must.

'You must ask your brother that question,' she said.

'Ask him what?'

She had not heard the door open, nor the silent step of his feet on the thick carpet, but there he was beside her and immediately her pulse raced simply to be close to him. Awareness became a throb of desire. The proud carriage of his head, the austerely handsome face, the tall, loose-limbed grace.

'Luke…at last!' Adam Hallaston grinned.

'I trust you have welcomed my wife in a suitable manner. Your waistcoat is a thing of wonder, Adam.'

Painfully fashionable, Adam had the grace to laugh at the reference to the striped magnificence, confirming for Harriette that there was an affection between them. Perhaps after losing one brother they were protective of each other.

'Ask me what?' Luke repeated.

He looked weary, Harriette decided, on edge. The lines beside his mouth were deeply scored. The healing scar on his cheek stood out, as if his skin was tautly stretched in some hard-held emotion over the fine bones of his face. He straightened his shoulders as if he carried a heavy burden. Before she could think, compassion touched her sore heart, but exhausted herself beyond belief, Harriette brushed it aside and gave him no quarter. 'Your brother would ask you why you married me, so distant as I am from the ladies who usually clamour for your attention, but whose bait you have not so far taken. Lord Adam is curious. He informs me that the Hallastons never marry young.'

'Does he now? It's true. But as for my choice of a bride—there's no difficulty in explaining that.' Luke's level gaze held Harriette's challenging stare without compunction as he lifted her hand and carried it to his lips. His mouth was as cold as his face. 'I saw Harriette in a storm, near the sea. She was wet to the skin and her hair drenched and whipped by the wind into a tangle. Apart from her gown, she looked like a mermaid. I felt a need to wed her immediately.' He did not smile. 'She saved my life that night, and so I was bound to her, and she to me, irrevocably and for ever.'

A ridiculously romantic picture to save her from

humiliation. A pretty confection, little of which was true except for the proximity of the sea and the danger to his life. And the picture was coldly drawn as if it held no pleasure for him. To her horror, Harriette felt emotional tears threaten to well and fall. She must be more tired than she had thought. She swallowed hard against them and summoned the brightest smile.

'A mermaid?' Harriette tried to smile. 'As for saving your brother's life—' she kept the smile intact as she addressed Adam '—it was merely a matter of rescuing him from a fishy grave.'

Later, when she climbed the stairs to her new bedchamber, Harriette felt the full weight of that long day in her heart. She might feel bound to Luke, *irrevocably and for ever* as he had so charmingly put it, but his response to her on their journey from Old Wincomlee made it unbearably clear that he saw her as a burden. A misjudgement on his part. An alliance that was not to his taste.

What had she done to change his mind?

But perhaps she had done nothing, perhaps he had always viewed this marriage with regret and she had merely misread his kindness and generosity when he had taken her to bed. He had wed her because he had to and now, returned to his life in London, wished he had not. She could think of nothing she had done or said to make him revise his opinion of her, but he had, so presumably she had misread his opinion in the first place. She could not fault his good manners, but there was a withdrawal, as impenetrable as a physical barrier, between them.

He had found her unsuitable and had rejected her.

A shaming thought crept into her mind. Had he also found her not to his taste in bed? How could she judge? His kindness might mask displeasure, disgust. Telling her she was beautiful—they were only words after all.

And in that moment Harriette made a silent vow. She would play her part in this marriage, conduct herself with appropriate dignity as Countess of Venmore and make no demands whatsoever on the Earl. He had wed her, given her respectability and an entré into society whether she desired it or not. That was as much as she would ask of him. That ridiculous infatuation—it could not possibly be love!—that had been born when had seen him broken and filthy at her feet, that crippling emotion, would be buttoned away within her heart for ever. And if sometimes she wept at the death of her hopes, then it would be entirely in private. Cool. Polite. Reserved. Because that was what he wanted from his wife—or at least from her. She would be grateful, but would preserve a formal distance, never demanding his time or his presence, not expecting him to dance attendance on her. She would never be a burden to him.

It is not my intention to inconvenience you in any way. She practised her words silently in her head as she accompanied him up the staircase to her new suite of rooms. *You have fulfilled your duty towards me. You have given me so much, I cannot ask for your time, as well, can I?*

She would never say, *I want you. I love you. Hold me, Luke, kiss me as you did at Lydyard's Pride! Touch my body with those clever, elegantly skilful hands that make me burn for you. Tell me again that I am beautiful. Make me feel feminine and desired.* She would never say that.

Luke came to her room. No doubt from his well-bred sense of duty and honour, she decided bitterly. Harriette had taken herself to bed, dismissing her new maid, staring unseeingly at the pages of a book of poetry that did not hold her attention.

Luke knocked, entered, walked forwards slowly to stand beside her. After a wordless moment he sat on the edge of her bed. Yes, she had been right, his features fine drawn, but this was no time for sympathy.

'Do you have everything you need?' he asked courteously.

'Of course. You are most generous.'

Harriette put the book face-down and looked at

him, searched his face, trying to read the thoughts behind the stern expression. What did he want from her? It would be so easy to open her arms, to allow herself to be held and kissed. How easy it would be to slide breathlessly into his embrace, to curl her fingers into the thickness of his midnight hair, to ask no questions. Simply to be and to enjoy. But that was not possible and not in her nature to ignore the distance he had put between them.

'Did you wish to talk to me?' she asked.

Reaching out, he lifted her hands and turned them palm up, smoothing his thumbs over them as if he would read the message written in the lines.

'Do you want me to stay?' he asked, all impeccable courtesy.

He would rather not be here, she thought, even as her heart shivered at his caress. *He is magnificently polite, but his heart is not in it.*

'No,' she replied. How hard the words were. How difficult pride was. Her hands stiffened in his loose hold. 'It was a long journey. I am tired.'

'Of course.' He dropped her hands as if they scorched him. 'I should have been more considerate. We will talk when you are rested. It is imperative that we…'

Luke did not move, or finish his thought, but drew his knuckles gently over her cheekbone, down her cheek, her jaw, down the length of her throat.

Harriette felt herself tense. Surely he would feel the pulse beating there under his fingers. Surely he would see the flush of colour as her blood raced.

Luke leaned and pressed his lips to the satin skin at the base of her throat, the fragile hollow where her heart beat so heavily, whilst Harriette held her breath.

'Goodnight, Harriette. Sleep well. We'll talk tomorrow.'

And Luke stood, bowed, enigmatic and reserved, turned away. Only when he had reached the door did Harriette speak to stop him.

'Why did you not tell me about Marcus?'

He stood motionless, his back to her. Nor did he look round. 'There is nothing to tell.'

Then he was gone. She heard his footsteps die away along the corridor to his own room. He might not care about the rift between them, but she did. His instinct, for whatever reason, might be to push her away but it took all her willpower not to beg him to stay and hold her in his arms. It broke her heart.

Turning her face into her pillow, Harriette wept as she had not done since she was a child.

Luke closed the door of his room and leaned back against it, head thrown back, eyes closed against the emptiness of the room. The silence round him was agonising. Had he wanted her when he had gone to her room, despite all his doubts? Would he have stayed if she had smiled at him? Yes, he would. The fragility of her arms, her slender hands demanded that he cover them with kisses. The curl of her neatly combed hair, the gleam of pale flesh above the lace of the robe roused an urge to stroke. She had looked lost in the expanse of the elegant bed with its flower-sprigged hangings. Instinct had urged him to strip off his clothes and take her there. To press her naked body into the sheets beneath his, and sink deep, forgetting past and future in her arms as he had at Lydyard's Pride. To let her surround him with soft arms and thighs. She called to some basic primitive need in his blood to make her his. To awaken her nipples with tongue and teeth, to plant open-mouthed kisses all the way down the soft valley between her breasts towards the dark secret place that he could claim for his own by right.

He had wanted all of that, and did so now. Luke bared his teeth as his erection strained for release. He should have stayed with her and turned her cold words into cries of searing passion.

But it was better this way. There was too much between them to simply step over and ignore. So this was better. Wasn't it?

Then since he was so sure, why did he feel torn, his heart rent in two? It wasn't as if he loved her or even felt anything more for her than a duty, a heavy responsibility. And yet the urge was there to open his heart to her, to tell her of the coils that trapped him, constrained him. To explain why, in her eyes, he must apparently play the role of traitor and spy.

He could not, must not.

He had told Harriette that he had a brother in London. What he had not told her was that he had a second brother, who was now dead. Marcus, fighting with the British army under Wellington in the Penninsular War. Marcus's death was a raw wound that refused to heal, a death with lasting consequences that no one could have possibly foreseen and that now presented him with the most difficult choices of his life.

Luke felt alone and without counsel. Pushing himself away from the door, he scrubbed his hands over his face, tunneling his fingers through his hair, and groaned as he tried ineffectually to block out the image of his dead brother's laughing face.

'Oh, God, Marcus.' His harsh voice broke the silence. 'Why did you have to die?' And then, 'How do I deal with this woman who pulls at my emotions but whom I dare not trust?'

Chapter Seven

Breakfast in Grosvenor Square was a quiet affair and this one, two days later, was no exception. Adam was—well, Adam was wherever a young man might be at that early hour in the morning. Which left Luke and Harriette to share the breakfast table.

The London Season was well over. The *haut ton* had decamped *en masse* to the cooler rooms of its country homes, to rural watering places, or to the coastal attraction of Brighton. All of which Harriette saw as to her advantage. She need not attend Almack's and exhibit her lack of expertise in dancing. She did not have to curtsy to the polite world at some ball or drum or fashionable al fresco breakfast where she would be under the scrutiny of the blue blood of England. Nor did she have to preside over her own event in Grosvenor Square to stamp her presence on London society.

No one who was anyone remained in London in August. Except for the Venmore household. Which surprised her. Surely this was not the usual pattern of life for the Earl of Venmore? What could keep Luke in London, as short of company as it was? There was definitely *something*. Not only secrets hung in the air at Hallaston House, but an unease, almost a sense of waiting—and she thought it was not estate business that kept Luke occupied. Was it all tied up with Luke's abortive mission to France? She remembered in Luke's senseless ravings the woman that had caused him such distress, the woman he sought and could not find. Marie-Claude. Was this unknown lady the cause of Luke's coldness towards her? He had denied it, but did Marie-Claude stand between them? Did Luke actually love this unknown? He had not come to her bed again after her less than elegant rebuff.

Harriette was lonely and heartsore. She longed for Luke to repeat the intimate demands of their wedding night, but he would not. She considered abandoning her pride, taking his elegant lapels in her hands and pressing her lips to that sternly beautiful mouth, but dare not.

She sat and contemplated her husband. Across the table from her, Luke buried himself in the *Morning Post*. Harriette watched him covertly. In her mind she saw herself spread out before him on his bed.

She saw Luke kneeling naked beside her, as his hands and mouth began an exquisite exploration… If only it could be so.

She closed her eyes against the image. For now there were other priorities.

'Luke…'

Graves brought in a silver salver bearing a single sheet of paper, folded. He bowed, offering it to Luke. A thin line developed between Luke's brows as Harriette watched him read. He gave an imperceptible nod. A severity touched his mouth, a distinct tightening of the muscles in his jaw, across his cheekbones.

'Harriette…' Luke folded the note carefully and stowed it in the breast pocket of his beautifully cut coat. And there was the cool, unbridgeable distance between them again, as if his mind was elsewhere. She could see it, sense it, almost taste it, a harsh metallic tang, as if he had withdrawn into some distant place where she had no right to encroach. As if his thoughts were still with the contents of that single page. What had he read there? Was it a woman's hand—that of Marie-Claude's? Or was it all connected to dealings that he must keep secret from her? The name of Jean-Jacques Noir flitted into her mind, to lie alongside that of Marie-Claude.

'Who is the note from, Luke?' she asked, lured by her unhappy suspicions. 'Is it from France?'

'France? No, why should it be? Harriette, I shall be away for a few days.'

'To The Venmore?' Would he take her with him?

'No. I'm going to Bishop's Waltham.' It meant nothing to her. 'It will take me from home for two days, three at the most.'

'Oh.' Disappointment lodged in her throat. Before she could stop herself she asked, against all her determination not to make demands on him, 'Can I go with you? I have never been to Bishop's Waltham.'

But Luke was already on his feet, throwing down his napkin. 'No. Not this time and it's tedious work. I won't have the leisure to escort you round the town and you might find time heavy on your hands. Much better to stay here. I know it's flat, but…' For a moment she thought he would leave with no further explanation, then halfway to the door, he spun on his heel and returned. To lean down to where she still sat, to cradle her face between his hands. Gently, with exquisite tenderness, he pressed his lips against the soft skin between her brows, then to her lips. 'Forgive me, Harriette. I did not want this, but I have no choice… But when I return…' He ran the pad of his thumb along her bottom lip, following the caress with another kiss, prolonged and sure, a firm demand to set her pulse racing, then he released her. A courteous little bow and he strode across the room.

'Luke…' How driven he was, by some dark and dangerous compulsion.

He stopped, one hand on the doorknob and looked back almost, she thought, with impatience, as if he could not bear to be held back. It left Harriette with nothing to say other than. 'Take care.'

'Of course.' His quick smile she considered perfunctory. 'You'll enjoy spending money on some new gowns in my absence.'

Harriette stayed in the breakfast parlour, sinking back into her chair, listening to the rapid sounds of departure. Then he was gone and she had no idea what he was doing. How easy it was to allow hurt to well up and nearly choke her. She would miss him appallingly, yet could do nothing but accept that he would not miss her! All he could do was encourage her to improve her wardrobe! Furthermore, all her suspicions of Luke had been resurrected by the delivery of that one letter.

Struggling through low spirits that threatened to smother her in an impenetrable fog, Harriette stepped into the entrance hall just as one of the footmen—Charles, she thought—was making his way up the staircase, carefully balancing a tray of food, heartily loaded. It snatched at her attention.

'Charles! Where are you taking that?'

The young man stopped on the landing, spun

round to the danger of the tray, startled as a rabbit facing a huntsman. 'It's a breakfast tray, my lady.'

She smiled. 'Yes. I am aware. But where are you taking it? Do we have guests staying?' Would Luke not have told her if that were so?

'It's—it's for Lord Adam, my lady.'

'Then don't let me keep you.'

Charles, swallowing visibly, continued on his upward path. Harriette was left to consider that she did not believe a word of what was obviously a spur-of-the-moment explanation. So much food. Adam might wade through it, but he would not ask for a tray to his room.

Harriette considered Charles's retreating shoulders, then discreetly followed, taking refuge in the first guest room on the corridor, leaving the door ajar, from where there was no difficulty in discovering the destination of the loaded tray. Once Charles had retreated down the stairs, Harriette walked smartly to the now closed door and opened it.

Who was the more surprised, Harriette could not say.

'*Madame…*' A young man, seated at the table in the window embrasure, the tray before him, a fork in his hand, leapt to his feet.

'Who are you?' Harriette asked in astonishment.

'I…' He froze, fork in one hand, napkin in the other.

'This is my house and you appear to be staying in

one of my guest rooms without my knowledge, eating breakfast from my kitchens, sir. Who are you? What are you doing here?'

'*Madame… Je m'appelle…*' He stammered to a halt again, eyes widening in dismay. 'My name is Henri, *madame*. Captain Henri.' He struggled with heavily accented English.

The young man's obvious French birth stirred Harriette's already simmering suspicions to a fast boil. 'We can speak French if you wish it, sir. You will be more comfortable with that. My mother was French.'

'Ah, *madame*…my gratitude.' The young man lapsed immediately into his native tongue. 'But I should say nothing. It is not wise.'

'What is not wise? I should introduce myself. I am the Countess of Venmore.'

'Madame la Contesse.' Dropping both napkin and fork on the table, the young man executed a neat bow with military precision. '*Enchanté.*'

Refusing to be distracted by his excellent manners, Harriette demanded, 'Why are you here?

'I await the return of Monsieur Luke. I am not at liberty to say why.'

'Why not?'

'It would be too dangerous. It would not be safe for my presence to be known here.'

'Dangerous? For you or for my husband?'

'For both, I think, *madame.*'

Harriette struggled to come to terms with her discovery. 'But who are you, Captain Henri?' She knew exactly who—or at least *what* he was.

Captain Henri shook his head, his whole bearing beseeching her to have pity. And Harriette took a moment to examine her guest. Young, little more than twenty years, she estimated. And thin. Thin cheeks, a haunted expression. His clothes were of good quality, but hung on his spare frame as if they had not been made for him. Harriette also saw that he stood awkwardly, as if he carried a recent injury to one arm or shoulder. There was a pride there, an innate dignity, as well as impeccably good manners, but at this moment he was fearful and unwilling to be indiscreet. She thought he might have been a handsome lad before war had taken its toll in stark grooves between his brows and tightly stretched skin over sharp cheekbones.

'Were you a prisoner?' she asked.

Again he bowed. 'I was, Madame la Contesse. Regretfully. What use in my denying it? That's all I will say. Except to thank you for your hospitality. And beg pardon for my ill manners. But in the circumstances, you understand…'

No, she did not understand at all. What was a French prisoner of war from Napoleon's forces doing in her guest room? She feared for the answer.

204 Compromised Miss

'Does the Earl of Venmore know you are staying here?'

'Ah, Monsieur Luke? He does, *madame*.'

So what had Luke to do with a prisoner of war? Treachery…treason…spying. The terrible words danced once more before her eyes. She knew that prisoners escaped back to France, slipping into a French port with forged papers, carrying with them news for Napoleon's ears of England's defences, English war plans against their enemy.

The logical explanation—surely the only explanation—was that Luke was involved in the return of this young man to France. But why? Was Luke himself in the pay of France, was he feeding delicate information to Napoleon through the auspices of French prisoners of war? The evidence against him grew stronger. And in that moment of shocked revelation Harriette would have wagered any consignment of contraband that the man Jean-Jacques Noir was somehow involved.

But Captain Henri was not going to enlighten her.

'Madame la Contesse…?' His anxiety was self-evident. 'What do you intend to do with me? Will you hand me over to the authorities?'

She discovered that she had been frowning at him and forced her face into a softer expression. She could take no such action until the proof was incontrovertible. Her whole being, mind and soul, reacted against branding Luke a traitor.

'You are safe here, Captain Henri,' she reassured him. 'Eat your meal in peace.'

And she left him to his solitary breakfast and closed the door softly.

Striding round to his stabling to order up his curricle, Luke was far too aware of the sense of desolation he had left behind in the breakfast parlour, and of his own making. Married for less than three days, no understanding between them, rather a deep and threatening abyss, and here he was planning to abandon her. He had read Harriette's disappointment, wanted more than anything to reassure her and restore that sparkle of happiness he had seen on the night of the hidden contraband, but until this damnable matter that plagued his whole life was settled, he could not. The early morning air cool on his cheeks, he was conscious only of the warmth of her mouth on his and suddenly, shock-ingly intimate, her limbs entangled with his, her body hot and welcoming. It brought him to halt, a frown between his brows. Harriette called to some basic element in him, yet he was deliberately walk-ing away from her and the hurt he saw in her eyes. With a set jaw, Luke squared his shoulders and forced himself to honour the call of duty before he threw caution to the winds and returned to kiss the colour back into Harriette's pale cheeks.

For the next two days Harriette kept her secret. The one certainty in her solitary existence was that, apart from her pleasure in a number of fashionable gowns, she missed Luke with a sharp loneliness she could never have imagined. Her heart was no longer her own, nor her dreams, which were troubled with high storms and shadowy figures that claimed to be Jean-Jacques Noir. Luke, too, was there, but could not hear her when she called to him, but disappearring into the mist over the sea, leaving her alone. Harriette was relieved when daylight gave her an excuse to rise, unrested and anxious. From her bedchamber she prowled the rooms, her thoughts constantly worrying over what it was that Luke might be doing in Bishop's Waltham. Even in the library, Lukes own preserve, she found no sense of his presence. The heavily masculine room was still, silent, with only the scent of lavender polish and the faint aroma of candle-wax. It gave her no sense of Luke.

It was there she found herself standing before two portraits.

One, an elegant little Kit Kat, three-quarter length, a younger Luke perhaps, until she saw the obvious differences in the more rounded cheeks, the curl in the dark hair. A young man who lacked Luke's gravity. So this would be Marcus. The grey-green eyes looked out of the portrait with a direct confidence that she immediately recognised. So lifelike, it seemed impossible that Marcus Hallaston was dead.

Next to the Kit Kat, the more formal portrait took her eye. This was Luke. Definitely *Lucius* here, standing before a handsome rambling property, a spaniel at his feet, the parkland and trees of what was clearly The Venmore stretching behind him. Luke stared down at her, stern, handsome, authoritative. Harriette felt that those green eyes pinned her to the Aubusson carpet, knew her, owned her, yet there was no humour in them, no trace of affection. The Earl of Venmore was cold, judgemental. Reaching up, she ran her finger down the unblemished painted cheek.

An excellent portrayal of the man she knew, but she did not like it.

The door opened behind her. Harriette spun round, almost as if she would see Luke in the flesh, smiling at her as he once had and as he did not in the portrait. Instead Adam halted on the threshold, then came in.

'Harriette. Where's Luke?'

'He's gone to Bishop's Waltham,' Harriette replied. 'Did he not tell you?'

'No. Luke tells me very little.'

She tilted her head, acknowledging the brusque reply, considering how much she might ask. 'Why do you suppose Luke would wish to go to Bishop's Waltham?'

'I have no idea. Or at least…' Adam's brows knit. 'The name's familiar. I think I've heard it recently. I know!' His face cleared. 'It's a parole town.'

'A parole town?' The connection for Harriette with what she already knew was a matter of terrible simplicity. Her head began to throb with a dull ache.

'Yes. Problems there, prisoners of war absconding, breaking their parole, escaping back to France. That sort of thing.'

'And what will Luke be doing in a parole town, do you suppose?'

'Well—I don't suppose his visit had anything to do with that. Perhaps he's gone to look at a new stallion.'

So Adam knew nothing. It seemed that Adam was just as much in the dark as she. Harriette found herself turning back to the portrait and Adam came to stand beside her.

'It was painted late last year,' he said.

'It's very good. It makes him look…' She hesitated.

'Very proud?' Adam finished, sliding his eyes to hers.

'Well—I was going to say arrogant!'

'Yes,' Adam agreed and sighed. 'And he's not.

This was painted just after Marcus's death. He was unhappy….'

As one, they turned to the Kit Kat, the laughing face of Marcus Hallaston.

'Adam—will you tell me about Marcus? Your brother does not speak of him. All I know was that he was killed. Tell me—unless it would be too painful for you.'

'I'll tell you what I can.' Adam folded his arms, considering the likeness as if he could still see his brother, alive and vigorous, in this same room. 'Marcus was a half-dozen years older than I, closer to Luke in age, so we did not grow up together, but I know he was always Army mad. Couldn't wait to purchase a commission in the 11th Hussars.'

'He was fighting in the Peninsula?'

'Yes. He was killed at Salamanca last July. It…it devastated us. Luke just clammed up. It's always in the back of your mind that it can happen in war, but you just never believe it.' He lifted his shoulders uneasily. 'Everyone liked Marcus. I still expect him to come home, full of far-fetched stories of his adventures as he did when I was a lad. I miss him. Luke does, beyond bearing.'

Harriette contemplated the scant outline. A tragic story of a young man dying before his time, infinitely regrettable but always to be expected in times of war, a situation that could be echoed in any number of families the length and breadth of the land.

'I'm glad I know.'

Then the words poured out, as if Harriette's interest had loosed a stopper in a bottle. 'Something's troubling Luke. I don't think it's Marcus, but he won't say. We've been close, he's had a care for us, with both our parents dead. Now it's as if…I don't know. Luke's always been reticent, reserved, I suppose, but now he's distant and preoccupied. He won't explain. He was never so unapproachable.'

'I know.' She touched his arm. 'I can give you no advice, Adam.'

'Sorry!' His voice was gruff. 'I shouldn't have burdened you with my problems—not that they are problems. It's just that I wish he trusted me, you know. I expect he talks to *you*.'

'Why?'

'Because you are his wife.'

'No, Adam, he does not.' Harriette laughed softly, sadly. 'I cannot help you.'

Harriette could find no other reply to make to this troubled young man. *I expect he talks to you because you are his wife*. How tragically ironic. Adam could not be further from the truth. What hope was there for her in such a marriage? Staring at the austere painted face of the Earl of Venmore in which she could see neither compassion nor understanding, merely an implacable determination, she knew that she had made a terrible mistake. Love was not enough. Her skin might burn at the thought of his touch, her heart might desire to heal and soothe whatever rode him with such sharp spurs. But only if he would allow it. If he was a traitor without principle or honour—how could love deal with that?

Harriette assessed her next move. It crossed her mind to visit the guest room and force Monsieur Henri by means she could not yet envisage to tell her all he knew. She had made up her mind to do just that when the hammer of the knocker on the front door heralded a visitor, an individual in neat black who had just been ushered into the entrance hall by Graves.

Graves immediately approached, bowed. 'This is Mr Harvey, your ladyship. From Hoare's Bank. To see his lordship. As I have explained, the Earl is away from home.'

'Thank you, Graves. Can I help you, Mr Harvey?' A matter of financial affairs between the Earl and his banking establishment could wait until Luke's return. Harriette's interest was polite but perfunctory.

'I have an important delivery for the Earl of Venmore, my lady. It is expected.' Mr Harvey smiled discreetly, indicating the wooden travelling case tucked beneath his arm.

'Perhaps you would care to place it in my lord's study for the Earl's attention, sir.' She looked around for Graves, but he had vanished in the direction of the servants' quarters, expecting Harriette to deal with it. 'If you would come with me, I'll show you where you might leave it in safety.'

Mr Harvey followed her into the small parlour with its escritoire and rosewood cabinet where Luke stored estate documents. 'I'm sure I can leave so valuable a box in your care, my lady. And if you would be so willing as to sign this receipt? And here, my lady, is the key into your safe keeping.'

A travelling case and a key. Tension hummed through Harriette, tingling to her fingertips, but she merely smiled and signed the receipt. Mr Harvey bowed himself out. Harriette was left to look at the plain box with its domed lid and the insignia of Hoare's Bank stamped clearly below the escutcheon and the ornate lock. Although not very large, it was obviously quite heavy. The key suddenly felt hot in her hand.

Would it matter very much if she opened the chest to see the contents? It had been given into her possession in her husband's name after all. The urge to see the contents grew with every second.

This is not your affair. You should trust him.

'I do trust him. It's just that…' The prisoner of war and the parole town nudged at the doubts that tumbled through her mind.

Without conscience, Harriette acted. The key slid with ease into the lock, turned with well-oiled precision. Harriette lifted the lid. Inside a number of red velvet purses were tucked neatly together. She had to guess no longer, the contents were written clear within their velvet cushioning. Loosening the drawstring, she emptied one of the purses on to the shining wood of the desk. The bright gold of the guineas rolled and fell.

Harriette stood perfectly still before the bright evidence, her heart beating riotously against her ribs. Funds for the Earl of Venmore's everyday expenditure? She doubted it. A special delivery under lock and key? And so many bags of coin? She could not imagine how much wealth lay before her.

Harriette slowly scooped the coins into her hand and restored them to their tidy nest. Beside the chest a pile of unopened letters had been left by Graves for the Earl's attention. Harriette's hand strayed towards them, halted, her conscience suddenly returning. Was she really going to riffle through her husband's correspondence in his absence?

Yes, I am. Then stared at the letter on the top of the pile. Quite obviously it was from France. *Yes, I definitely am!* She opened it with trembling fingers.

It was a brief letter with the simple inscription to the Earl of Venmore.

Our business is not yet complete. I will set time and place when this can be remedied and inform you of them. It will be on French soil. You already know the terms.

The pain you experienced at my hands was through your own intransigence in attempting to trick me. Next time I shall not be so conciliatory in my dealings.

Don't disappoint me. You know the price. The outcome will be to the benefit of both of us. And to the third party whose name you know.

I know I do not need to warn you to speak of this to no one.

Jean-Jacques Noir

Harriette did not understand the references, but then she did not need to. The signature confirmed all the fears in her troubled mind.

'What is he doing?' she demanded of the silent room. 'How can I love a man who appears to be wading through so much murky water?'

You can love him simply because you do. Illogical and regrettable it may be, but you lost your heart to him the moment he fell at your feet, broken and bloody. And you can love him because you are hoping that you have misjudged him. Praying that his connection with France and the creature Jean-Jacques Noir is perfectly innocent. The voice whispered in her ear. Harriette shook her head to dislodge it.

'Of course I pray that my suspicions are unfounded. Just as I'm praying that I've misread the reason for a box of gold and a letter from a French rogue,' she replied tartly, refolding the incriminating letter. 'Just as I'm praying that I've misread his deliberate retreat from me. But I haven't.' Head bent, she surveyed the unpleasant missive, letting it fall back on to the pile as if it soiled her fingers. 'Something has changed between us since the day we stood in Old Wincomlee church together. Since he took me to bed with such care and yet such fire in his blood. I have not imagined that! Nor am I imagining all of this…' she swept her hand over the items on Luke's desk '…nor that the Frenchman is still under my roof!'

Harriette brushed a wayward tear from her cheeks.

Chapter Eight

Luke returned home from Bishop's Waltham and shut himself into his study, letting the silence of the house settle around him. It had been a hectic few days, but the necessary papers and a passage to France for Captain Henri, in disguise, had been arranged. Harriette fortunately was not at home. At this moment he had no wish to face her, no wish to face anyone. Trivial words of greeting, enquiries about how she went on in his absence, simple, sensible words, or even smooth excuses for his absence, would not seem to form in his mind. As for taking her to bed... She would rightly condemn him if she knew he had returned to her from arranging the escape of one of England's enemies.

Captain Henri, at this moment hidden in one of the guest bedrooms, an officer and a prisoner of war on parole, billeted with a local family on the strength of his oath that he would make no move to escape, had found his honour compromised in a need to return to France. It was not Luke's place to discover the man's reasons. Honour was a costly commodity, as he had discovered. And if Captain Henri would not afford to consider every nuance of the word *honour*, neither to his shame could he. Luke was trapped in a web of intrigue and dishonour running contrary to every tenet of his upbringing. But he banished the desperate line of thought to the deepest recesses of his mind, even though he knew it would return to haunt him in the dark hours of the night. Marcus dead. Jean-Jacques Noir manipulating events. Luke had been so used to determining the direction of his own life, now he appeared to be pulled in every direction by invisible strings. And like a fly in a spider's web, he could see no way out without some measure of pain and distress for those he loved. How could it all have happened?

Trusting people had becoming a major issue in his life.

And then, of course, there was Harriette. Harriette… Luke rubbed his hands roughly over his face. She haunted his mind in an insoluble tension of admiration straining against a fear that she had lied to him, respect coupled with a lurking dread that she was not what she seemed. All overlaid by a strong physical desire. There was no doubt that he felt an unquenchable need for her, nor that she responded to him with equal passion.

Hell and the devil! Luke did not know where to step next in this lethal morass of contradictions.

The clatter of horses' hooves outside in the square brought him back to the present. Luke pushed himself upright, focusing on the strongbox with its hoard of guineas, the pile of letters with the familiar black script of Jean-Jacques Noir on the top—so unlikely a pseudonym, damn him! Would there ever be an end to this nightmare? The visit to Bishop's Waltham had achieved everything he could have desired, but whether it would bring him any closer to ending this horror, he was not prepared to wager. Luke scowled at his inability to order events to his liking.

Luke's thoughts re-focused. Marcus. Who would have thought that Marcus's death at Salamanca would have cast him into this maelstrom? Even now Luke could remember the exact day they had finally heard that Marcus was dead, the intensity of the grief and loss that had still not loosed its grip.

But that loss of a loved brother was not to be the end of it.

Restless now, Luke pulled open a drawer in the little writing desk and lifted out an official sheet of paper, roughed folded, and a miniature. Pushing aside the travel-stained document whose content he knew by heart, he studied the pretty face. Expertly painted, beautifully framed, the woman who looked out at him was very young when the likeness had been taken, hardly more than a girl. Limpid blue eyes, fair curls held with ribbons to fall from her crown to her shoulders. A delicate lace edging to her dress emphasised the youthfulness of her almost flat bosom. She looked little more than a girl still in the schoolroom, but even at this tender age there was a decisiveness about the chin and mouth. A sharpness to the eye. Here was a girl who knew her mind and would act upon it. And there was a joyful, mischievous humour there.

Marie-Claude de la Roche, inscribed on the back of the portrait.

For a long moment Luke tapped the document on the edge of the desk, then slammed the drawer closed on both paper and pretty miniature. What could he do, more than the shady negotiations that he had already instigated? He would arrange for Captain Henri to return to France. It appalled him that he would willingly hand over the box of gold to a man so devoid of honour as Noir, but he would do it if he had to. He had risked his life once in Port St Martin and he would do it again. What a mess it all was.

As for Harriette, she was already knee-deep in suspicions that he was a spy in the pay of Napoleon. His mouth curled in what was not a smile. The thought of Harriette brought him up short with a sudden urge to lay it all before her. Dare he do that? He was in desperate need of someone to whom he could unburden his fears, who would give him an unbiased opinion. Luke feared he could no longer be objective in something that touched his family so closely. Harriette would give him cold, clear advice. If he told Harriette…

His heart, leaping with a sudden, outrageous hope, plummeted once more. It was far too danger-ous to tell Harriette of his predicament, smuggler as she was and perhaps even a Wrecker, too. If she told her cousin of what she knew, and there was no guar-antee that she would not allow a chance word to fall in the ear of Alexander Ellerdine… Luke scowled. He would not trust Ellerdine to keep his mouth shut. And then it would be so easy for that knowledge to spread through the smuggling fraternity, and then all the world would know. What would Noir do then? Luke knew exactly what he would do—had he not been warned? He dare not contemplate the mon-strousness of Noir's vicious threat.

So now he sat with the obscure letter from a French criminal, a chest of gold and a French enemy in his house, waiting for the next set of instructions, which he knew he would not like, but would have no choice but to obey. Self-contempt roiled in his gut that he should be so quick to question Harriette's honour. Where had his own code of honour gone?

Dead and buried under the weight of family loyalties! Was there no way out of this impossible entanglement? There was a light tap on the door. Harriette stood on the threshold as if his thoughts had conjured her there.

'Luke. I didn't know you had returned.'

'An hour ago—no more.'

Desire took him full in the chest, a vicious blow, a caress of delight. It speared through him, stroked over him. His heart, his loins. He wanted her, to hold her and kiss her, to strip her and pleasure her into mindless surrender beneath him. Was she unaware of how pretty a picture she made? So far removed from the windswept, salt-encrusted young man in boots and breeches, in this delicate muslin gown, her hair arranged into feathery ringlets that drew his eye to the intoxicating column of her neck, rather than stuffed under a woollen cap. He smiled at her because he had no choice. And after the smallest hesitation—was it even there?—she smiled back.

And how could he have mistrusted her, believed her guilty of death and destruction. Of course she would help him. She was his wife and he was free to pour the dilemma of Marcus at her feet, to ask her clear-eyed advice.

He pushed the chest and the letters aside, rose to his feet, crossed the room to her, giving himself no more time to think, only to feel, to savour this moment after their parting. Without a word, cupping his hand on the back of her neck, he drew her forwards, letting his fingers tangle in her hair. She was all softness, all beguiling desirability. Luke bent his head, all other concerns obliterated, and brought his mouth down on hers. At first he felt the tension in her, but deepening the kiss, changing the angle, he lured her on until he felt the release of her breath, sweet against his skin. His tongue explored, took possession and Harriette sighed against him. She would not repulse him this time. Need built fast in his loins, his erection hard against her as he held her strongly so that she would know his desire. His tongue tasted the dark excitement of her mouth. He would take her to bed, forget all issues that divided them, simply sinking into her warmth, her delectable body.

'I've missed you. I want you… Do you know how much you are in my thoughts?' he murmured against those lips that parted beneath his with such sweetness. Luke raised his head, studying her face, the delicate flush, the shy curve of her mouth kissed into softness. Her lips begged to be kissed again—but not now, not yet. Not until he had made an attempt to smooth the path between them. He eased his fingers from her shoulders, pushed her gently away but not too far, keeping possession of her hands, keeping her close enough to touch.

'Harriette—I need to tell you something…'

He saw it at once, the tension returning immediately in her, fingers clenching around his, an unwillingness to meet his gaze. The grey eyes were quickly masked by dark lashes, as if she feared his confession.

'Harriette…'

'I need to ask you something, too,' Harriette replied before he could continue. And he saw trouble in her eyes, now raised defiantly to his, and suffered a bleak premonition that lodged as a fist of ice in his chest.

'Then ask me.' Resigned, his fingers tightened around her wrists where her pulse beat so heavily against his palms.

'I don't think you'll like it,' she admitted gruffly.

'Well, ask it anyway.'

It was not to be. Graves knocked softly and entered.

'My lord. There is a Mr Ellerdine here. To see her ladyship. I've put him in the gold parlour.'

'Alexander…!' He felt her reaction under his hands, saw her instant smile. 'Why would he be in town?'

It could not escape Luke's notice that Harriette instantly pulled free from his clasp. Ellerdine, her cousin, her friend, her partner in despicable crimes. 'Perhaps you should go and see him,' Luke advised coolly, evenly, turning from her to pick up the correspondence from the desk again. Refusing to admit to the huge sense of disappointment. Or even more the surge of sheer male jealousy that this man had a place in her life.

But Harriette did not move. She looked at him, a frown returning. 'Should I go to him? Or we could tell him to wait—until we are finished here.'

'Why would we do that? I'm sure you wish to see him.'

'Well, yes. But you said you needed to tell me something. And I—'

'It's not important.'

'Oh.' A shadow touched her face.

'It can wait, Harriette. Go and speak with your cousin. I'm sure you have things to tell him.'

'Yes.' Still she did not move.

'We'll continue this conversation later, Harriette.'

'Of course.'

Then, with the faintest of sighs, she was gone, leaving Luke shattered by the strength of the emotions she stirred in him. Harriette's connection with Alexander Ellerdine did not please him at all. It was impossible to deny the bite of jealousy at the smile that lit her eyes when his name was announced. And considering it, it forced him to a decision. He could not tell her about Marie-Claude de la Roche, could he? What an unequivocal mistake that would have been! All he could do now was to sit and wait for further communication from Jean-Jacques Noir, unless his French prisoner of war could discover something of the girl's present whereabouts. He'd be damned if he'd give in to the rogue Noir—but he might not have any choice in the matter if Mademoiselle de la Roche could not be discovered... And Luke swore as his thoughts came full circle, ending once again with his helplessness and probable failure.

But he would not think of that now. Nor would he think of the reason for Alexander Ellerdine's presence in his house. Or the worry in Harriette's face when she admitted he would not like the question she must ask. And certainly not her pleasure at the prospect of setting eyes on her cousin again.

Except what else was there to think of?

Harriette discovered Alexander leaning his shoulders against the wall to gaze out of the window over the smart railed gardens of Grosvenor Square, a glass of port in hand.

'You look flustered.' His first remark, not particularly friendly.

'Yes,' she responded, instantly wary. 'I ran downstairs too quickly.'

Harriette closed the door carefully at her back and simply stood there, grasping at her composure. Her cheeks felt to be on fire and her fashionable curls were undoubtedly disordered from Luke's possessive fingers. It even felt that her lips were soft and bruised from the power of his kisses. As for her heart, it leaped and bounded against her muslin bodice, so much that it compromised her breathing.

She forced herself to take a deep breath. Running her tongue over dry lips, Harriette ordered her thoughts back into line. And failed. How devastating was Luke's presence. Five minutes in his company, in his arms, and all her self-control was awry. His hard mouth capturing hers, his hand caressing the nape of her neck, his arms pinioning her against his body whilst his tongue plundered her mouth with such urgency, for a brief time she could imagine that nothing could come between them. How weak she was that she could forget the presence of Captain Henri and a box of gold, seduced by strong arms and searing lips that captured her soul from her body.

And then, given the most trivial of excuses, he had dismissed her, whilst she had escaped from him with ridiculous speed. But it would have been far too dangerous to remain, far too easy to forget to keep her emotions hidden from his searching green gaze. How humiliating for her if Luke should discover that her heart was his, when he had no desire to possess it. Kissing her was one thing; loving her was quite another.

Whilst his need to talk to her had not been so very urgent after all. He had almost ordered her from the room, as if he had regretted his hot kisses.

Harriette's heart hurt.

'Is the enforced leisure of town life robbing you of your energy? I recall the time when you could sail all day without losing breath,' Alexander remarked.

Harriette sensed the implied criticism, but merely shook her head.

'Too much pleasure, too much champagne. Too much the Countess of Venmore, I would say. I told you you'd regret it. But you wouldn't listen, would you? You were always too headstrong for your own good.'

There was the sharpness again in his words. Harriette's spine stiffened. 'I don't regret it. And I don't like your implications that I made a mistake, Alexander!'

But he was close beside her, abandoning the glass of port so that he could lean to kiss her cheek with easy familiarity, gentling his voice. 'I meant no harm. Perhaps I've missed you more than I realised, Harry. You look charming, different.'

Puffing out a little breath, relieved that there was no ill will between them after all, Harriette smiled in quick forgiveness. 'Zan—it's good to see you. What are you doing here?'

'A lucrative little sale that you'll approve of.' He took her hand in a companionable hold. 'A valuable cargo. You'll soon be seeing some of our silks and laces clothing the backs of the *haut ton*.'

'So business is good.'

'It is. And I couldn't resist visiting my pretty cousin to enquire after her good fortune, could I?'

Harriette felt a comforting warmth blooming in her breast. Unlike her edgy dealings with Luke, here was someone uncomplicated whom she had known for ever. No tensions or difficulties in their relationship, no need for her to hide her thoughts or her feelings, no need to keep up a permanent pretence. No need to question her loyalties for a man whom she loved but dare not love. Zan was a friend, knew her faults and strengths, just as she knew his. There was no deceit in Alexander, no attempt to hide his shadowy dealings outside the law, and she found that she had missed him, the ease of their conversation. To her dismay, her horror, she felt tears gather and begin to track down her cheeks.

'Harriette—what is it?' Alexander demanded at once. 'What has happened to make you weep?'

Before she could wipe away the tears and assemble a suitable answer, she was surrounded by his arms, and faced with such immediate compassion she found herself weeping on his shoulder. Thoroughly embarrassed, she resisted, but his arms were warm and comfortable so that the tightness in her chest eased and the tears continued to flow. Until

Alexander drew her to a little gilt-legged sofa and settled her there. Finding a handkerchief in his pocket, he sat beside her and dried her tears with competent strokes.

'Nothing can be so bad as to reduce my brave cousin to tears. Tell me, Harriette.'

'Nothing.' She took the linen from Alexander and sniffed, mortified, contrite. 'I shouldn't have done that. I don't know what came over me.'

His voice was as soothing as a feather eiderdown on a winter's night, wrapping her round in reassurance. 'Why should you not lean on my shoulder? Who else would you turn to? Have we not always stood for one another, even as children?'

'I know.' Her smile was watery.

She felt Alexander's fingers tighten on hers. 'What has he done to you?'

'Luke? Why, nothing. He doesn't beat me, you know.' She tried for a gleam of humour. 'Luke treats me with all consideration and gives me all I could possibly need. I've received nothing but kindness here. I have no complaints.'

'No one understands you as I do. You should never have married him, Harriette. As I said, you always were foolishly headstrong.'

But I love him. I'm just no longer sure that love is enough! Harriette shook her head and could not answer.

'Tell me,' Alexander repeated.

How tempting it was, because she was vulnerable, because she could speak of her suspicions to no one in the Hallaston household, and because he was her cousin. How tempting to tell Zan of the Frenchman in the guest room. The box of guineas. The letter and what she knew of a villain called Jean-Jacques Noir. Luke's visit to the parole town.

She could not. How could she put into words, even to her cousin, that Luke was in communication with the enemy, perhaps in the pay of France, passing information or gold coin—or both—to Napoleon? Helping French prisoners of war to break their terms of parole so that they might escape to fight again.

Her words dried on her lips at the enormity of it all.

Besides, could she believe that Luke had the makings of a traitor? He had rescued her from the consequences of scandal and cruel gossip. Surely then his whole life could not be guided by *dishonour*. Yet why not? Had he not bargained for the use of the *Ghost*? How well that would fit with a life of spying and the passing of secrets to England's enemies.

'There's nothing to tell.' And Harriette sighed.

'When I offered you a means of escape from this, you should have taken it. You should have wed me, Harriette,' he chided gently.

'Perhaps.' She found that she could no longer meet his eyes. 'You are very kind.'

'Not kind. I care about you. I always have.'

'I know.' *But I don't love you—and you don't love me.* Harriette swallowed against the tears that threatened again, covering her face with her hands.

With one hand he lifted her chin so that she must look up. 'We could have lived together at the Pride. Made a life there.'

She tried a smile. 'And done what? Seen it fall down around our ears? Neither of us has the money to put it to rights.'

'No, we don't. Not even with the profits from smuggling.' He hesitated. 'Not yet, but one day perhaps…'

Harriette smiled damply. 'It's only dreams, Zan. It would take a fortune.'

'Poor Harriette. So torn by doubts.' His hand was warm on her cheek, his voice soft in her ear. 'Leave it all. Come back to Lydyard's Pride with me. I can't promise you wealth and luxury but you'll know all my sins. Venmore will divorce you and you can wed me. As you should have done in the first place.' His thumb stroked her lips. 'Just do it, Harry.'

His seductive tones, his use of her childhood name, destroyed her composure anew and Harriette wept again, until Alexander drew her in his arms. 'Don't weep,' he murmured, his head against the top of her head. 'He's not worth it.' She felt him touch his lips to her hair.

The door to the parlour opened softly.

Venmore stood on the threshold.

Harriette sprang to her feet, cheeks flushed in a wash of guilt, furious she should feel so compromised at receiving comfort from her cousin. She wiped her eyes ineffectually on a scrap of lace and linen. The tensions in the room screamed within her. She lifted her head and faced her husband.

'I see I have interrupted,' he remarked, cold as a January night. 'How remiss of me. I should have realised that there were issues between cousins that were not my affair.'

How to answer that? Harriette quailed before the glacial chill in Luke's face, the proud arrogance of his stance, even as she resented his entirely wrong conclusions. 'No…indeed, my lord, there are none.'

'We are cousins, Venmore. There is a lifetime of connection between us. Harriette—I must go.' Alexander bowed to Harriette, deliberately, as provocative as his words, lifting her hand to his lips, and then to the Earl. 'Forgive me for trespassing on your time, my lord.' And he walked to the door before looking back over his shoulder. 'You know my advice, Harriette. It's your choice if you act on it.'

Then Harriette was alone, to face Luke with all the stark suspicion between them, as solid as a newly constructed redoubt between opposing armies. The air between them quivered as taut as a wire. Harriette waited for what he would say. All she could see was the banked fury in his eyes where fire burned and flickered, a tight anger in the lines of his face, under control but only just. Standing rigidly to his full height he looked magnificent, but it was the face of an avenging angel who would strike and wound without compassion.

Luke kept a fierce hand on his temper. To walk in on Harriette and find her in the arms of her damned cousin—it pulled him up short as a fist to the jaw. Not five minutes after he himself had held her and kissed her and had contemplated the blessed release of laying his insurmountable problems at her feet, he had discovered her in appallingly intimate discussion with Alexander Ellerdine.

And just what advice had the flamboyant Mr Ellerdine been giving her? Luke bared his teeth in the approximation of a snarl. How could he have been so misguided, so completely taken in by her? She did not seem in any degree contrite. Guilty, of course, springing to her feet with consternation shadowing her beautiful eyes. At least he had had the sense to keep his tongue between his teeth and not rage at her as impulse had prompted. He had not pounced to seize her shoulders and shake her and demand why she could not find comfort in *his* embrace, from his body. It took a masterly degree of control, of which he was cynically proud.

And he had been crass enough to consider telling her of the fate of Marie-Claude de la Roche and his own duplicitous attempts to rescue her. He might as well have put a notice in the Morning Post. And if, through Ellerdine and the smuggling fraternity, Jean-Jacques Noir got wind of it…

How could Harriette have betrayed him in this blatant manner? He supposed it should come as no surprise to him that there was a closeness between Harriette and Alexander Ellerdine. But for her to fall into that man's arms at the first opportunity… And she had been weeping. If she was in trouble, in distress, then she should have come to *him*. Wept on *his* shoulder. Allow *him* to kiss away her tears, not Alexander Ellerdine.

Had the man dared to kiss her?

Which centred his thoughts back to the heart of the problem. The two were close. In blood and in business dealings. Smugglers and Wreckers.

By God! She had allowed that man to touch her, to kiss her!

Footsteps and the murmur of servants' voices beyond the door came to his ears and prompted a decision. 'We will continue this conversation in the privacy of your room, madam.'

'I have nothing to say to you.' She faced him, refused to look away.

'But I have much to say to you. And you have much to explain!'

'No. I will explain nothing.' Harriette took a step in retreat, but with a stride that closed the distance between them Luke grasped her wrist. Ineffectually Harriette tried to wrench free.

Luke felt her shudder, but she was not afraid of him. Her eyes were wide and fearless on his, and he thought she might just defy him. 'If you do not come with me, I shall carry you. I would rather you saved us both the humiliation.'

She stood perfectly still for a moment. 'Very well.' Without another word Harriette accompanied him up the stairs, conscious of his fingers hard round her wrist. Once in her room, released, she went to sit at her dressing table with her back to him, but able to watch him in the mirror.

'Well?' Luke demanded.

'I have nothing to say.'

'I don't care to see you in the arms of another man. Understand me, my lady. I will not have it!'

Harriette's fingers had clenched around her ivory comb, anything to give her fingers something to do to prevent them from trembling, as she lifted her chin to return that uncompromising regard in the mirror. If there was to be a confrontation between them, she would not retreat from it. She kept her voice low, even.

'I was not *in his arms*, in the manner that your words imply, my lord. Alexander is my cousin.'

'As I am aware. Of what importance is that? He is an attractive man.'

'I have known him all my life!' she retorted.

'That, too, I know. An association of long standing.'

Distressingly formal, cold as winter but with an undertone of scorching heat beneath the sneer that curled his lips. A heat that might at any moment leap out of control. Meeting those brilliantly furious green eyes now, she shivered. Luke had seen her in Alexander's arms. She could well guess his thoughts on being faced with that incriminating little tableau. His face had become a mask, his words short and brutal, as if he suspected her of the most shocking of betrayals. Perhaps she was not altogether blameless… But did that give him the right to address her in this peremptory manner? To actually threaten to carry her to her room? She continuted to sit before the mirror, unaware and uncaring of the attractive picture she made, all her good intentions to *explain* about Alexander draining away.

'My *association* with Alexander, as you put it, is from the day I was born.' Harriette took a steadying breath. 'How would he not comfort me?'

'I am also aware, for it was common knowledge

in Old Wincomlee, that you and your cousin would make a match of it.'

'Common knowledge?' Harriette spun round on the stool to face him, brows raised in disbelief. 'Who told you that? It is a lie.'

Luke shrugged aside the denial. 'I presume you wish you had. The appearance in my parlour would suggest that.'

'I wish no such thing!' Now she was on her feet, the comb discarded with a clatter. 'You have mis-judged me entirely. How dare you have suspicions of my integrity? How dare you question the sanctity of my marriage vows?' Anger trickled dangerously through her blood. Conciliation had been abandoned with the comb.

In a stride he was there, so close that the silk eau-de-nil ruffles of her gown brushed his thighs. Before she could retreat, his hands were on her shoulders, holding her. His eyes raked her face, his fingers gripped savagely. There was no softness in him, no laughter, no tolerance.

'I won't have it, Harriette.'

'Nor will I have you putting a burden of guilt on me that I do not deserve.'

'You are my wife. You will behave with discretion.'

'You said I should be free to order my life as I wished.'

'It was not my intent that you take a lover!'

'Nor have I!'

'Nor will you. I'll not allow it. You are my wife. You are mine.'

She saw the change in his face, a shiver of something more than anger, more dangerous than fury, the moment before he lowered his head and covered her open lips with his. Heated, passionate, he gave no quarter, until she was aware of nothing but the power of his body against hers, the force of his tongue taking possession. It set light to the emotions in her own blood and she clung, responded, arched demandingly against him, in spite of all her misgivings.

'Harriette…' he murmured against her mouth as he stooped to lift her, to carry her to her bed.

'No…' She forced herself to push against his shoulders. Panic rippled through her at the conflict in her feelings. How easy it would be to let him take her, fill her with pleasure. It was what she wanted, what her mind and body desired. How easy it would be to rip to shreds all the accusations and suspicions that lay between them and bury them beneath the sheets of her bed. But when he left her the cold divide would still be there, the weight in her heart would remain. So, wife though she might be, she would not. 'No!' Harriette repeated more forcefully.

Luke lifted his head, his lips, as if she had struck him. Allowed her to slide to her feet. And Harriette, in her distress, allowed all her fears to transmute into words. She expressed, fatally, the first thought that came into her head.

'I won't go to bed with a man who is engaging in espionage, or, even worse, treason!'

'What?' His hands fell away.

'I said that I won't share my bed with a traitor,' she stated with as much composure as she could muster, as her throat dried in trepidation, her heart fluttered.

'I am not guilty of such a crime.' His brows were a black bar.

'But you did not tell me the truth, Luke. Don't deny it.' Harriette lifted her hand, fingers splayed against his chest, when he would have interrupted. His own heart beat as hard as hers. 'I know about Captain Henri, your prisoner of war, waiting to be transported back to France. He would not tell me about the agreement between you, but I think there can be only one reason.'

'I see.' Luke's face was an essay in bitter betrayal. 'I was away too long, it seems. In my absence you have tried and condemned me.'

'Yes. For I must.' She must say what was in her heart. She could hide the facts no longer. 'I know about the gold waiting for you in your study from Hoare's Bank. I know that you have been visiting a parole town—how can that not be in connection with your prisoner of war?' When she received no response, she continued. 'And I know about the letter from Jean-Jacques Noir. You are still in league with him.'

From her list, Luke homed in on one detail. 'You've been reading my correspondence?' His mouth tightened in a disdain that, she discovered, could match hers.

'Yes.' Refusing to feel shame, yet silently begging him to refute all her accusations. 'In the opinion of the Monsieur Marcel in Port St Martin, Noir is a man of neither morals nor principle.'

'Ha!' The bark of laughter was harsh. 'Morals? Principle? A fine condemnation coming from the leader of a gang of smugglers.'

'Perhaps. But Marcel does not sell his country's secrets to the enemy. Nor does he help his enemy's army with gold and escaped prisoners.'

'Which is what I do, I suppose.'

'Why not? Since you refuse to explain to me, I have to presume that you are involved in some terrible treachery against England's welfare.'

Luke fought to find his breath, stung almost beyond control by the accusation, yet astonished at how much she had discovered of his carefully disguised secrets. But that was not important! He stoked his own temper. She had the temerity to accuse him when he had discovered her in Ellerdine's embrace. The bright memory of Ellerdine's smile destroyed the last vestige of control. Fired by pure male jealousy, without thought for the words he chose, he uttered the one accusation that had been a burr against his skin since that morning at Lydyard's Pride.

'And are you any better, more righteous than I, Harriette? If we are to speak of morals and principle, can you put yourself on a high pedestal? I think not. You might be beautiful when in the grip of temper.' Once again he closed the space, dragged her to him and kissed her, suddenly, shatteringly, all force and fire. She was his. She would never belong to her damned cousin! He captured her mouth again. 'But beauty can be a mask for all manner of deceits.'

Harriette gasped at the unexpected. 'I don't understand you. You have always known my connection with the Free Trade.' She felt the flush rise in her cheeks. He was suddenly so close to her, so angry. So magnificently furious! A sudden premonition of disaster flooded her, but still she replied calmly. 'My smuggling has never been a secret between us.'

'You are ridiculously naïve if you would have me believe that's all you're involved with,' Luke spoke, smooth as silk, deadly as the edge of a knife. 'Are you willing to stand there in such lovely innocence and deny that you are a Wrecker?'

It was as if a bolt of lightning charged the atmosphere in the room. As if a bottomless abyss, dark and deadly, opened at Harriette's feet.

'A *Wrecker*?'

Luke watched the effect of his accusation with a

tightening of a band around his heart, yet closed his senses against the swim of horror in her lovely eyes. 'My education was extended to remarkable lengths in my short stay in Old Wincomlee. When too stormy for smuggling, there are those who would think nothing of attracting a vessel into an unfriendly bay, on to the rocks. Who consider the safety of the cargo to be paramount compared with the safety of the crew, who can be left to fight for themselves, to sink or swim. A welcoming light on a dark and stormy night would seem to be a sign from God for a foundering vessel. I think the Tower Room at Lydyard's Pride could be used for any number of distasteful activities.'

Harriette was stunned. This was beyond belief, that he should believe her capable of such atrocities. *But you think him to be capable of treason. What difference?* Harriette banished the voice.

'How dare you!'

'Do you deny it?'

'I do. And I will as long as I have breath in my body! What possible proof do you have that I might be a Wrecker? Who would make such an accusation? No Lydyard would ever give their assent to such an operation. I would *never* do such a thing.'

'No? What about the *Lion d'Or*?'

'I recall it. It foundered in the bay.'

'And the crew?'

'Lost. In spite of all we did.'

'What happened to the cargo?'

'Alexander sold it.'

'So you saved the cargo, if not the lives of the crew.' The lines around Luke's mouth were deeply sardonic. 'Who lit the lamp in the Tower Room, Harriette?'

'It was not lit.'

'George Gadie was not as sure as *you* appear to be.'

'It *shouldn't* have been lit—not on a night like that…' The heat of anger in Harriette's blood was suddenly replaced by a deep chill. Breath was ripped from her lungs.

'So you say. But the question is, do I believe you? You have no difficulty in distrusting me, Madam Countess.' It ripped at her heart, cruel claws.

So she retaliated. 'Do you blame me, all things considered? Why, even when you asked for my hand in marriage, what was it you said? We will make a business contract. My reputation in exchange for the use of the *Ghost*. Was it to smooth your negotiations with your French contacts? You refused to explain, as I recall.'

'I have not used the *Ghost*!' Luke snapped.

'But that doesn't mean that you won't. Nor does it explain Captain Henri. And I am no Wrecker! I was not there when the *Lion d'Or* came aground.' Harriette found her anger melding with an intense grief, to leave her distressingly tearful. 'I was at Whitescar Hall, at the celebration of the birth of Sir Wallace's first child, with all the county present.' She smeared the tears from her cheeks. This was no time to weep.

'Yes. I left the reception—Wallace was furious, I remember—to launch the *Ghost* to try to save lives. I don't suppose you'll believe me, but that's the truth. Damn you, Luke,' she whispered. 'I am no Wrecker. Have I ever lied to you?'

It filled Luke with shame. Harriette's simple explanation. Her final simple question. Luke took in the effects of his accusation with a gut-churning mix of guilt and contempt for what he had allowed himself to do. The catch in Harriette's voice, the sheer misery in her face despite the sternly braced shoulders, struck home and shame coated Luke's skin. Even in the face of such distress she had the strength of will to face him, even when tears transformed her eyes to silver and marked her delicate skin.

Luke swallowed painfully. How despicable had he been? He had gone too far; far beyond honour or decency, spurred by sheer brutal jealousy that his wife should choose to find solace in Ellerdine's arms. And who could blame her when he treated her with such lack of consideration. Did he believe her? Yes, he did. Here, in Harriette's brief account, was no artfully hidden guilt, of that he would swear.

Whatever Ellerdine's carefully aimed inference that morning at Lydyard's Pride, Luke found that he simply could not believe it of her. How could he ever have believed it? How could he doubt her transparent integrity, or the devastation in her eyes? His vicious words had reduced her to tears and he should be ashamed of causing suffering to a woman of such high spirit. Whatever else was between them, he would stake his honour on the truth of her denial.

'Have I ever lied to you?' Harriette demanded again.

'No. Never.'

'And yet you would believe some vicious gossip before you would believe me. Who would say such lies about me?' She pressed her hand against her breast. 'It hurts me—so much pain—that you should think it.' And the tears that she would give anything to control began to slide down her cheeks once more. But still she held his gaze. As if allowing him to see into her heart. 'On my honour I am not guilty.'

And Luke, wishing that he could turn back the hands of the ormolu clock on the mantelpiece, responded to his conscience. 'Harriette—I know. It was unforgivable of me. I should never have accused you of that.'

Harriette would have turned from him, but he stopped her, fingers burning into her shoulders. She risked a glance. The fury was no longer there, but overlaid by something far more immediate that caused her heart to throb, her skin to heat. Before she could draw breath he had dragged her to him so that the delicate ruffles were crushed between them. His mouth was so close to hers, his eyes blazing with green fire that was no longer temper.

'What do you want of me, Luke?'

His eyes swept her face. How sad she looked. Wounded and confused. It was his doing. Self-blame layered itself on his skin, a slick and unpleasant sensation. He could tell her that his doubts had been fired by Ellerdine, but that would be shrugging the blame from his own shoulders. At least he had enough honour left to him to refuse to do that. The shame was his for believing Ellerdine before his own wife. The shame was his for accusing her. He had allowed his jealousy to overcome his sense of judgement.

He did not know what to say to her.

And at that moment Harriette raised her hand and touched his cheek in an open plea. The most intimate of little gestures.

'Luke…' Her voice broke.

It stole his breath and suddenly the jealousy and shame were swept away. Desire became a fast flood, centred on his awareness of her slender body hard against his.

'Harriette—can you forgive me?'

She stood motionless in the circle of his arms. 'I

don't know,' she admitted on a sob. 'I feel as if I am wounded beyond healing.'

'And the fault is mine. All I can ask is your forgiveness. I have no excuse for my behaviour.'

'What do you want of me?' she repeated, as his arms remained encircling her.

Then his lips were hard, bruising, the powerful muscles of his arms banding.

'This!'

It robbed her of words, of thought. Only sensation remained, a desperate thrill from the crown of her head to the arch of her feet. As overwhelming as it was horrifying that she had so little command over her response to him. Her lips parted beneath his demand, she could do nothing but press herself against him.

Luke raised his head.

And Harriette, more angry with herself than with Luke, felt emotion build and spill over until she raised her hand, instinctively, to strike out at the arrogance of him. But Luke caught her wrist and pulled it to his lips.

'No! You'll not strike me. And I still have enough honour left to me, no matter what you think.' He trailed his lips in open-mouthed kisses from wrist— where her pulse rioted—to her soft palm. 'Tell me to go, Harriette, and I will.' Desire curled low in his belly. His muscles tightened in painful urgency.

She stood, arrow straight, ashamed of herself, resentful of his power over her. 'I should not have done that.' And took a deep breath that pressed her breasts against his chest. 'Do you still want me?'

'I'll not force myself on you, Harriette. Do you think me so lacking in integrity?' His mouth captured hers again, forcing her lips to part, his tongue owning her, awakening all manner of sensations, stirring a response that shivered through Harriette, a need that destroyed all her defences.

'Well?' he gasped at last, eyes raking her face. 'Do I go or do I stay?'

She should refuse him. She knew it, and *would* refuse him. But Harriette's blood had sprung into flame, her skin on fire with it.

'Damn you, Luke,' she said, and allowed desire to rule her. With the smallest of steps so that the hair's breadth between them was obliterated, she locked her arms around his neck and allowed him to push her back on to her bed.

It was a breathtaking acknowledgement of desire oversetting willpower. Time and place, even the bitter words of the past moments, held no meaning. Clothes were ripped aside, wilfully discarded in the heat of demand to be flesh to flesh as Luke's hands and mouth devoured her. It seemed to Harriette that every inch of sensitive skin was prey to the intoxication of his body. They rolled, entwined, breath ragged, his muscles bunching, rippling beneath her sweat-slicked palms. Tensing when her nails gripped, bit. Until he covered her, the weight of him holding her motionless, thighs spread and open to his avid gaze. Harriette stilled in breathless anticipation, every thought, every response, dominated by his superb body.

Luke reared above her, her body finally subject to his, his sex straining. His fingers dipped between her thighs and she cried out as they penetrated. As her belly tensed in a curl of anticipation, she reached up to press open-mouthed kisses over his throat, his shoulders.

'Harriette…!'

Luke looked down at her, the lovely flushed face, the tender bruised lips. The silver of her eyes shining as brilliantly as any diamonds. He was beyond reason, beyond control, lured on by a need to bury himself between the slender thighs, a primal desire that overrode every other sense.

'Look at me!' he demanded.

And she did, so that he could see his own reflection in her eyes.

'You are mine, not any other man's. I'll have you. And you'll have me—all of me. You are not Ellerdine's—and never will be.'

Perspiration sprang on his brow, his chest, as he still held tight to the reins. Yet at the core of his mind there remained the essence of a consideration that he must have a care of her. She was ready for him, impossibly hot, enthrallingly slick and yet he must not use her as if driven by thoughtless, indiscriminate lust.

The decision was stripped from him when, in a sinuous, silk-smooth action Harriette ambushed him, arched her body against his, against the heel of his hand. It was enough to drive out every thought but the lure of the passion that speared between them. One hard thrust and she was his. No languorous coupling, no gradual building of urgency, but an overwhelming driving on to the end because he had no choice. Because she held him, nails scoring into his hips, teeth nipping at his shoulder. He felt her muscles tense and shiver beneath his, stoking his erection. With a final shuddering he emptied into her, a hot spill.

'Harriette…you destroy me…'

As breathless as he, shattered by the emotions in the room, by her own compliance in such wanton desire, Harriette could only hold on. Compliance? No, she had been as hungry for fulfilment as Luke. Duty and obedience? Is that what it had been? Never. It had been the fiercest of desires to touch and be touched, to possess and be possessed. Words, her own unspoken—*don't let him take you, it makes you too vulnerable*—his recalled—*Harriette, you destroy me*—spun in her brain.

She regretted it, or did she? She did not know, only that she had been unable to stand against the force of the wild, untamed demands that had arced between them.

She stared into his eyes, so close that she could see the reflection of the candle flames. He had not asked her, this time, if she wished him to blow them out. He had not had the courtesy, and yet it had not mattered. She had not noticed in the frenzy of longing. As shame returned, Harriette turned her head aside so that he should not see the regret that he should take her in the heat of anger rather than affection. With lust rather than love.

Wordlessly, raising her hands, she pushed with her palms against his chest.

Luke's heart still thundered in his chest, his body still astonishingly hard, desiring her all over again, but he answered her silent signal and lifted himself away, to his knees, washed by a return of that sharp surge of guilt. Never had he wanted a woman as he had wanted this furious girl, and still did. If she had raised one word of rejection he would have left her, but she had not and he had been seduced into an act of uncontrolled, unbridled physical need. Why had she not refused him, pushed him away, as she was doing now? It was as if she had been driven to it as much as he, against her wishes, against all her doubts in him.

Luke lingered for one moment to wind his hand into her hair, gently, turning her face so that she must look up at him and spoke the one thought in his mind.

'You are mine, Harriette. Whatever is between us, whatever divides us, you are mine.'

Abruptly he left her, the fine linen of the sheets tumbled beneath her, her hair spread over the pillow. Magnificently naked, still aroused by the sight of her flushed beauty, he stood for a moment at the door between her chamber and his dressing room, sharply aware of the trace of tears in her lovely eyes, tears he had put there. How cruel the words, the accusations between them, and his without foundation. And despite his apology there had been no healing in his possession of her. That, too, must be laid at his door. Could he have not soothed her heart? Self-contempt stabbed hard, so that his tone was more curt than he intended.

'I shall be at Brooks's tonight, my lady. I will send your maid to you.' There was no vestige of expression on his face. 'Tomorrow I shall be away, taking our French guest with me. It will delight you to know that his presence in Grosvenor Square will no longer be on your conscience. You can at least pretend you have no proof for your suspicions over my integrity towards my country.'

'And will you be able to pretend the same, my

lord?' Harriette replied on a sob. 'Will you pretend that I do not lure men to their death?'

'No. There's no pretence,' he murmured softly on a sigh. 'I don't believe that. I don't think you capable of taking a man's life so indiscriminately. You have too much honour, too much integrity for that. You had the compassion to save my life when many would have thrown me overboard and good riddance to a man with questionable loyalties. No one would have blamed you. Whereas I have treated you with such lack of consideration… I can only ask for your forgiveness. If you cannot, I can hardly blame you, can I?'

She was unable to reply. With pride springing to her defence, Harriette made no attempt to wipe away the telltale moisture from her cheeks nor to cover her body from his uncaring contemplation. Luke's words meant nothing to her in her distress. The contrast to the heat of his body, the fire of his kisses shocked her into a bleak reality. Distrust lay heavy between them, and always would, a dangerous shifting sand of suspicion and doubt, waiting to drag them in. It lurked, a third entity in the room. Like a ghost in the shadowed recesses of a ruin.

Chapter Nine

Harriette could not sleep. She heard the opening and closing of the front door, a murmur of voices in the hall, later heard Luke's returning footsteps on the stair. The door of his own room opened and closed softly. Silence fell on the house. And when cool grey began to lap at the edges of her room, Harriette pushed back the covers and opened a small travelling case on her bed, staring hopelessly down into its empty exterior, his words stamped in her memory as if in blood.

'Do you deny that you are a Wrecker?' Luke had asked her, and disgust had marked his voice, his face. He might have rescinded his allegation, but how had such a suspicion become fixed in his mind in the first place?

She could not live with such a slight on her honour.

Her fingers closed on the edge of the little case. It was too difficult to decide what to take with her,

her brain refusing to function with its usual clarity, but she was not to be deterred. Faced with what appeared to be proof of Luke's involvement in something clandestine, she had once believed that her love for him could remain strong despite the conflicting pull of rogue tides between them. Just to be with him could surely be enough. How wrong she had been—it was too painful. Luke turned her bones to water, her blood to fire, but if he could not trust her with the truth, what future did they have together? Perhaps there were ways out of this entanglement, but for the present they eluded her.

She must put some distance between them. If not, she would either accuse him again with unforgivable words, or she would weep on his chest and tell him she believed everything he said. What a poor creature that would make of her, turning a blind eye to the issues between them. It was not in her nature. No sailor closed his eyes against a fast running tide or storm-lashed shore, but set the course and sail to weather the onslaught. A distance between them might help them to see if there was anything to be salvaged from the wreckage. She could not stay, her heart broken that he should so misjudge her, believing her guilty without evidence.

Is it not possible that you *are misjudging him? But there* is *evidence. Too much of it!*

There was only one place to go where she might

find some measure of peace. Once there, she would be able to think. She began to place the necessities for her journey into the case. But first… Harriette opened the door to the adjoining dressing room, entered, walked through and listened, head bent at Luke's door. She would not leave without seeing him one more time.

Harriette turned the handle softly, pushed the door ajar, breath held. He was asleep. Abandoned, a book lay face down on the cover. Arm outflung, face turned into the pillow—Luke's chest rose and fell with a steady rhythm. From her safe distance, Harriette simply stood and looked, swept back to those first days when he had been under her care. Wounded and vulnerable, there had been no cruel burden of secrets between them then. She had been free to love him.

Harriette slipped off her shoes and walked across the thick carpet, to stand beside the swagged and curtained bed. Her eyes took in every beloved detail of his face, the contours of his shoulders, the elegant hands, the scar on his cheek almost invisible in the soft candlelight. Luke! She loved him still despite the forces that drove him, despite all that tore them apart.

'Luke.' She framed the word silently, raising her hand as if she might smooth his hair, but in the end dared not. 'Goodbye, Luke. I loved you no matter what—I still love you. Why could you not love me? Why could we not make a life together without lies and deceit?'

Her heart ached, a physical pain.

He stirred a little as if aware of her closeness. It forced Harriette to retreat, with one final glance over her shoulder at the door. If he told her the truth, then she would come home again.

And if he would not?

Then she would sever the ties for ever, whatever the cost.

It had taken two long days of negotiation and the exchange of gold for Luke to dispose of his French prisoner. At last it was done. With a fair wind and a modicum of luck, without a need of *Lydyard's Ghost*, Captain Henri would now be on French soil. Luke could only hope that the Captain bring him the vital information.

But all such concerns were wiped from his mind. He forced his fingers to remain steady as he opened the folded single page he discovered waiting for him on his desk. The definite strokes raced across the page with a furious energy. Much like her, he thought, but could not smile. He read the whole of it at a glance with a peculiar lack of feeling as if its content were of no importance, without emotion, with no suggestion that his life was in the process of falling apart. All his senses were frozen. How could he react, when Harriette's thoughts, expressed in these few short lines, were of no surprise to him? Had he not anticipated just such a desolate emptiness waiting for him, every minute of his journey home?

I have written this in case you should worry about me. It would be wrong of me not to tell you.

Why did those two lines stir his guilt to outrageous pain? Did she think he would care so little? Did she not realise that his memory of his harsh words were a sharp pain that gave him no rest?

I have gone to Lydyard's Pride. I know that you regretted your cruel words, but they still hurt me more than I can say. Forgive me if you feel that I have returned your generosity with less than gratitude. I know you meant to rescue me from a difficult situation. With so much unresolved between us and no way that I can see of achieving that resolution, I have left you. I had hoped that you might tell me the truth, but I see that you feel unable to trust me. I cannot hope your affairs come to fruition. I fear for them.

You will always have my thanks—and my sincere affection. I cannot write of that.

I am not a Wrecker.

There were the faintest of smears on the final line as if she had caught the wet ink with her sleeve or her hand in an impatient gesture.

He folded the paper carefully, tucking it into the breast pocket of his coat, somewhere, he thought, in the region of his heart. If he still possessed one. It felt at this moment as if it were turned to stone.

I have left you.

The words hammered in his brain.

I am not a Wrecker.

She had not accepted his apology. Perhaps in the deluge of emotion she had not understood what he had said, that he had seen his mistake. Perhaps he had not made his regret plain enough. Or perhaps she never could forgive him for doubting her. One fact was clear—he had hurt her beyond measure. So Harriette had returned to her old life, and how could he blame her? Luke recalled with humiliation what he had done, the accusations he had flung at her, the implication that she would take Ellerdine as her lover. It had not been to his credit. And she had answered him, fire with fire, blistering him with her knowledge of his most private affairs. As they had faced each other, damned each other with bitter words, all he could think of was how beautiful she was with temper flashing in her splendid eyes. How desirable she was and how much he had wanted her. So, at the end, he had drawn the sting and he had taken her, loved her with his body. And then, by God! What had he done? Walked away from her, in his own mind before any more wounding words could be said to tear and divide. But Harriette would have thought he had abandoned her.

I have left you. You will always have my sincere affection.

Luke stared down into the empty fire grate, forehead resting on his arm, feeling the pain of loss, as strong even as when he had learned of Marcus's death. For Luke had learned one true fact out of the whole mess of lies and deceit. He loved her, and he should be whipped for causing her distress. It seemed impossible that he could know a woman for so short a time and yet love her as if she were his soul mate. Harriette was, quite simply, essential to his happiness. Somehow, without his realizing it, she had slid beneath his skin, made a place for herself in his mind, in his heart, in the marrow of his bones, so that he was conscious of her presence even when they were apart. Even now he could taste the sweetness of her lips, smell the insistently soft scent of lavender that she used on her hair. How had she done that when a matter of weeks ago he had not even known she existed?

Perhaps he had always loved her, he thought, from the day that he had discovered she was

Harriette Lydyard rather than Captain Harry of *Lydyard's Ghost*.

Had that admiration been love all along?

What miraculous turn of fortune had brought Harriette to cross his path? She was everything the Hallaston family would have rejected as a bride for the Earl, and yet she was his choice. The only woman he had ever met that he would wish to stand beside him. And he had treated her with callous disrespect, driving her away. He could not blame her.

Luke took out the note to read it again. She was desolate, despite the calm brevity of her words, and it was his fault. Had she not believed him when he had admitted his fault and exonerated her? He could imagine her courage in writing the note, blotting away the tears, removing herself from a situation that gave her too much pain. Of his own making.

By God, he had made a mess of it! He slammed his fist into the smooth marble, ignoring the pain in his knuckles, then poured a glass of brandy, drinking it down in one vicious swallow as if the heat in his belly could melt the ice in his heart. So what now? Luke took cold consideration of the facts.

He could not allow this impasse between them to continue. At least he knew where she was and that she was safe—it was the only comfort in the whole damned business, the only bright light in a murk of cloud and shadow that made it easy to plan, to think clearly. His first thought was to order up the curricle and go straight to Lydyard's Pride and bring her back. Every bone in his body urged him to go to her and heal her pain. But in his hand, also left on his desk for him to read on his return, was a message even shorter than Harriette's, a note that demanded his immediate attention. He did not need to read it again.

Port Les Villets. First Wednesday in August. Twelve Noon.

Jean-Jacques Noir had replied at last. One week from now. The game of cat and mouse was on again, a game that Luke was determined to win—because he dare not lose it.

If Harriette had not been so low in spirits, she would have been overjoyed to see Lydyard's Pride again, its proud tower visible for miles, its stonework gleaming in the clear light from the sea. It should have been a moment of intense joy, returning to a much loved home, but Harriette was forced to acknowledge that her heart was no longer here. Her heart was still in Grosvenor Square—a formal rigid residence for which she had no affection and would not be sorry if she never saw again—but her heart was still there with a difficult, intransigent man who would not open the door in his own heart and let her in.

Harriette walked up the steps, lifted the latch and

pushed, entering the hallway with its cobwebs and dust motes. She opened the door into the library. How quiet and empty it seemed. Then one of the parlours. Why did all the rooms, even though she had rarely used any of them, remind her of the time she had spent here with Luke? Next the shabby withdrawing room. She opened the door.

And came to a startled halt on the threshold, unable to take in what faced her. The furniture under its holland covers had been pushed back, chairs stacked against the walls, the threadbare carpet rolled before the fireplace. In their place stood a pile of barrels and bales and boxes of what, to her experienced eye, could only be contraband. Spirits and wine. Silk and lace and tea. All stacked in her withdrawing room.

She advanced to inspect the hoard. The barrels were stained with sea water, but well packed to preserve their delicate contents. Contraband, all openly stored with no attempt to hide or even conceal them under the covers. And what was it doing here, of all places? Removing it would be a whole morning's work, so that one chance visit from the Excise men would mean instant discovery—and then they would all be in the mire. The whole venture would be closed down by heavy-handed justice to the loss of the whole community, with bars and shackles for those involved.

Was she to be the first Lydyard to find herself in Newgate?

What had happened here in her absence? Whose plan was this?

Harriette lifted her skirts and ran up the stairs with foreboding in her heart, as she climbed to the Tower Room where she discovered signs of recent occupation. The bed was made up. A ruffled shirt flung over the seat of a chair. A candle, well burned down, and a pile of books on the nightstand.

She knew who was guilty of this encroachment on her property.

Turning on her heel, Harriette ran back down, to search out George Gadie. Better to get the facts before she started flinging accusations. Puzzlement warred with anger at so careless an organisation. Had they no sense? Using the double cellars at the Pride in an emergency was one thing; filling her withdrawing room with such blatant evidence was dangerously foolhardy. And if there had been an emergency, why not use any number of other secret caches—in the church crypt, in the rafters of the Silver Boat. She stalked round the front of the house. By what right did anyone take up residence in her house in her absence without her consent?

Harriette marched through the archway into the stable block—to see that she had a visitor. This was not what she had wanted, not at this precise moment, but faced with the inevitable she did not flinch. Perhaps it was for the best to accost the leader of the enterprise and discover just what was afoot.

'Alexander!'

He had his back to her, in the act of dismounting, and turned his head in obvious surprise at her voice. Alexander Ellerdine leaped to the ground, let the reins fall and strode across to her.

In the seconds it took him to cover the short distance, Harriette watched his face. By the time he reached her his eyes were lit by a warm smile of welcome, his lips curved. Had she imagined the tightening of skin over his jaw, the momentary flash of impatience in his eye?

He took her hands, holding them wide to appraise her. 'Harriette! Very fashionable for Old Wincomlee. Fine feathers indeed.' He flicked his fingertips against the flirtatiously curling feathers of her bonnet. 'I didn't expect you quite yet, my lovely cousin.'

'No. So I see.' She returned neither his smile nor his flattery. 'What is that in my withdrawing room?'

'Contraband, of course.' Alexander, kissing her fingers with a broad grin, like a small boy caught out in some mischief, was completely unruffled. Entirely unrepentant. Overwhelmingly charming.

'I know that. And *you* should know that I would not approve of it stored so openly in my house. I don't like it. I warned you not to do so when I left.'

'I know you did. And it's my fault. I can't deny

it.' He waved it away, now a wicked glint in his eye. 'A false alarm. We thought the Excise men were about—but it proved not to be the case.'

Harriette felt her unease growing rather than subsiding under the smooth answers. 'You shouldn't have done it, Zan! I don't want the Pride to become the target of Preventive measures. It is my home, not a smugglers' den!'

'Soon mended.' He drew her hand through his arm, turning her to lead her towards the house. 'Don't let it disturb you. I have everything in hand.'

'Are you living here?' Harriette demanded, realising that she would never get her cousin to admit his fault.

'No, of course not.' His head tilted quizzically, considering his words. 'You mean, the Tower Room, I suppose. I *have* spent some hours there. It was necessary to light the lamp.'

'Wiggins is perfectly capable of following orders.'

'As he did.' The slightest frown between his brows. 'You're very suspicious suddenly. Have you lost your taste for smuggling? Do you no longer trust me?' His sharp glance swept her face.

Perhaps she was making too much of it all. Harriette sighed, feeling no inclination to argue with her cousin and set herself to make amends. 'Forgive me. It's just that I didn't expect to find the goods quite so—obvious.'

'It'll be moved tonight, I promise.'

'I don't want it to happen again, Zan.'

His expressive brows rose. 'And what has happened to put you in so bad a frame of mind? Have you quarrelled again with the noble Earl?'

Pain struck her heart anew. 'No.' She would not, could not talk about it.

Alexander kissed her cheek, patted her hand where it lay on his arm. 'Come on, then. Let's sample a glass of our Gentlemen's endeavours and you can tell me why you're here and how long you intend to stay. I knew you'd come back. Venmore's not the man for you, you know. We'll run the contraband together again. You and me, just as it was.'

But as she retraced her steps back into the Pride, Harriette decided that she would not tell Alexander too much, just enough to keep him satisfied. Why should she have to explain why she had returned to her own home? Furthermore she did not believe him that the contraband had been hastily stored in open view through necessity and false alarm. There was more than one consignment here. If her suspicions were true, this was part of a planned campaign.

So why not push the issue? Too tired, too wary of Alexander's flippant mood, Harriette chose careful retreat, at the same time damning herself as a coward. But now she was back she would put it all to rights.

It would take her mind off Luke.

Although one of Alexander's accusations had hit home. Smuggling and contraband had lost their interest for her. Even so, it would be good to take *Lydyard's Ghost* out and let the wind and sea obliterate her sorrow.

What was Luke doing now? Would he miss her? Harriette doubted it.

With a glass of brandy at his elbow and a pen in hand, Luke tried unsuccessfully to banish Harriette from his mind and concentrate on the necessity of his being in Port Les Villets in three days' time, at noon.

Lydyard's Ghost!

The image of the smart cutter swam into his mind. It could be the answer to all his problems after all. He tried to imagine what Harriette would say if he asked her to launch it for him and allow him to sail to France.

He could imagine all too well!

His uneasy musings were interrupted by Adam's arrival. Luke considered telling his brother to go to the devil, but one look at his face dried the words on his tongue. The boy looked uneasy, his hand white-knuckled on the library door as if unsure whether to enter or retreat, and it struck Luke that he has spent little time in—well, how long?—in paying any attention to his younger brother. On the other hand this was not the best time for Luke to have to deal with some youthful prank that had gone awry. So he would put him off.

'Adam? Did you want me? I'm too busy at the moment unless it's urgent.'

'It is. Or so I think. Whether you'll tell me, I've no idea.' Adam scowled, tight-lipped. 'You're always too busy.'

Arrested by the tone, Luke eyed his brother. His face was set in mutinous lines, an unexpected and entirely unusual snap of anger in his eyes. 'What should I tell you?' he asked carefully.

'Whatever's going on that you're keeping from me.'

'I'm not sure I understand…'

'Yes, you do.' Adam advanced. '*Something's* going on. I've waited, hoping you would take me into your confidence, but you won't. And where's Harriette? Harriette's been gone for days and you haven't said where, or when she'll be back. What's going on, Luke?'

'Ah…' Taken aback at Adam's vehemence and uncanny accuracy, Luke was lost for a suitable explanation.

Adam seemed not to notice. 'And now I'm accosted by some foreign ruffian, on my own doorstep would you believe, embroiled in God knows what. Is it spying, Luke? Is that it? I can't believe it of you, but…'

Luke breathed out slowly. Where should he start? How little could he say?

'Why won't you talk to me, Luke?' Adam demanded, dragging up a chair and leaning his elbows on the desk before him. 'You're too damned unapproachable! I'm not a child to be cosseted or fobbed off. I've kept silent this far because it's as plain as day you're in trouble, but I can't any longer. And don't tell me I'm too young!'

With a sigh, Luke rose from his chair, poured another glass of brandy and handed it to the young brother who had suddenly grown up without his noticing.

Adam took the glass, but did not drink or let up on his attack. 'Are you going to tell me? Where's Harriette?'

Recognising the inevitable, admiring the courage that it must have taken for Adam to challenge him in this manner, Luke resumed his seat. It was all true. He had been taciturn, withdrawn, often unavailable, something he must put to rights. His lips curved in sardonic contempt. 'Yes,' he replied bluntly, facing his demons. 'I've already lost Harriette. I daren't push my brother away, as well.'

'Harriette? Lost her?' Adam stared at Luke's face. 'She's *left* you?'

Unable to sit, Luke put down his glass, to stand at the uncurtained window, to look down unseeingly into the dark of the Square. 'She's gone back to Lydyard's Pride.' He fought to keep the announcement flatly unemotional. Instead it sounded bleak and final.

'She couldn't stomach the secrecy, either, I suppose?'

'No.' There was nothing else to say. And then he remembered and swung to face Adam. 'You said you were accosted on the doorstep. Who stopped you?'

'I've no idea. A man was waiting in the Square. He watched me, and followed me until he saw me about to open the door. He stopped me on the steps.' Adam hesitated. 'I think he might have been French by his accent. He said I must give this to you—and only you.' He held out a twist of paper. 'What's going on, Luke?'

Without answering, Luke opened it. Then clenched his fist over it, crushing it.

'This changes everything.'

'Who's it from?' Adam demanded.

Luke looked across, reading the new lines of cynicism in his brother's face and relented because he had run out of options. 'Well, you wanted to know, so here's the truth. This is what your honourable brother is involved in. The note is from a French prisoner of war called Captain Henri, a man who broke his parole and whom I helped to escape back to France.' Then watched as the look of horror crept over Adam's face.

'You didn't! You helped a Frenchman on parole to escape?'

'I did.'

'For God's sake, Luke!' Now Adam was on his feet again. 'Are you out of your mind? Are you indeed in league with the enemy? I would have denied it with my last breath, but—'

'Yes, I helped a French Captain to escape,' Luke broke in. Suddenly he was desperately weary of the whole affair. He picked up his own forgotten glass of brandy and drank deeply.

'Luke!' Adam was aghast. 'You would help them? When Marcus was killed by a French bullet?' Then, seeing the pain in Luke's eyes, 'What does Captain Henri say that's so important to you? And I warn you, I'm not leaving this room until you tell me what's going on.'

'Adam…'

'I'm your brother, and if you're in trouble, then you can't expect me not to want to help, can you? I know I'm not Marcus—' his voice almost broke '—but I'm as old as he was when he joined the Hussars. I'm old enough to play my role in whatever *this* is.'

'I know you're not Marcus,' Luke replied gently. 'You are a man in your own right.' It was just another wound in Luke's heart that he had not taken Adam's loss into account, and had played his hand so badly in this game. Unable to think of any argument against it, Luke sat his brother down, another glass of brandy to hand for both of them, and told him all.

Before retiring for the night, Luke ordered up the curricle for the next morning. What does Captain Henri say? Adam had asked. It was the faintest light on the horizon, contained in that one brief note. It might make his subterfuge all worthwhile.

Jean-Jacques Noir was not to be found in Port Les Villets as he had stipulated for the meeting. Instead he was putting up at the inn in Port St Martin. It seemed that Monsieur Noir was planning another wild goose chase to lure the Earl of Venmore and his guineas to France, another ambush.

But Port St Martin might just be the key to turn the lock. Because Port St Martin was the base of Harriette's French smuggling connections. Harriette could get him there, without Noir being aware of it. And she could get him out again.

But to achieve that, Luke would have to tell her the whole, abandon all his pride, all his so-called good reasons for carrying this burden on his own shoulders, and ask her for her help. It meant his using Harriette, where previously he had refused to involve her in something so redolent of deceit and treachery. It would also mean that he must trust her, perhaps with his own life, and with that of an innocent young woman whose future happiness rested in his hands.

What about Harriette's own life? Would you so cavalierly put that in danger?

Luke trod the stairs to his room, wishing he would not find it empty. No, he would never put Harriette's life in danger. He might consider stepping into a trap himself, because his conscience demanded it. He might risk his own life, he might fail to rescue Marie-Claude de la Roche. The whole outcome was uncertain and shadowed in doubt. But of one fact he was adamant. Harriette's life must not be risked. The thought that she might be hurt in any way was more than he could tolerate.

'Will she do it?' Adam had asked.

'I don't know.' It was a harsh admission. 'I don't deserve that she should believe me or come to my aid. I have not treated her well.'

For his pride and his intransigence, Harriette would be justified in consigning him with a few well-chosen words to the devil. He could only hope that she would be magnanimous enough to listen to his offer, an offer he would make to her in return for her help. He detested it, it would bring him no happiness—nor did he deserve that it should—but it must be done. Need, sharp and edgy, to hold Harriette in his arms and heal her hurts, crawled under his skin, but Luke knew that he must make amends and give her what she desired, whatever the cost to himself.

Chapter Ten

Harriette climbed the steep cliff path to Lydyard's Pride, enjoying the freedom of loose jacket, boots and breeches. To dress à la mode was impossible if she wished to launch the cutter, with a hand to sails and tiller. She smiled grimly—the blue taffeta with its ribbons and delicate lace would just not *do* as, with Gabriel Gadie's help, she had sailed *Lydyard's Ghost* across the bay and along the coast, glorying in it, with no one to watch or criticise or question her actions.

What would Luke say if he saw her…?

Abruptly she turned her thoughts away, watching a pair of kittiwakes diving and tumbling together in the stiff breeze. It was nearly a week now, since she had left Grosvenor Square. Which had been entirely her own choice, so how could she not accept the consequences of her action? If she had ever harboured any secret longing that Luke might come to find her, they had long since died. Harriette shrugged her shoulders under the rough cloth of the jacket, as if she could dislodge its weight and the weight from her heart. The moisture on her cheek owed nothing to the sharp cold as the wind buffeted and tugged at her garments, or to the spray from the rocks below.

Harriette entered the house through the kitchen quarters where Wiggins, enjoying a glass of port at his mistress's expense, struggled to his feet in consternation and Jenny, blushing, dropped a rapid curtsy. She continued along the corridor towards the entrance hall, pulling off her cap to shake free her hair.

'Harriette!'

She halted, suddenly breathless, at the voice. 'Adam?'

He loped forwards, as full of easy confidence as if he were greeting her at Grosvenor Square, to salute her cheek. 'You look windblown.' He chuckled, eyes alight with mischief. 'And *different*! Shall I admit it? I didn't truly believe you when you told me you were a smuggler. Now I do! Will you let me sail with you in your cutter?'

'Yes, of course. I've been… But what are *you* doing here?'

'I brought him.'

Luke.

At the sound of his unmistakable voice, cool, smoothly confident, devastatingly attractive, Harriette's breath caught in her lungs, her heart leapt with a dazzling rush of sensation. It seemed to her that all the blood drained from her skin to leave her cold and shaky. Even her bones felt brittle. Slowly, she turned to face him as he walked towards her. And saw immediately that his habitual air of self-assurance was not as firm as she had expected. There was a tension in him. A wariness, an uncertainty.

But then all she could see was the familiar elegant figure clad in a superbly fashionable blue coat and well-cut breeches. His boots were polished to per-fection, but no darker or more polished than the rich dark hair, black as a raven on the cliffs. Harriette allowed her gaze to travel over the austerely handsome features. The many-caped greatcoat that bushed his heels, drawing her attention to the height and breadth of the man who had haunted her dreams and her waking hours. His presence filled the room, as he filled every one of her senses. How could this have happened in so short a time? A month ago she had not even known him. *I know you*, was all she could think. *I know your touch, your taste.*

'We have just arrived.'

'Luke…' She could think of no appropriate words. For a moment she had thought he had come for her. For what other possible reason could he come to Lydyard's Pride? But all was now clear. Or not clear at all. If he had come, as she had so foolishly dreamed, to declare an undying love and heal the wounds, he would not have brought an audience, would he? Nor had he made a move to approach her, having stopped far more than an arm's distance from her with a politely formal bow. His mouth was stern. It was Adam who had smiled, kissed her hand. Luke stood with a distance separating them. She was his wife, but he could not bear to touch her. Where had the ridiculous notion of an undying love come from? So Harriette, the perfect hostess despite her unconventional attire, fixed the vestige of a welcoming smile on her lips.

'Come into the library. There should be fire in there. Has no one looked after you? Ring the bell, Adam, if you will, for Wiggins. I can offer you brandy or port. Food will take longer…'

She opened the door, hearing the flood of inconsequential words as nerves chased through her, and closed her lips. Luke had come to her. There was no need for her to take the initiative, to smooth over the social discomfort. Let him explain.

Adam hung back. 'I'll go and see what the kitchens can offer,' he ventured with a glance at his brother. 'Leave you two together.'

They were alone in the library as she had often imagined over the past days. But nothing like in her imagination. In her dreams there had never been this impenetrable barrier.

'Well?' She turned to face him, seeing immediately that Luke looked tired, but beneath the prints of a draining weariness she recognised a bleak determination. His eyes were steady and cool on hers and he did not look away.

'I don't believe you are a Wrecker,' he stated bluntly.

'No. You said. I remember.'

'I was wrong to say it, even more appallingly wrong to think it. And I know I hurt you.'

'Yes. You did. It no longer matters.' Surprised, unsmiling, Harriette took a breath, proud of her control.

'It does matter.' She saw muscles along his jaw tighten. 'There are things that I must tell you, Harriette. If you will listen.'

'So I presumed, since you have made the journey here. I thought we were done with talking. As I recall, our last conversation was…not amicable.'

'No, it was not.' She saw his hands clench at his sides, the tiniest of movements before he forced them to relax. His spine was rigidly upright. 'I want in part to put that right. I need to tell you the truth. I should have told you weeks ago.'

'Truth? What is that? Do you know the meaning of the word?'

Even to her own ears Harriette sounded unreceptive, but she was not of a mind to make this easy for him. What could he possibly say that would make things any better between them? Why tell her the truth now? Luke had still not touched her, not once. Not even taken her hand in formal acknowledgement, when it was her ridiculous desire to throw herself into his arms and cover his face with kisses.

But she would hear him out. Harriette sat, wishing briefly that she had skirts that she could dispose elegantly about her, but, hands folded neatly, she resigned herself to listen as he began to speak, as controlled now and glamorous as she had remembered him, the scar fading to no more than a silvery line, his voice low, deliberate as if he weighed every word.

'What I would say will not excuse my refusal to take you into my confidence, but I hope it will go some way to explain it. I think you should see this first.'

Taking it from his pocket, he handed her a little miniature in an intricate frame that fitted into the palm of her hand. The woman—hardly more than a girl—smiled back at her with the bluest of eyes. Her fair hair curled in artless ringlets from her crown to her shoulders, held there by a blue ribbon. Just a pretty girl with joyful laughter in her painted eyes. Harriette turned the frame over. *Marie-Claude de la Roche.*

'Marie-Claude. So this is the woman you sought. She's lovely.' Harriette looked up, puzzled, cold fingers gripping her throat. 'Who is she?' Would he tell her, at last, that this was the lady who owned his heart? She ran her tongue over suddenly dry lips. 'Is she your lover?'

'She is—' Taking the miniature, Luke placed it on the desk, hesitated, then began again, choosing his words carefully. 'It's possible that she is the woman Marcus married. That she is my brother Marcus's widow.'

Harriette found that she could breathe again. Marcus's widow. Luke's sister by marriage, not his estranged and lost love. Yet what did that matter now? Marie-Claude de la Roche might claim no place in Luke's heart, Harriette acknowledged with hard cynicism, but then neither did she. Then she remembered.

'But Adam said that Marcus was not married.'

'So we thought. Yet I am told that this is the young woman whom Marcus inexplicably married at some point in the campaign in Spain before he met his death. Without telling any member of his family who she was, where he had met her or why he had felt the need to wed her in haste in such difficult times. This has come into my possession, too.'

Luke placed before her a document, stained, travel worn. Opening it, Harriette read the proof of marriage between Marcus Hallaston and Marie-Claude de la Roche.

'I don't understand why you must keep this secret,' Harriette stated flatly.

Luke prowled restlessly to the window and back

again to lean against the carved marble of the fire surround, hands dug deep in the pockets of his breeches.

'At some point after Marcus died, his wife—Marie-Claude de la Roche—fell into the hands of a Frenchman who goes by the name of Jean-Jacques Noir.' He nodded as Harriette drew in a breath. 'Yes, the same. A man who made it his business to discover her history and her connections. Those connections led him to me. It was Noir who sent me the miniature and this.' He pushed himself upright, walked to her and held out a letter. 'You see it is addressed to me specifically.'

And Harriette, smoothing the much creased document, read:

This is Marie-Claude de la Roche, the legal wife of Captain Marcus Hallaston. There is a child from this marriage. A boy. The woman and her child are at present living under my protection. If you wish to make contact with her, there will be a price to pay. If you are not willing to pay my price, you will never see her or the child, your brother's son.

Harriette raised her eyes as the words struck home. 'So there is a baby, as well?'

'So it seems.'

'And this is blackmail?'

'Yes.'

'But…' she frowned, unwilling to accept the truth in the brutal words '…how do you know the truth of this? Could it not just be a mercenary ploy to gain money from you?'

'It could. Read on.'

You might consider that this is all falsehood, the document a forgery, and that I have no proof of my claims. Dare you risk it? Do you dare to allow the child, your brother's son and your heir as it stands, to be brought up in my care?

'Monsieur Noir knows how to twist the blade, does he not?' Harriette shivered at the thinly veiled threat in the words. 'Do you think the marriage licence is genuine?'

'It could be a forgery—but dare I take the chance? He holds all the cards. And, to change the image, I am working blind, dancing to every tune he plays because, as he says, I dare do no other.'

'I understand that, Luke. But why did you not tell me? Why did you allow me to think you were engaged in something so despicable as spying for Napoleon?'

'Read on to the end,' Luke advised heavily, turning his back to stare unseeingly at the view of cliffs and sky from the window.

Harriette did so, blood chilling to ice as the tone of the letter grew infinitely more threatening.

It will cost you heavily to release Marie-Claude de la Roche from my control. I will inform you of the terms in due course. I advise you not to speak of this to anyone or instigate a search. If I hear any evidence of this, I will have no compunction in taking immediate action. It would be no difficulty for me to hide a young woman and her child from you. She could be very useful to me. There are valuable opportunities for so pretty a girl and her protector in a town where the French army is billeted. Her youthful attractions would fetch a high price. I am sure that you understand me.

And Harriette—as must Luke—understood the threat very well. She ran her eyes down the single page once more, taking in the vicious cruelty behind it. From the moment this package had been delivered, Marie-Claude de la Roche must have filled his mind. Who she was, where she might at this moment be, if there was indeed a child from a legal union with his brother—Luke would have no true idea. But Jean-Jacques Noir had the right of it. Luke dare not risk it being the truth. The girl being at the man's mercy, with her youth and innocence being offered for sale to soldiers in an army town, and Luke doing nothing to prevent it—well, that was too terrible an outcome to contemplate.

'So that's why the gold was delivered. Monsieur Noir's price for the girl's freedom.'

'Yes. I would buy the woman and her child, even at Noir's extortionate price, if I could rescue them in no other fashion. And if the marriage lines are genuine… Well, I have no choice, do I?'

'And his letter to you—the one that I read?' Harriette had the grace to blush.

'Fixing time and place for the deal to be done.'

Harriette frowned. 'So why did you need Captain Henri? I presume he is tied to this?'

Luke cast himself into the chair opposite Harriette, leaning forwards to stare at the floor, arms resting on thighs, and began an explanation in curt, flat sentences. Hiding a tight anguish that wrung Harriette's heart.

'I had to do *something* to take back the initiative in this appalling game. Hence Captain Henri Lefebvre—the young man hiding out in the guest bedchamber until a passage could be found for him to cross the Channel. He was more than willing to break the terms of his parole and his word of honour, to return home to France and freedom with a purse of gold and a set of instructions to travel the

Channel ports to seek out a man who might be Jean-Jacques Noir, travelling with a woman and baby.'

He looked up at her, face a mask. 'Should I have felt guilt on my conscience at asking a man to break his word of honour? Many would say that I was guilty of treachery, helping the enemy, but had I a choice? The boy was driven by a need to return to his mother and sisters who had no one to protect them or fend for them.' Luke shrugged, his voice hard-edged. 'I should feel guilty, but I cannot. And, yes, I would do it again tomorrow if I could discover and rescue Marie-Claude de la Roche and her child. It was a deliberate decision on my part. I don't choose to make an excuse since I decided it was worth any risk, even if it tainted my own honour and name. Even to embark on that disastrous episode at Port St Martin.'

'So that was why you were in France,' she murmured at the end. 'Noir had promised to negotiate the handing over of the girl.'

'Yes. And what a débâcle that turned out to be. Noir played with me, luring me to meet him, only to rob me and have me set upon by club-wielding brigands. A sharp warning for the future, I surmise. The bullet in the arm was not to kill, but to warn.' He laughed, a harsh sound in the quiet room. 'I admit I was disastrously naïve in going there and expecting to bring the girl back safely with no violent confrontation. What had I expected to achieve on my own? I was not even certain that she was there with Noir. It was an appalling mistake on my part. But now Noir has raised the stakes and I dare not refuse.'

'I can see why you have no choice but to go along with the demands.'

'Not if there is any chance of the girl being Marcus's widow. If I did nothing and she was abandoned or used by Noir as he threatens—then the responsibility for the loss of Marcus's widow and child would be on my head.' He surged to his feet again, striding away from Harriette, but she could hear the raw emotion in his voice. 'I could not bear it. Losing Marcus was bad enough. I couldn't lose this young woman and her child if there was the least chance of their being Marcus's genuine wife and son.'

Flooded with compassion for him, Harriette still chose to play devil's advocate. 'It could be that you are being played, a trout on a line, because Jean-Jacques Noir knows you to be rich enough to bleed and honourable enough to rise to the bait.'

'Do you think I have not told myself that? I know all the arguments that he is merely a rogue whom I should consign to the devil.' Disgust lay heavily on Luke's tongue. He turned his head to look at Harriette and added simply. 'I can't ignore his threats and possibly condemn an innocent young woman to a life of whoring and menace.'

'No,' she admitted softly. 'Of course you can't.' He had too much honour, as she had always known in her heart. Too much care for those he loved. Harriette folded the letter carefully and placed it on the table with the miniature. 'Why have you told me this? Why have you told me the truth now?'

'The letter that you read. Noir sent to inform me that I could make a deal for the woman at Port St Villets. But since then I have had news from Captain Henri who has fulfilled our agreement admirably. That Noir is not in Port Les Villets, but at this moment he is staying at the inn, Les Poissons Rouges in Port St Martin.'

'Port St Martin. Ah…I begin to see.'

'I can only presume that it is an ambush, sending me to the wrong place, to strip the gold from me when he has no intention of handing over the woman who is being kept elsewhere under some form of restraint. If I could get to Port St Martin without drawing attention to myself…'

Harriette finished the line of thought for him. 'And I have connections in Port St Martin with Marcel and the smugglers.'

'Yes.'

'You need my help.'

'Yes, I do. Will you help me, Harriette? Will you organise a run in the *Ghost* as a disguise, a cover for my movements? So that I can be in Port St Martin on the night before Noir's assignation, and Noir will suspect nothing. If it comes to Noir's ears that there's a contraband run, well, he's unlikely to make a connection with me.'

Harriette sat silently, eyes focused on her clasped hands, running over all Luke had said, all his revelations. Yes, she understood his dilemma . The heart-wrenching anxiety of it all. The fact that he had told her—but only because he needed her help. They were as far estranged as they had ever been.

Suddenly he was there on one knee before her, stilling her fingers beneath his. His eyes were dulled with shadow. 'Look at me, Harriette. Tell me what is in your heart.'

'In my heart?' No She could not do that. At last she looked up, only to lose herself in his gaze, but she forced herself to reply with magnificent composure. 'You should have told me all this at the beginning.'

'Yes. I should.'

'But you did not trust me.' Her words were severe.

'I have no excuse. Other than to protect the lady.'

'Did you think I would betray your trust?'

'I have dared trust no one.'

'Well, I suppose if you believed me to be a Wrecker, you would consider me far beyond trust, wouldn't you?'

An agonising silence fell between them, finally broken by Luke.

'All I can ask is your compassion for a young woman who is being used as a pawn in a game that could lead to her humiliation and ultimate destruction.'

Her lips twisted, 'I cannot refuse, can I?'

Luke rose, to stand before her. 'I would offer an inducement. Something I think you would find hard to reject.'

'What could you offer me, Luke?' If he heard her sharp phrase, he did not react, unless it was by a deepening of the lines that bracketed his mouth.

'I will give you your freedom. To live the sort of life you choose. I wed you to save you from slanderous gossip and innuendo. I will set in process a divorce and take the blame, so there is no guilt attached to you. And I will give you a settlement sufficient to restore this house, so that you might live here in comfort.'

It came to Harriette with the shock and suddenness of a thunderclap. A slap to the cheek. 'You are very generous,' she managed. Cold planning, icy cold. So sharp and precise like the blade of a knife to sever, to divide. To cast her adrift.

'I don't think you want to be tied to me any longer.'

'No?' A query. 'You have not asked me.'

'I said things to you that were—are—deplorable. I cannot expect you to consider life with me, can I? I think I have wounded you too much for you to accept any excuses I might make. You left me—and I know the blame is entirely mine.' The tension in the room wound tighter yet with the slick of bitterness.

'As you said, I left you.' She took a breath, held it until she knew she could control her voice. Harriette dare not even blink, certainly not when Luke momentarily lifted a hand to her as if he had heard the catch in her voice.

'Harriette…'

Adam opened the door and came in, ending whatever might have been said.

'Have you decided, Harriette? By the by, I've arranged for some food—probably when your ancient butler has finished his port.'

'Decided?' Her smile for the young man was bright, her emotions held miraculously in check. Pride put an edge on her voice. 'How could I refuse? To rescue a young woman and with such inducements as my freedom and a substantial settlement.' She slid a glance to Luke, whose face was turned to stone. 'With such an offer, of course I will do it.'

He sighed, a slow exhalation, and at last took her hand and raised it formally to his mouth in a stark caress. 'You can't know what this means to me.'

'Oh, I do know what it means to you. Marcus's widow and son rescued, your duty to your dead brother fulfilled—in return for your freedom, as well as mine.'

'No! That's not what I—'

'That's not what you said, but I think it's what you meant.' Harriette was already moving swiftly to the door. She looked back over her shoulder. 'What did it take for you to swallow your reluctance, Luke, to ask a smuggler for help? How could your Hallaston pride stomach it? But I will do it because of Marie-Claude de la Roche and her child. I will take you to Port St Martin.'

'No!'

Harriette halted abruptly, brow creased. 'But surely that's what you wanted?'

'No… I want George Gadie to sail the *Ghost*. Your work is done when the run is set up. You do not come with us.'

'And why should I not?' Her voice flat calm, dangerously so, Harriette turned slowly round. Luke sensed her rejection, but knew his own mind.

'It's too risky, the outcome too uncertain. I'll not have your life put in danger, Harriette.'

Her spine stiffened, her eyes fixed on his. 'The *Ghost* is mine. *I* decide who captains her. If I do not lead this run, the *Ghost* does not sail.'

'I'll not allow you to put your life in danger.'

'Allow me? You have no choice in the matter.' Her eyes narrowed. 'If you want the *Ghost*, Luke, you get Captain Harry, as well.'

'Gadie can do it,' he insisted.

'Yes, of course he can. But you'll not dictate to me who sails the *Ghost*, Luke.' She hesitated, but only for the space of a heartbeat. 'I'll sail without you to rescue the widow, if I have to.'

'You wouldn't!'

'Will you risk it?' she snapped back. Her palms were damp with sweat, but Harriette was clear in her mind. Luke would not sail into the jaws of Jean-Jacques Noir's trickery without her.

And Luke, accepting that he had no power over her decision, drew in a deep breath. 'Damn you, Harriette! You leave me no choice, do you?' A wry smile, perhaps even with the hint of cold amusement at the trap he had found himself in, touched his features. 'So we sail together. But when we get there, you follow my orders. It is my operation. Do you understand?'

Harriette stared. Then nodded. 'I understand perfectly. I'll accept that. Now if you will excuse me— I'll go and chivvy Wiggins into action…'

With ferociously brisk steps, Harriette made her escape before she could howl her grief.

Luke watched her go, thinking as the door closed on her that it was as if he had lost the most precious thing he owned. He had done it all wrong. Here was the chance to defeat Noir and solve the mystery of Marie-Claude de la Roche, once and for all, and yet he felt no satisfaction in its planning. Harriette had leapt at the chance to be free of him with startling alacrity, but then he could hardly fault her, the manner in which he had offered her the bargain. What silent message had he delivered to her in his proposition? In retrospect, he knew full well.

Oh, I do know what it means to you, she had said. *Marcus's widow and son rescued...in return for your freedom, as well as mine.*

His freedom from her was the last thing he wanted. He had just destroyed his own chance of happiness, but he would try to redeem himself in her eyes, if not in his own, by giving her her heart's desire, a step that would cost him more than he could ever have imagined. To live the rest of his life without her.

'So we have our passage to Port St Martin,' Adam observed, stepping carefully through the undercurrents in the room. 'Will it be dangerous?'

'Yes,' Luke replied harshly. 'If the storms and tides and rocks don't get you, the Revenue men will. And now we plan to put into a foreign port in a country with which we are at war. Yes, it is dangerous.'

For all of them. For Harriette, since it appeared that he had been given no choice but to take her with him. That was yet another unbearable responsibility to weigh on his conscience.

Harriette shut herself into her room and sat on the musty cushions of the window seat to stare out across the bay, which she did not see because of the tears that coursed down her cheeks. Tears for the young widow and her child, abandoned and help-less, robbed of the man she had loved enough to wed in the midst of battles and conflict in Spain, now at the mercy of such a man as Jean-Jacques Noir.

Tears for Luke. For the decisions he had been forced to take, the need for secrecy balanced against the urgency to discover the truth and stay clear of Noir's mercenary clutches. Oh, yes, she understood perfectly. She wept for Luke.

And for herself. He had told her the truth. She had dreamed of all deceit being stripped away between them and so it had, but to what end? The truth might have given Luke back his honour, but they were further apart than ever. His offer had been more than generous. He would divorce her and take the scandal of it on his own shoulders, promising her freedom, a settlement, independence. What more could she possibly want?

'I want Luke! I want to be his wife, to love him, to be his until the day I die,' she informed the spider that spun its web in the corner of the window. As she had wanted him from the moment she had turned over his inert body on the planking of the *Lydyard's Ghost.*

Well, you can't have him. You've got everything else you wanted, haven't you? You have the truth. He's honourable, without the stain of treachery that you feared, but he's not for you. He doesn't want you. He only told you the truth because he needs your help.

Harriette scrubbed her hands over her face. How strange. How ironic. A bargain between them when they were wed, a bargain to end it. Her lips twisted in impossible sadness. Very well, she would set up a run to Port St Martin, and take *Lydyard's Ghost* into the harbour because Luke asked it of her. And because it might rescue an innocent young woman. Zan would arrange it. Then it was finished, her obligations to him complete, her connection with Luke Hallaston finished. And also her connection with the Free Trade. Alexander could carry it on if he wished, but she would not. There! She had made her decisions. Her life would be wiped clean of an unhappy interlude.

Why, then, did she feel so unutterably low? Why did it seem that she had condemned herself to a lifetime of misery? Why did it feel as if her heart was shattered, the pieces sharp as broken glass?

'No. I won't do it—I won't sanction so potentially dangerous a plan.' The temperature in the threadbare little library just off the hall of Ellerdine Manor rose as Alexander's temper flashed. His eyes darted from Harriette to Luke, and back again. 'What are you asking me, Harriette? It could put the whole enterprise under threat. It's not how we operate. If we are to continue to make money from these ventures—and God knows I need it—' he flung out a hand to indicate the signs of age and neglect on dull furniture, rotting furnishings '—why run the risk of capture?'

Luke had the sense to remain silent since it would be to no advantage if he became involved. What was it he had said to Adam, that very day? *It seems we have our passage to Port St Martin.* He couldn't have been more wrong. Harriette might agree, but Alexander Ellerdine had other ideas. The question was, could they execute the operation without Ellerdine's backing and involvement? Harriette thought not.

Hence the explosive exchange of opinion between his wife and her cousin.

'Yes, we will do it,' Harriette insisted. 'In two nights the tides and the moon will be at their best for a crossing. Marcel can always produce a cargo if given notice, however short, of a run. I want you to contact him, Zan. And we will go into the harbour to pick up the cargo. What's so difficult about that? Since we've never done it before, the French authorities are hardly likely to be lying in wait for us, are they? I don't see why you are so hostile.'

This was Harriette at her most authoritative, despite her demure appearance in aquamarine muslin with silk ribbons and restrained curls beneath a straw bonnet. Luke would have laughed at the contradiction between her alluringly feminine appearance and her dogmatic stating of her intentions if this were not so crucial an interview. If he had not offered this vivid girl, whom he wanted more than anything else in life, her freedom in exchange. Laughter could not have been further from his heart.

Alexander scowled. 'I don't like it. Why in heaven's name put into the harbour at all? Why not exchange the cargo out in the bay as we always do?'

'Because I wish it,' Harriette replied calmly.

'Marcel will not agree.'

'He will. Why would he not, with less risk for his men?'

'But that's my point. There might be less risk for him, but there'd be a lot more risk for you and our crew if you actually sailed into the harbour. If the alarm was given, how easy would it be for you to escape? Our operation with Marcel could be blown for ever.'

'I think the risk is not so great.'

Hands fisted on hips, Alexander stared at the floor as if searching for an answer. Fleetingly Luke wondered which came uppermost in the man's mind—Harriette's safety, or the security of the slick little enterprise that was operating under Ellerdine's hand? There was certainly nothing of the lover in him in his rejection of all Harriette's arguments. When Alexander looked up his eyes were sharp and focused on Luke, as if the man had read his thoughts, and Luke was surprised to see such venom there. Yet his reply, smooth as silk, was for Harriette.

'And does Lord Venmore come, too?'

'Yes. He does. And his brother.'

'By God! Do you want it to fail? Too many difficulties, Harriette.' The clash of wills continued. 'Too many involved, with no experience of a run. I can't understand why you are so intransigent.'

'Neither do I understand why you should stand against me.' Harriette put an end to the dispute mildly enough, but with an undoubted toss of her head. 'And *I* determine who will sail in *Lydyard's Ghost*!' She ended with soft finality. 'All you have to do is get the message to Marcel and arrange the cash for the exchange of cargo, then the dispersal and storage of the goods when we return.'

'But why, Harriette?' It seemed that Ellerdine would press one more time.

Harriette turned with grave eyes and tightly pressed lips to look at Luke, tilting her head as she considered some unpalatable concern, then back to her cousin. 'Because it's my wish. It's the last run I'll do. On this night, in this manner.'

Luke veiled his surprise. He knew nothing of this decision. Neither, it seemed, did Alexander

Ellerdine, for his temper once more lashed out, voice rebounding from the four walls.

'You're giving it up? But how can you do that? What ridiculous thought's got into your head now? We're a good team, Harry. Why throw it all up for no reason?' A sneer curled his mouth and his glance at Luke was savagely unfriendly. 'Has *he* persuaded you at last? Forbidden you? For shame on you, Harry, to cast aside everything we have built up together!'

'No. It is my own decision.' Harriette lifted her chin at the slur. 'I'm cutting my connection with the Free Traders and nothing you say will change my mind, so don't try. Will you do this for me, this last time?' She placed a hand on his arm, a little shake. 'Please, Zan. Don't argue against it. Just do it.'

Luke watched Alexander Ellerdine bring whatever emotions drove him under control. The muscles in his face were taut, but at last he laughed and shrugged his shoulders in acceptance of defeat.

'Since you are so set on it, then I must. But I warn you, Captain Harry, I'll not let you give it up without a fight.'

Leaving Luke to wonder if the warning was for Harriette or for him. No, Luke did not trust Alexander Ellerdine. Nor did he like how he presumed on his relationship to press his lips to Harriette's palm so intimately in farewell. That prerogative was his, and his alone.

The fact that Luke was giving up that prerogative entirely passed him by.

He would like to plant a fist in Alexander Ellerdine's laughing face!

Chapter Eleven

The moon, a mere sliver of silver, cast little light as *Lydyard's Ghost* slid along the French coast on a flat sea. Dark-sailed, no lights showing, no voices, only the creak of rope and timber. Harriette stood at the bow, excitement and fear, apprehension for what was to come, leaping along her veins. She had never felt so nauseous in all her days at sea, but then, there had never been so much to lose. Or to gain. They edged closer to the harbour of the little town of Port St Martin, hardly more than an overgrown fishing village, looking for the pre-arranged signal of four blue flashes of light. She had done this many times before, but tonight was different. They would go into port, to tie up at the dock with other fishing vessels, and the outcome would be far more crucial than the simple loading of a cargo.

She turned her head to see where Luke stood at her shoulder, his face a mere glimmer in the dark, his body shrouded in a caped greatcoat. She was conscious of Luke's presence in everything she did. Conscious that this was the last time he would need her or be with her. After tonight she need never see him again. Once returned to England, he would take the lady to London—if they were fortunate enough to rescue her—and then the settlement of their marriage would be placed in the hands of the Hallaston legal men. Harriette looked ahead again to the approaching port, concentrating on what lay ahead. Now was no time for self-pity, now she must use every skill she had if they were to return to England with cargo intact, without harm. If her crew ended up languishing in a French jail, she would never forgive herself.

Even Luke had been forced to admit, when he had laid down his damnably trenchant rules for this operation, that in the end he needed her skill to sail the vessel into port without raising any alarm.

Her eyes caught it. The flashes of a light, the signal.

'Lower sails,' she whispered, and George Gadie murmured the order. The cutter came softly up against the stone wall of the harbour in a deep patch of shadow. Harriette held her breath, all her senses strained in the silence broken only by the lap of waves, the friction of wood against the stone wall, distant shouts of drunken roistering from the inn in the town. And the thud of her heart in her own breast, thunderous in her ears.

'Captain Harry?' A hoarse whisper from the quay. 'A fine day for sailing.'

There was the password. 'Marcel? Could do with a warm wind from the south.'

And there the answer. The large figure dropped down from the quay into the boat, and clapped Harriette on the shoulder. 'Why the change of plan, Captain?'

Luke stepped out of the shadows. 'It was my decision. A private matter of business. A traveller to collect.'

'Well, *monsieur.* We meet again.' Marcel glowered in recognition. 'I'd not have sworn for your integrity—or your life!—last time we met.'

'I am the Earl of Venmore.' Spoken softly, but no one could doubt his authority. 'Tonight—it is *my* operation.'

Marcel's frown deepened into a scowl.

'This is my husband, Luke.' Harriette gripped the smuggler's arm. 'You can trust him, Marcel.'

'Well, milord Luke, if Captain Harry can vouch for you…' Marcel huffed, grinned, a flash of white in his bearded face. 'Let's get the cargo loaded.' He lifted his hand to alert a half-dozen men who began to manoeuvre the bales and barrels.

Harriette made to hoist herself on to the quay to where Adam already stood. Until a two-handed grip on her jacket pulled her back. 'What…?' She whirled round.

'You'll wait here for us—in the cutter.' Luke's order was urgent, low voiced but entirely implacable, his face set and stern. 'You're only here because you insisted and I couldn't get here any other way. You'll not set foot on land. One hint of danger, that we're taken, or that the run is in peril of failure, and you'll abandon it, set sail at once.'

'No...' Overwhelmed by fear, Harriette wrenched her coat from his grip. 'We'll wait.'

Luke was not to be moved. 'With or without the cargo, you'll sail. With or without Adam and myself. Gadie, do you hear me?' He lifted his voice, glanced across. 'Any danger to your Captain and you'll put to sea. Disobey Captain Harry's orders if necessary. But you'll not disobey mine.'

Gadie's brows rose, but he nodded at the fierce gleam in Luke's eyes. 'Aye, aye, y'r honour.'

Luke turned back to Harriette. 'I want your word on it, Captain.'

And Harriette sighed, seeing no softening in his regard. 'Very well. You have my word,' she relented. 'I'll stay on the *Ghost*. This man...' she beckoned to one of Marcel's smugglers, addressing him rapidly in French and getting a nod in reply '...will take you and Adam to the inn, Les Poissons Rouges. He'll help you.'

Luke stayed, momentarily, as Adam followed their guide at a fast trot. The planes of his cheeks and jaw were stark in the moonlight. He was as grim as she had ever seen him. 'God keep you, Captain.'

'And you.'

Surprising her, he seized her hand from where it curled round one of the ropes, raised it to his lips in a courteous little gesture, as particular as if they were in a fashionable drawing room in Mayfair. 'Keep safe, Harriette. This is a damnable situation! I'd never forgive myself if you were hurt.' Then he was gone, swinging up after their guide, and Harriette forced her mind from the heat of his mouth against her skin, to the matter of the cargo.

George shuffled distractedly at her side. 'We can't wait too long, Cap'n. Tide'll turn soon.'

'Just a little while.'

An eruption of voices towards the town. 'Silence!' Harriette brought her arm down smartly and all crouched where they stood, both French and English, in the boat or on the quay, merging with the shadows. To any who might be inquisitive, it was just an empty fishing smack and a waiting cargo. Harriette's pulse beat in her throat like the wings of a trapped bird. What danger, what trap was Luke stepping into? Fear was a black void in her heart.

They moved rapidly along the quay, halting now and then in the shadows, listening.

Then in front, windows lit, door thrown open, was Les Poissons Rouges. Luke huffed in a mix of dismay and relief. Cannon fire in the harbour would not disturb the customers of this sailors' tavern. Raucous voices, tuneless singing, the squall of fiddles and a pipe. A woman's screech of laughter. They were carousing with a bottomless barrel of spirits. No one was aware of their approach in the general racket, but how the hell would he discover the whereabouts of a woman and child in this?

He waved Adam forwards, joining him in the final dash to the side of the inn. Mustn't think of Harriette waiting on the *Ghost*. Difficult, opinionated, head-strong Harriette. Infinitely dear to him. If anything should happen to her, he would never forgive himself. As long as she obeyed orders…

They flattened themselves against the wooden walls in the dark overhang of the tavern roof. Two men on guard at the door. Both sprawled on stools, the worse for spirits. Not difficult to get rid of them. Luke gestured to their French guide to approach to distract them, whilst he drew pair of pistols from the deep pockets of his greatcoat.

The smuggler shrugged good-humouredly, swag-gered forward, '*Bonsoir, messieurs*. Here's a pretty girl to keep you company. Come and look…'

Foolishly inebriated, the two men staggered to

their feet, lurched across to where Luke and Adam waited. They could barely stand. In disgust, Luke grasped the collar of the nearest, reversed the pistol in his grip and felled him with a blow to his head. Adam dispatched the other.

'The brandy did our job for us. If only the rest could be so easy!' They dragged the inert bodies into the deep shadows. No time to tie or gag them. Pray God they could find the woman fast. Luke bent to peer through the filthy window. A heavy fug of heat and drink. By the fireside sat a man, whom he instantly recognised, with a glass in his hand, an arm round the waist of a giggling serving wench. Jean-Jacques Noir. No sign of a girl with a baby. How would there be?

'Monsieur Luke.'

'What?' His head whipped round, his grip on the pistol tightened as the whisper behind him rattled his nerves.

'What took you so long?'

A recognisable shock of dark hair. A broad grin. 'Monsieur Henri, by God!'

'The same. I've been waiting for you since I sent the news of the lady—three nights now, I've waited. What kept you? But no matter…' He beckoned. 'Here's someone for you.' At his signal, from the dark alley at the side of the inn a slight figure with a bundle clasped to her shoulder stepped out.

Luke breathed out slowly. 'Marie-Claude de la Roche?'

A faint voice, barely more than a whisper. '*Mais non, monsieur.* Marie-Claude *Hallaston.*'

It was enough. No time for more, Luke decided. He would act first and ask questions later. 'Let's move,' he ordered, taking the girl's arm. And they were off down the quay towards *Lydyard's Ghost* and freedom.

'Listen!' From the deck of the *Ghost*, Harriette lifted her head, sensitive to every noise.

'What is it?' Marcel was at her side in an instant. 'What's this business milord Luke's engaged in?'

'To stop Jean-Jacques Noir from the kidnap of an innocent lady.'

Marcel grunted. 'Do you say? Then it'll be a pleasure to stop a man like that.'

'You may have to.' Harriette heard the echo of running footsteps. 'Alert your men, Marcel, if you will.'

With a brusque nod, Marcel began to give rapid, low-voiced instructions. Footsteps growing louder with every second. The insubstantial outline of a little knot of people approaching. Heart thudding, mouth dry, a long-bladed knife appearing in her hand from its snug hiding place in her boot, Harriette turned to face them. So difficult to recognise. She strained her eyes as a shredding cloud allowed the faintest of moonlight. And there was Luke, leading the way, pistol in one hand. The French smuggler carried a bundle clasped to his chest whilst Adam had an arm round a shrouded smaller figure, urging it on. And another man. Jean-Jacques Noir? No—Luke exchanged a quick word with him over the cloaked figure's head and the man nodded.

Then they were all on the quay, beside the *Ghost*, breathless.

'We have her.' Luke gently thrust the cloaked figure towards Harriette on the waiting boat, offering a hand to the man who accompanied them. 'Captain Henri—you have all my thanks.'

'Delighted to be of service, Monsieur Luke.' He bowed smartly with military precision. 'Easy enough to warn the lady to be ready. Otherwise—luck played her hand, keeping Noir and his associates interested in a keg of brandy.' His smile was cynical. 'How miraculous that so large a keg of such excellent quality should find its way to Les Poissons Rouges for three nights running at this precise time! You owe me for it, Monsieur Luke. Now go, before—ah! Too late!' Shouts reached them. A warning pistol shot. 'Someone saw us and raised the alarm,' Captain Henri remarked laconically. 'To be expected…'

'Let's get them aboard…' Luke ordered. But

shots rang out again, closer now. 'Too late for that. Get down!'

He pushed the lady to her knees behind the bales of tea, also the smuggler cradling the child as he focused in intense relief on the figure of Harriette, still aboard as he had ordered, crouched in the shadow of the mast. As long as he could protect her… Then all Luke's concentration was on the approaching rabble, standing to confront them with Adam and Captain Henri at his side. Could they escape out of this, getting everyone to safety? But then there was no time to think of anything because there was his enemy, Jean-Jacques Noir. Short, thickset, wrapped in shadow, a pistol in his fist, a group of thickset individuals with clubs and knives at his back.

Breathlessly, Noir threw back his head and laughed.

Luke's muscles tensed, but he simply stood, waited, a silent challenge.

'Very clever, my lord,' Noir hissed in smooth English. 'Was it your idea to plant the brandy?' His face broke in an animal snarl. 'But you'll not take her, Venmore. Not without payment. I'll make you pay for your trickery. And you know the cost if you refuse to hand over the gold.'

'I'll not put gold in your pockets,' Luke snapped. 'The lady goes with me to England.'

'If you resist, I shoot her first, then the child.' Noir

raised the pistol. 'And then I might just shoot you for putting me to so much trouble with no reward.'

'But if you shoot the lady, where would be your bargaining tool?' Luke enquired as calmly as if discussing the purchase of a horse, but he raised the pistol in his own hand. 'I wager my bullet would find your black heart first.'

'Ha! You won't risk it, Venmore. Not if the child is your brother's cub. Give her back to me, and I might just let you go.' For the first time a hint of unease crept into Noir's voice. 'I might even renegotiate the value of the pretty widow—to your advantage.'

'And I should trust you?' Cold, deadly cold. 'I shall never give her into your keeping.'

'Enough! We have nothing more to say to each other. Get her. Now!' Noir's patience snapped. He waved the pistol, indicating to his men. 'Kill any who stand in your way.'

As Luke leveled his pistol at Noir, he was suddenly aware of a movement at his shoulder. Harriette! A knife in her hand, catching the moonlight with an evil gleam. Fear for her gripped his belly as admiration for her courage swamped him. She had come to his aid despite the threat of death, despite his orders. By God, he should beat her for her wilfulness…! By God, he loved her!

'Before you do something so foolhardy, Monsieur

Noir…' her voice ran out fearlessly '…you and your rabble should see that we are not alone here.'

'An old trick,' Noir snarled, 'that would fool no one.'

'Do you think so, *monsieur*? Would we be so ill planned as to allow ourselves to fall into a trap? Look around you!'

The shadows moved to become dense figures. Luke held his breath as he saw what Harriette and Marcel had arranged. Behind Noir, moving swiftly to encircle him, stood the stalwart bodies of Marcel's smugglers.

Luke laughed softly as relief and respect surged through him. Not only had Harriette leapt to his side, but she had set up this neat trap. He caught her glance, held it as the heat of awareness tightened between them.

That was for later. But for now… 'Attack, *mes amis*!' Luke growled.

The quay erupted into a mass of heaving figures. Shifting his weight, Luke thrust Harriette unmercifully into the safety of the waiting bales before wading into the mêlée. Blows were struck and landed with shouts and groans and curses, but there was no doubt of the ultimate victory. Captain Henri's brandy had done its work and the drunken rabble were disarmed by enthusiastic smugglers. When Noir in desperation raised his pistol, without compunction Luke fired his. Struck above the elbow, Noir howled and dropped the weapon as he was seized and held struggling, at shoulder and wrist, by two smugglers.

Luke rescued Noir's pistol from the floor.

'You lost this game, *monsieur*,' he observed. His voice was soft, his actions ferociously controlled. 'The prize is mine. You talk of trickery, yet last time we met you robbed me and put a bullet in my arm. You were a fool to try to trick me a second time.'

'Damn you for a treacherous Englishman!' Noir spat on the quay.

'What do you wish us to do with them, milord Luke?' Marcel asked with a glint in his eye. 'Do we kill them all?'

'Why not?' Luke replied, relishing the fear that ran round the group. 'They deserve no less for the wretched misery they have caused.' For a moment cold fury turned his eyes to grey-green ice, and in that instant he was quite capable of cold-blooded killing. But only for a moment. 'Let him go,' Luke ordered.

'Not so.' Marcel shook his head, his grin widening. 'He deserves some entertainment for our inconvenience.'

'Let him go,' Luke repeated.

At the authority in the tone the smugglers released him, stood back.

'What will you do? Shoot me in cold blood?' Noir said, face ashen in the moonlight.

'No. By God, I've an urge to do it, but, no, I won't.' Luke walked slowly forwards. There would be no more blood on his hands. 'Monsieur Marcel wants entertainment. I hope you can swim.'

The blow of his fist to Noir's chin connected with a wicked snap, sending the man staggering back, and off the wall into the filthy water of the harbour with a splash. A roar of appreciation went up from the smugglers, who tossed the rest of Noir's men into the water with him.

There was no time to be lost. No time for Harriette to admire the final humiliation of Luke's enemy. Not blood, nor captivity for a martyr to feed on, but a foul drenching in the scum and refuse of the harbour and an ignominious clamber on to the quay. Harriette felt her blood heat and race through her veins as she took the lady's arm to help her on to the *Ghost*, seating her as comfortably as she could in a nest of canvas in the stern before taking the whimpering bundle from Adam and giving it over into the care of its mother.

'Merci, monsieur,' the lady managed hesitantly.

And Harriette squeezed her hand whilst on the quay Luke made his farewells to Captain Henri.

'When the war is over, contact me in London. I'm in your debt and always will be.'

'I will, sir.'

'No time…' George interrupted, an eye on the swirl in the water. 'The tide's on the turn.'

Then Luke was there at her side, eyes blazing, her calculated disobedience forgotten in the thrill of success. 'We did it. Thank God we did it!'

Marcel raised his hand, a final signal. '*Au revoir.* Always good to do business with you, Captain Harry. Milord Luke. We enjoyed the scuffle! *A bientôt.*'

'Farewell, Marcel.' Harriette raised her hand in response.

There would be no next time.

Lydyard's Ghost sailed out of harbour, for home. Harriette turned her face to the wind. The crew was safe, the lady rescued, Jean-Jacques Noir over-turned. She should be rejoicing. So why did she feel as if her whole world was disintegrating at her feet?

The bay might be invisible in the darkness, but the lamp from the Tower Room at Lydyard's Pride beamed steadily, beckoning them home to a safe berth. A wind stirred the sea into an uneasy swell, growing stronger by the minute. Luke fixed his sight on the light, relief sweet in his veins that the lady and her child were safely in his care. Whether she was Marcus's widow, he had yet to discover—a dangerous voyage in an open boat being no place to exchange information—but she was no longer under the dominion of Jean-Jacques Noir.

But the sweetness of relief was short lived, replaced by the bitterness of loss, as his gaze moved to the figure standing before the mast. He might have solved the one burden that had plagued him through weeks of gnawing anxiety, but another, far greater, far more personal loomed. A weight of regrets pressed down on him. He made his way forwards through the piles of contraband.

'Harriette.'

Startled, she swung round. Lifted her hand in denial. 'No…not here.'

'Captain Harry, then, if you prefer.' He could not smile.

'What?' Her attention was elsewhere, on the state of the sea, the strengthening wind, the approaching landing. He knew he should retreat, but could not. 'Can't it wait?'

'No. It has to be said now. Whatever happens—'

'I know. You're grateful. You've told me. Now, I'm busy.'

He would not have it. 'Yes, you have my gratitude, but I need—'

'There's no need to say more.' Her eyes were brilliant, hard as diamonds. She wore her command easily, her words clipped, spine straight, every inch the captain. 'You have the lady and the child. If she's Marcus's widow, then you have victory indeed.' She would have pushed away from him towards the prow.

Beneath the natural frustration that she would not listen to him, all Luke could think of was how magnificent she was, how determined to bring this enterprise to a successful conclusion—and for him. How had he never noticed how sensuous her mouth was? Awareness of her chased through his body without mercy, filling every part of him with love. It sank, a spreading warmth, into the very marrow of his bones and, for that one moment, coated the strains of the past days. Without thought of their surroundings, the crew around them, he reached out to take her wrist, held on when she yanked hard, and instead pulled her into his arms.

'No…!'

'Yes! Captain Harry.' He was aware of the outrageously grim humour underlying the moment as his mouth took hers, hard, as need slammed into his body. Battered by the increasing wind, doused with spray, he held her to him as her lips parted beneath the elemental force of his, his tongue claiming hers. He tasted the salt on her face, the honeyed sweetness of her lips, the heat of her mouth. As on their wedding night in the Tower Room, molten fire, a searing energy, ran through him that he poured into her. His arms were bands of steel that left no spaces between them. And Harriette clung to him. He felt her respond, her body plastered against his.

Until a lurch of the boat beneath their feet made them stagger and forced him to raise his head. Yet his eyes captured and held hers, fierce as a hawk, dark with desire, even as they struggled for balance.

'Whatever happens next—' his voice harsh above the roar and thwack of the wind and sea '—don't forget. Don't forget what has been between us. How I made you feel.'

What made him say it, he had no idea. To remind her of the fire between them, of the passion they had found in each other's arms, the storm of desire that could overwhelm them, even as they were planning their ultimate separation.

Obviously stunned, Harriette clung to him with one hand, raising the other to her lips. 'I can never forget that…'

I love you, Harriette. I adore you… The words appeared in his mind and he would have said them with the approaching storm as a backdrop.

'Cap'n Harry!' George Gadie coughed discreetly. 'There's lights on the cliff—and on the path down to the bay—but the signal from the Tower's constant—still says all's well.'

Luke felt every muscle in her body tense. Harriette pulled away from him, and Luke let her go.

'Look.' George pointed at the pinprick of lights. 'What d'you think, Cap'n?'

And Luke felt her hand close convulsively over his arm. Her reply might be matter of fact, but he felt a knot of fear form in his belly. 'I think Captain Rodmell and his dragoons have come to meet us.'

'I thought Ellerdine's job was to warn you,' Luke spoke the thought in everyone's mind.

'It is,' Harriette snapped.

Harriette turned from the string of bobbing lights, back to Luke. 'We've got to get this boat and its crew—and the cargo—to safety. It's too late to sail along to the next bay—a storm's approaching. We've some hard work ahead of us if we're to pull it off right and tight.'

George was already laying hands on rope and weights, lashing them to the barrels. Harriette stepped to help him. Luke put out a restraining hand.

'Captain,' he requested formally, 'tell me what you want of me and I'll do it. I may be no sailor, but I can do more than sit and wait.'

A flash of a smile to break the tension. Luke felt the warmth of it. She held his hand in a cold slick clasp for just a moment. 'Grab that rope and do what George tells you. The next hour is going to be as fast and dangerous as any you've ever known. Welcome to the Brotherhood of the Free Traders, Lord Venmore!'

* * *

Harriette fought to keep a clear head and considered her options She didn't have many. None, really. Anger and astonishment warred within her. Never had a run gone so wrong, never had the signals been so dangerously contradictory. The lamp from her own Tower shone safety, whilst the lights on the cliff, so many of them, could be none but the Revenue men. The safety of all of them, her crew, the French widow and her child, Adam, and of course, Luke, was in her hands.

What in Heaven's name was Zan thinking? Why had he not given her some warning? If *she* could see the Preventive men, then so must *he*. All he had to do was send a lad to Wiggins who would immediately flash the warning.

No time to think of that now. She nodded to George, who needed no advice from her. He, too, must have seen the necessity.

'Sow the crop?' he asked.

'Yes. And fast. We must get to the beach and away, before the Preventives.'

She had done it only once before, but had every confidence in her crew. And now she had extra hands to tie and lift. She found the time to glance back to the woman and child cowering beneath a boat cloak in the stern. Safe enough. And there was Luke, cursing as the loops of wet rope tightened around his fingers, as he staggered to keep his balance against the thrust of the waves. He would do well enough, following orders as any seaman. Her throat tightened as she watched him brace and haul against a recalcitrant barrel. Could she really agree to live alone, without him? Later…that was for later… She turned away to keep an eye on Adam, whose queasy belly had abated under the excitement of action.

Then there was nothing to think about but the task in hand.

Anchor dropped, the cutter lurched and wallowed in the waves, as one by one the barrels, lashed one to the other, a heavy stone at one end, were hoisted and tipped over the side so that they sank anonymously into the water.

'How do you know where they are?' Luke gasped from his exertions, drenched to the skin as they all were, hair plastered darkly to his head, but heart-stoppingly beautiful to her eyes.

Adam answered, his hands full. 'This. Gabriel says to use this.'

'Let me tie it, lad.' George elbowed him aside without compunction. 'If it comes adrift, we lose everything. It needs firm lashing, and you're no smuggler yet! Another dozen years, perhaps, under my hand…' And as Adam grinned, George grasped the end of the rope attached to the barrels and lashed the inflated bladder with a tuft of feathers to it.

'So the bird marks the spot.' Luke watched it bob and dip in the waves.

'Exactly.' Harriette nodded in satisfaction. 'We come and reclaim it when the danger's past. Now we land. We've those to dispose of.' She eyed the dozen small bales with concern.

'Can you not do the same?'

'No. It's lace. Too fragile, and the bales not waterproof enough. But too valuable to abandon unless we must. We need to hide them. Don't worry. The dragoons are always slow—they don't know the cliff paths.' She hoped she sounded more confident than she felt. 'If luck's with us and Zan is to hand, we'll land and be gone before the Revenue men even reach the shore. Your widow will be safe.'

They ran the cutter up on to the beach before a squall of wind much as they had done many times before. Harriette leapt off into the shallows to help her crew drag the boat as high as they could. Within minutes the bales were exposed on the pebbles, the widow and the child carried in stalwart arms. A thoroughly disreputable group if Captain Rodmell caught them, Harriette acknowledged.

She looked around, her eyes telling her what she had feared. No ponies. No tubsmen. What had gone wrong? What was Zan doing? Her mind tried to snatch at possibilities, but failed entirely. The dragoons were still making their clumsy way down the cliff path. She could hear the roll of stones, the smothered curses off to the left. They still had time to hide the evidence. The clouds broke, shifted, the moon illuminating them, making them too easy a target. Couldn't be helped.

George and Gabriel were already lashing two small bales to each smuggler, looped efficiently on back and chest. Harriette grabbed Luke's arm to get his attention, the wind snatching away her words.

'Luke! Adam…you, too… Help them carry the bales…' She felt the resistance in him even as she issued her order, heard his furiously edged reply that left her in no doubt of his opinion.

'You'll not do it, Captain Harry! Send me off with the contraband to save my skin whilst you wait for the Preventives? Do you think I will leave you here alone to face the weight of the law?' Temper was vivid on Luke's face. 'I won't do it.'

'I need you to carry the bales,' she stated as calmly as she could as the crunch of pebbles on their left grew nearer, and the lack of aid for the smugglers lit a fear that lashed at her.

Luke's hands were tight on her shoulders. 'I can't leave you here.'

'You must. I know what to do, and you don't. You must go…'

Luke remained unconvinced and intransigent.

'You'll be found with the cutter—and in male attire. What will Captain Rodmell presume? You're no fool, Captain Harry. You know that you'll be taken under suspicion.'

'No, I won't. I have a plan.'

The crack of a pistol sounded loud, close, too close, startling them. It came from the right. A spurt of sand and pebbles leapt up at their feet. Then another flash and crack of sound, both from the base of the cliff on the right. Another shower of sand from a spent bullet.

'By God! What's…?' Luke gasped, head whipping round.

And Harriette found herself almost lifted from the ground, swung round so that the bulk of Luke's body covered hers, standing between her and the invisible marksman. Again the crack of a pistol. Too close, too close! And not from the direction of the dragoons… No sooner had the idea slid into her mind than all thought was driven out.

'Get down!' Luke ordered.

And Harriette found herself pushed to the floor, dragged into Luke's arms and pinned to the ground beneath him, just as a fourth shot rang out. Pain flashed along her side, screamingly along her ribs, but she set her teeth and her mind against the darkness that swam before her vision, making no sound other than an indrawn breath.

They waited for the next shot.

Seconds passed. It did not come.

Held tight in Luke's embrace, her face buried against his chest, breathing in the salt sweat of him, Harriette felt ridiculously safe and protected against all danger, despite the flaring pain. For a long moment she just held on, unable to think, only to feel the vital heat of him and the agony of her ribs. Then carefully, gently, he eased his weight from her and lifted her until she was seated in his arms.

'Are you hurt?' He ran his hands from shoulder to wrist, returning to cup her face, to draw his fingers gently over cheek and jaw, tucking her escaping curls back into the stocking cap.

'No,' she lied without compunction. 'But you— were you hit?'

'No.'

She touched his face, marvelling that he was unharmed. She had had Luke's blood on her hands before, before she loved him. How much more terrible would it be now that he was her love, her life.

'Harriette—if you should be hurt because of this…'

'Well, I'm not hurt,' she managed in a low voice, managing an impressive edge of irritation to mask the pain. 'Let me get up. You're crushing me on the pebbles.' He stood and then pulled her to her feet, sweeping the sand from her until she stilled him with her hand, a plea in her eyes. 'I know what to do here. Go with George to the churchyard. Adam, too. If you want us to come out of this unscathed, keep out of the way until it's over. It will do no good for the Earl of Venmore to be taken with contraband goods. *Luke*! I don't want you here!' Harriette's heart shuddered at the thought that he could even now be lying dead at her feet.

'Very well.' His temper flashed. 'I'll go—not because I want to, but only because I see the sense of it—or I think I do. When this is over…'

'When this is over, we'll talk about it,' she finished. 'But go!'

His hands were hard on her shoulders, then arms firm about her, making the pain so intense she could hardly bear it, his kiss on her mouth hot and full of temper so that her blood sang with it, before the smugglers were off, moving quickly, well laden. Briefly she followed him with her eyes. Surely he was in no danger now. Then deliberately Harriette turned her back.

She and the French widow had a role to play.

Harriette pulled off her cap and pushed her fingers through her hair so that it tumbled lankly to her shoulders. It would have to do. Spying what she needed, she swept up the discarded boat cloak and wrapped it round her so she was covered from chin to toe, hiding her inappropriate garments and the blood that stained her coat. It might have gone unnoticed so far, but she could feel the wetness of it spreading against her skin, and Captain Rodmell had eagle eyes. Tensing her body against the pain, she stepped to crouch in front of the lady who was looking at her in some form of awe. Silent throughout all that had gone before, yet she must have seen Luke's embrace. Harriette smiled a little at the shock on the lady's face as she lapsed into French to make the explanations easier, and prayed that Mademoiselle de la Roche possessed both nerve and imagination.

'*Bonsoir, madame*. My name is Harriette. And you are Marie-Claude?'

'A *woman*… Ah…*madame*? Forgive me, I did not realise…'

'No matter. Can you weep—in abject fear and gratitude, Marie-Claude?'

'Yes.' She shuddered grimly. 'I can certainly do that.'

'Then that's what I want you to do. Listen now. When the Revenue officer arrives, convince him of your helplessness. Weep on his chest if you have to.' She patted the girl's hand, hissing a breath at the protestations of her ribs. 'It could all depend on you.'

'Yes. I can do that.' Accented English, but perfectly correct. 'But you are injured, *madame*!' The girl's eyes widened.

'Not enough to signify. Will you do it?'

'I will.' Quick colour tinted her cheeks, her eyes sparkled.

And, pressing a hand to her side beneath the enveloping cloak, Harriette rose to her feet to face the dragoons as the crunch of booted feet on pebble reached them. Then they were surrounded by armed soldiers.

And Captain Rodmell. 'Don't move.' He shouldered between their ranks, a pistol in his hand. Stopped as he saw the two women standing alone on the beach. 'What's going on here?' His eyes flickered from one to the other, making Harriette glad of her cloak. Then at the empty *Lydyard's Ghost* beside them.

'Captain. Thank God! Can you help us?' Shrill, anxious.

'Help you…?' He cast a glance around, obviously for contraband, disbelieving when he saw none.

Harriette drew herself up as if her dignity had been wounded. 'I am the Countess of Venmore. Perhaps you did not recognise me.'

'I know very well who you are, my lady,' he snapped. 'I recall our previous unfortunate meeting on the day of your wedding. What are you doing here?'

'This is my cousin, Marie-Claude.' Harriette drew the already weeping lady forwards. 'We have just rescued her from a cruel confinement in France, by her husband who robbed her of her inheritance and threatened to take her child from her. I have to get her to the Pride, but she's too weak to walk on her own.'

The Captain glanced suspiciously at the cutter. 'Where's the crew that brought her here?'

'Gone!' Harriette all but wrung her hands. 'Left us, demanding more money that I did not have to give them. I can't help Marie-Claude and the child on my own. I don't know what to do, unless you can help me.'

A sob from the lady. *'Monsieur le Capitaine, s'il vous plaît…'* Drenched eyes of lucent blue were lifted to the Captain's face, and he was lost.

'Madame…' Chivalrous to the last, the Captain took the delicate outstretched hand.

'I am so happy to be here. Help me, Monsieur le Capitaine. You cannot know how cruel my husband was. How he beat me. I know that Englishmen would not treat a lady so vilely.' And she duly cast herself on his breast in a storm of emotion, as if her legs would hold her no longer.

As if on cue, the baby, abandoned for the moment on the shingle, began to wail.

The Captain looked at Harriette, a vestige of panic in his face. 'What do I do to help you, my lady?'

'Get us to Lydyard's Pride. That's all we need.'

The Captain issued orders to shepherd the helpless women and the wailing infant up the path to the house on the cliff. All Harriette had to do was set her teeth against the pain, ask herself what in God's name Zan was doing, and give thanks that Luke would be well away and safe.

Chapter Twelve

Luke shuffled over on to his back, attempted to stretch cramped limbs, and discovered yet again that he could not. Close, confined, the stone walls hemmed him in all round. Like being in a tomb. Which it was. Dust, cobwebs, spiders shared the space with him, but no bones. Thank God! Also with him a number of bales of precious French lace, tucked under shoulder and thigh, that restricted his movements even more.

Hell and the devil! He eased the stiff muscles in neck and shoulder. He'd not wish this on anyone, even his worst enemy. Was this living incarceration, enclosed in a table-tomb, a price worth paying?

When they had crept into the churchyard, breathless with the weight of contraband pressing against back and chest, under George Gadie's instructions they had put their shoulders to the stone cover and levered it enough to make an opening. It took no time at all to hide the packages. But then, without apology, George had indicated that he, too, should climb into the hiding place.

'Better to hide you, too, y'r honour.' Luke could see the appreciative grin. 'What would Cap'n Harry say if I was to let the Revenue take you prisoner?'

With a sigh of resignation, Luke had complied.

'Don't worry.' George and Gabriel had manoeuvred the heavy lid back into place, leaving him in total darkness. 'We'll come and get you out when the coast's clear. We'll be sure to drink a glass to your health, m'lord!'

No light pierced the stonework and time stretched endlessly. Luke settled his head against a packet of lace and let his thoughts fly free. It was easy to feel a heady sense of relief. He had the young woman and the child safe in England. Noir's hold over him was destroyed. If the lady was not Marcus's widow, and there was still no proof that she was, he would set her up in a little house in London, or wherever she chose to go. She was as much a victim, he suspected, as he.

For now, Harriette and the French widow were safe at Lydyard's Pride.

But his thoughts quickly swooped away from relief to naked concern, to worry about the loose and worrying ends that did not tie up. Or perhaps they did, in which case—danger loomed frighteningly clear. With a shudder not only from the cold seeping into his damp clothes, Luke considered the very real possibility that Harriette was not safe at all, a thought that raked his heart with bloody claws.

Who had informed Captain Rodmell against them? By Harriette's own admission, they rarely saw a Preventive officer on this stretch of the coast, so why now, on this particular run? Even if good fortune had thrown her hand against them, they should have been warned of the danger, early enough to sail along the coast and put into another cove. So who had ordered that the lamp be kept burning in the Tower Room, and left burning with its false message when the Revenue men were almost upon them? And why were there no men or animals to move the contraband, to get them all off the beach as fast as possible? Harriette had certainly expected them there, even though she drew no attention to their absence.

Luke frowned into the darkness, straining against despair at his incarceration. Had Harriette been able to dupe Captain Rodmell to get herself and the widow to safety? But what if she hadn't? What if she was taken under duress, regardless of her sex and social standing? What if, at this very moment, she was locked in a cell in Lewes? He was trapped here and could do nothing to help her. Whatever her orders, he should never have left her alone on the beach.

Of one fact, out of the whole stinking morass in which they almost sank, Luke was quite certain. The near disaster of the previous night had been no accident. And to Luke's mind there could only be one source of their misfortune. As soon as he was free of this prison, he would bring the culprit to book.

At last! The solid cover of the tomb was pushed aside with much sliding and grating to allow grey daylight to flood in. A hand was thrust in and Luke, accepting it, climbed stiffly out to see George and Gabriel Gadie. Adam, too.

'My wife. How is she? Is she safe?' His first words as he grasped George Gadie's arm.

'Haven't seen 'er for myself, y'r honour, but she'll be safe enough.'

'I've spent the last—how many hours?—imagining her clamped in irons!' Luke stretched his stiffened muscles and allowed himself a deep breath as at least some of the fears of the last hours drained from him. She would be unharmed. Harriette would be home at Lydyard's Pride. And there was Adam, filthy, rumpled and disreputable, grey from lack of sleep, but with a gleam in his eyes. 'And you came out of it unharmed, little brother. If I look anything like you...' He managed a grimace as a pretence for a smile as blood flowed painfully into cramped limbs.

'You do,' Adam admitted with a grin. 'Worse. I

spent the night in the rafters of the Silver Boat. It's got to be better than a tomb.'

'You have all the luck.' Luke stretched his arms, shoulders, stamped his feet until life returned. Then, as they turned to follow the path to Lydyard's Pride, he grasped George Gadie's shoulder and pulled him to a standstill. 'We were meant to fail last night, weren't we?'

'Seems so, y'r honour,' Gadie admitted with a lift of his shoulder.

'I'll tell you one thing,' Adam broke in. 'The shots that were fired at us—they came from the opposite direction. Not where the dragoons were on the cliff path. The Revenue men didn't fire them.'

Luke stared, attention caught. 'Adam—are you sure?'

'Yes. I saw the flash of fire. And they were pistol shots. A dragoon's rifle wasn't used, I'd swear to it.'

'Pistols!' The idea spun in Luke's mind. 'Why didn't I realise that?'

'You were a bit preoccupied,' Adam reminded him drily. 'Too busy picking yourself and Harriette up from the pebbles.'

The implications chased each other through Luke's thoughts, until he became aware that Adam was looking at him with eyes widening in horror.

'Luke?'

'What is it?'

'Were you hit? Did one of the bullets hit you? I didn't think…'

'No. Why?'

Adam took hold of his lapel, pulling the coat aside. 'Look—on your shirt—and your coat.'

Luke looked down. He was damp and filthy, covered with sand and grime. But in the grey light of dawn, the stains could be made out. Dried blood, dark and encrusted on his chest and arms, on his thighs. But not *his* blood. Breath backed up in his lungs as fear curdled in his belly. His chest felt bound in iron bands. He had not known. All this time and he had not known.

'Not mine… Harriette! Harriette was hit. It's her blood.'

She hadn't told him. Rather she had denied it. He had pushed her to the ground, out of the path of a bullet, but it had still found her instead of him. Then she had sent him off to safety with the contraband and all the time she… How badly was she hurt? Had he, after all, saved the life of his brother's widow, only to lose his own wife?

With a terror such as he had never before in his life experienced, Luke took off at a run along the path between church and Lydyard's Pride.

The night's storm had blown itself out. Lydyard's Pride glistened on the cliff top in the morning mist, almost watchful, as if some vital development must still unfold within its walls. Luke took the steps at a run, threw back the door and came to a halt in the shabby entrance hall. Still too early for the girls from the village to be there. Nor was Wiggins obvious. So he must search for himself, and did so. The withdrawing room, the library, the parlours, staying only to sweep a glance around each. Nothing, all unoccupied. No sign of blood or some terrible tragedy from the early hours.

How could he live with the blame that she was hurt? How would he live the rest of his life without her if she were dead?

There had been enough blood to stain his own clothes liberally, now shockingly clear in the light of day. He felt it as he climbed the staircase, stiff on the linen of his shirt, rough against his skin. Who knew what damage some local inexpert doctor might not do to her? She might have bled to death through the early hours, whilst he had been shut up in that god-forsaken tomb. Why had he allowed her to dictate his movements? True, she had the experience, but he should never have countenanced it.

She might even now be lying dead in her bedchamber....

Which thought took him up the stairs straight to her room. He did not even stay to knock on the door, but flung it back.

And stopped on the threshold, chest heaving.

* * *

Harriette looked up, lips parted at the intrusion. Then relaxed on a fluttering little laugh. She had known he was safe—George, considerately, had sent word to Wiggins—but with the problem of Marie-Claude and Captain Rodmell to demand her attention she had not thought of how much the night would have taken its physical toll. His face was stark with strain and lack of sleep—there would have been as little rest for him in the tomb as there had been for her. His hair disordered, smudges on his face where he had brushed cobwebs from his skin, he was as far from the elegant and polished Corinthian of the London *haut ton* as it was possible to imagine. Clothes ravaged from salt and water, his cravat in a stage of magnificent disintegration, his boots stained and dull. And there on his breast, on coat and waistcoat and shirt was the ugly rust-brown of her dried blood.

She had, she decided, never loved him more. He was alive, he was safe, he had thrust his own body between her and the bullets, and now he had come to find her. He was out of breath. He must have run up the stairs. Was it concern for her? Was it to find her, to know if she was safe? A tiny flame of hope flickered into life in her heart.

Despite everything, all the danger they had been through, energy still vibrated from him. His eyes were alight with fire in their depths. How splendidly masculine he was, how impossibly good to look at. How she longed to walk into his arms and be held there. To touch his face, his hair, to drink in the familiar scent of him.

But she could not.

Reality set in for Harriette. Did they not have a bargain that was now close to fulfilment? He would have come back to the Pride to complete the deal, to claim Marie-Claude. That was why he was here. Then he would leave her.

He had come to end it all. How foolish for her to have any other longings. The little flame of hope died.

Luke found his voice. The only thought in his head. 'I thought you were dead!'

'No. As you see.'

Harriette was seated by the fire in a loose robe of fine lace. Meggie hovered at her side with pinched lips. On a little table stood a bowl of bloodied water. A roll of linen. Meggie held a pair of scissors.

'I know you were struck by the bullet.'

'Yes.'

Her face was as pale as the wax of the candle at her elbow. The shadows beneath her eyes were too heavy, deep as bruises. Her lips were tightly pressed, too pale, and her eyes were laced with pain.

'She should rest, my lord.' Meggie frowned at him.

'Not before I know she is safe.' An outrageous relief left him almost light-headed, and with it an unexpected brush of anger. She might have been dead and he not know. Why could she not have told him that she was hurt and in pain? The thought that she had suffered—was still suffering—without his knowledge simply fuelled the fire.

'I think you should go to bed, my lady.' Meggie turned her frown on Harriette.

'And I will ensure that she does. But not before I have spoken to her.'

'Please go, Meggie,' Harriette urged. 'I'll come to no further harm.'

Passing him on the way to the door, bearing the bowl and linen, Meggie cast a disapproving glare in his direction. 'She's lost too much blood. Don't hurt her or worry her, my lord,' Meggie admonished.

'I've no intention of doing either!' But he closed the door quietly. Then strode across the room to sink to one knee at Harriette's feet, taking possession of her hands, holding on when she struggled to free herself.

'Humour me.' He folded her hands tightly within his own. 'Let me look at you. Let me be sure that you are safe.'

'There's no need, Luke.' Harriette flushed to her hairline. 'Meggie exaggerates.'

'But you are hurt.' He did not release her. Could not.

'A bullet grazed along my ribs—that's all. Meggie has bandaged it.'

'You lost a lot of blood. You didn't tell me! Why didn't you tell me you were hit?'

'What good would that have done?' Now her fingers clung to his in a need to make him understand. 'The Preventives were almost at the beach. We were only just in time. We had to get you, the crew and the contraband away.'

'And so you did.' Luke bent his head, his forehead against their joined hands, and breathed deep, accepting the truth of it. She had seen the need and acted on it. He still did not know how she had created her own escape, and that of the widow, without raising suspicion. 'Should I tell you how much I admire you?' He lifted his eyes to hers, slid his hands up her forearms and bent his head to press his lips to the translucent skin of her wrists, startled when she hissed in a breath. Pushing up the loose sleeves of her robe, his fingers stilled. Her inner arms were rough and grazed, both of them, the soft skin broken in places.

'What…?'

'The shingle,' she explained with the ghost of a laugh, that could have been a tearful catch in her voice. 'When we fell—I must have slid on it. It's sharp and unforgiving with the broken shells. It's nothing and will heal quickly enough.'

'Harriette!'

His eyes were captured by hers, to be held by them and he felt himself drown in their clear depths. There was pain there. All good sense told him to treat her gently. Sense warned him to keep her at a distance. But what power did good sense have in the face of this woman whose courage was beyond question? This woman whom he loved to the very depth of his soul and would until the final breath in his body. How could he have considered making so foolish a pact with her that would allow her to walk away from him? Driven by an absolute need to hold her, soothe her, reassure her and himself of the life-giving force that surged through his blood, Luke rose to his feet, lifting her to stand with him.

Holding her, hands lightly on her shoulders, his mouth took hers. Gently, softly, conscious of her fragility, until he forgot everything but his desire for her as her lips opened beneath his demand. Unconsciously, his embrace wrapped her closer, his mouth moved with fierce urgency in unrestrained kisses. Until she murmured, flinched.

'Forgive me, forgive me…'

He relaxed, but did not release her. Could not as her vulnerability flowed through his veins, as her lips again parted beneath his to allow his tongue to caress and soothe the wet, satin-soft skin. His blood was hot, his erection hardened in painful demand.

They were both alive and here was a need to celebrate that one simple fact.

With a superb exercise of will Luke released her, stepped back from her.

'You are too sweet and desirable. And you are so tired.' Her eyes were heavy lidded, the lashes falling to shadow her cheeks where the prints of exhaustion were even more evident, her face even whiter. 'You need to sleep.'

'I should tell you…about the bullets.'

'Tomorrow…' But dawn had already fully come. 'Later today—that will be soon enough.' Then added, 'Let your mind be at peace, Harriette. I know about the bullets.'

'Yes. I thought you might…' She did not argue, was too weary to do so, as she swayed on her feet. With extravagant care he lifted her in his arms, carried her to her bed and placed her there. Folded the covers over her, arranging the pillows to her comfort. She was almost asleep before he was finished.

'We did it, Luke,' she murmured. 'We rescued her…'

'*You* rescued her,' he amended. 'Tell me all about Captain Rodmell when you wake.'

'Will you be here?'

'Yes. I will be here. I'll not leave you.'

Her breast beneath the delicate lace rose and fell regularly, her eyes were closed.

Luke simply stood and looked at her, taking in every detail of her. She was alive and he must give thanks for that. His love for her, still so new when she had fled from him, had bloomed into full maturity, astounding him by its power. The seconds, the minutes, passed and still all he wanted to do was stand there and absorb the very essence of her as she slept. It was too late. Ridiculously too late. He had fallen in love with her, totally, irrevocably, yet had offered her her freedom in the same breath. As a man of honour he must keep his promise.

In despair, Luke forced himself into action, to draw the fall of the curtain to shield the bed from the intrusive sun. To pull forwards a chair—and damned uncomfortable it was—to sit beside her. He should leave her to sleep undisturbed, but he could not. Covering her hand where it lay on the coverlet with his own, he turned it over, smoothing his fingers over hers. Another contradiction here. He smiled briefly. Slender femininity coupled with the roughness from using rope and tiller, the sheer physical work of sailing a cutter. So practical, so pretty. Like the rest of her. He tucked a curl back from her face, letting his hand rest on the silkiness of it. Leaning to kiss her brow, her lips. He would stay with her for a little time. She did not need him, but he would remain on guard. Nothing must be allowed to disturb or harm his wife.

The horror of what had nearly happened struck him anew. She had nearly died, running the contraband for him, just so that he might rescue a woman who meant nothing to him, who might yet be a heartless impostor. Could he have borne it if Harriette had died? What would life be like without her? Unbearable. Unimaginable. Impossible.

Exhaustion got the better of him. Luke slept also, his head and arms resting on the bed beside her as she had once slept to keep watch over him. Until Meggie returned to wake him with a hand to his shoulder.

'What is it?' His eyes were instantly on Harriette. 'Is she…?'

'She's asleep. You should go and get some sleep, too, my lord.'

'You speak as if I have no right to be here,' he replied harshly. 'She is my *wife*.'

'Yes, she is. But she ran away from you. I don't know why—and I'm sure you'll tell me it's none of my business—but she would not do such a thing without reason.'

He stretched, touched Harriette's fingers fleetingly. 'She had every reason.'

For a long moment Luke lingered by the bed where Harriette was deeply asleep. Her life was in no danger and he thanked God for it. He had promised he would stay with her, but what use? She did not need him now and Meggie did not want him here.

'You should go and bathe, change your clothes. Rest, my lord.' Meggie's voice had softened a little. 'I'll take care of her for you.'

'I know you will. She has no need of me. I love her, you know.'

'Do you? Does she know?'

'It doesn't matter.'

'She did this for you. And was hurt. Will you break her heart, as well?' All in the fiercest of whispers.

Without reply, Luke left Harriette in Meggie's care, feeling as if his heart had been ripped from his body.

Then with one objective in mind, he sought out Wiggins to resurrect the elderly butler's memory over a bottle of brandy. To discuss with him the events of a distant night when the *Lion d'or*, a French vessel out of Dieppe, foundered on the rocks of the bay.

It was in the full light of morning that Harriette woke. The sun had moved round and she was dazzled by it, unable to collect her thoughts as she struggled to the surface. She recalled falling into sleep as if into a black sea on a stormy night. As she moved, stretched, her ribs drew a groan from her lips and she recalled all the events of the night. Luke had promised he would stay with her, but he had not.

She was alone in the room. Well, perhaps it was all for the best. A successful enterprise was one thing, a future together quite another. She touched her fingers to her lips, the memory of his mouth against hers. That had been no dream. But he had left her.

Harriette struggled to sit up, all hope quenched as neatly and completely as a candle with a snuffer, but her determination was strong.

There was a new day to be faced. To solve the riddle of Marie-Claude. To end her association with Luke Hallaston. She would dress her hair, put on a fashionable London gown, and then proceed to draw a line beneath this part of her life.

From his conversation with Wiggins, with no opportunity to put his appearance to rights, Luke's attention was demanded by the immediate problem waiting for him in the library.

'I know I have no proof. Perhaps you think I am an adventurer, a French whore, grasping at any chance of a future for my bastard child and myself.'

The lady standing in the centre of the library flung out her hand dramatically to indicate the sleeping child, wrapped in a blanket in Meggie's arms. Here was plain speaking. Luke had not expected that, all his own doubts put brutally and unequivocally into words by this pretty Frenchwoman. Small, neat, fair-haired, blue-eyed, her air of fragility was offset by a determination to argue her case in English far better than he had expected. Gone were the tears of the previous night when under strain. Gone was the frenzied panic when he had snatched her from the authority of Jean-Jacques Noir, unless that had been all a charade, too…

'You think I am in league with Monsieur Noir,' she continued, uneasily echoing his thoughts. 'I am not! He is a monster! Marcus said we should go home, to England, when he had leave. That I would be welcomed by his family. That was his plan, before he…before he was killed. But now he is not here and I am not welcome at all! It is clear you do not want me here.'

'But Marcus married you? In the middle of a bloody war?' Adam, leaning against the edge of the dek, arms folded, voiced the scepticism in Luke's mind.

'We met, we fell in love.' She raised her chin, her blue eyes challenging Luke's. 'Marcus would not leave me unprotected when my family was *assassinated* in a guerrilla attack on our lodgings.' She spat the word. 'He insisted on wedding me. A drumhead wedding, before a priest.'

Once Luke would have cast that aside—would Marcus do something so ridiculously impractical, so ill judged? Now he was not so sure. Love could hit hard and drive men to any sort of intemperate action. The door behind him opened quietly and he knew immediately that it was Harriette. Her hair fell in soft ringlets. A simple gown of cream-and-lemon striped muslin, lace trimmed, gave her an air of quiet fashion. But Luke thought she looked as if a breath of wind would destroy her.

'Harriette.' He discovered he was frowning at her. 'You should be resting…'

'I have rested.'

Her gaze was as cool as her gown, her tone brooking no argument, as if she had not clung to him, accepting and returning his kisses. Harriette walked over to touch the widow's hand.

'Marie-Claude. Have my people looked after you?'

'Yes. I can have no complaints on *that* score. But my integrity is cast into doubt!'

'Forgive me, *madame*…' Shelving his own problems, Luke concentrated on the immediate and sought for some path to follow. 'Do you have *nothing* of your…your alliance with my brother?'

'Nothing beyond my word of honour. And this. Marcus gave me this when we were wed. But I could have stolen it, couldn't I? Perhaps even from his dead body?' Lifting the chain from around her neck, shimmering with outrage, she displayed a ring from the bosom of her gown.

'Have you no documents?' Adam asked.

'No, Monsieur Adam. I have not. *That man* took my marriage documents, and now my dear Marcus is dead.' Marie-Claude's eyes were suddenly damp. 'I have no proof at all.' But she did not weep.

Impressed by her courage, Luke drew the document Noir had sent him from his inner pocket, held it out. 'Madame—is this the document stolen from you?'

With a gasp, Marie-Claude pounced to snatch the sheet. Opened it, tracing her fingers over the words written there. 'Yes. Oh, yes.' Now tears tracked down her cheeks as she pressed it to her heart.

Moved beyond belief Luke touched her arm in compassion. '*Madame*—would you tell me how you came to fall into Noir's hands?' he asked gently.

'*Bien sûr.*' The lady tilted her chin and dashed away the tears. 'When Marcus died I decided to come to England as he had wanted. I accepted help from the wife of an English officer who was returning home. So much mud—our horses foundering, our carriage broken and useless. I gave birth to my son—*Marcus's* son—in a hut with a mud floor.' Her fingers clenched white-knuckled at the memory. 'We sailed from Lisbon, but storms forced us to put into Bordeaux. There I made a mistake. I should have waited, but I was impatient. Our ship was damaged and I had no resources of my own. I had no patience to wait longer…' Her teeth dug into her lower lip as she remembered. 'It was there I met that villain Noir. My own countryman who was generous enough to take pity on me.' She laughed, the harsh sound at odds with her slight prettiness.

'And he offered to see you safe in England.' Luke saw the inevitability in the lady's careful account that described none of her obvious suffering.

'Yes. Kind he seemed, compassionate. He asked if he could help me because I reminded him of his daughter who had just died. *Mon Dieu*! I was stupid enough to tell him of my plight. He took me under his protection and promised to bring me to one of the Channel ports and see me safe to London. I trusted him. He treated me well, saw to my comfort when we travelled, with a private room for me at the inns. It was only when we reached the coast that I realised. Noir had no intention of letting me go. He would use me as a weapon to make his own fortune. He did not hide his plans from me. He boasted of them! And I could not escape. I had no money—my baby to protect. And he watched me. Every hour of every day. He set a serving woman to keep account of my every move, to sleep in my room.'

Marie-Claude took a deep breath, fixing her accusing stare on Luke. 'And now I am here and it seems to me my plight is no better. You do not even believe that I was Marcus's wife!' She wiped at stray tears. 'Perhaps I understand your reluctance. But I have been through so much and I don't know what to do or where to go if you will not help me.'

'Forgive my apparent harshness, *madame*. Whatever happens, I will not leave you destitute.'

'But you don't believe me.'

Perhaps he did. She was just the sort of girl that Marcus would have fallen in love with. Pretty as a picture, but with a decided sparkle in her eye, at this moment directed at him with patent hostility. Yet what proof was there that, as she herself said, she did not have an eye to wealth and status, alone with a child out of wedlock, put up to it by Noir?

Meanwhile the lady drew herself up to her small height. 'I offer you my thanks for setting me free from *that man* and bringing me to England. You, Madame Harriette, were kinder than I could believe, despite your strange clothing. We fooled the brave Captain, did we not? But now I will impose on you no longer. I will not inflict myself or my child on you when I am neither believed nor wanted here.' She walked purposefully towards Meggie and the baby, clasping one of his flailing fists. 'If I could beg transport to a town nearby… I will find lodgings and work. I will be a burden on no one. Nor my child.'

'No! Not that!' Luke did not know if it was the right decision, but he acted on what his instincts told him. The lady did not deserve to be vilified or abandoned or manipulated for a second time. Whatever the truth of her story, he would not turn her out on to the streets. 'No, *madame*! I believe you were used despicably by Noir and I will not allow you to make your own way. You are clearly of gentle birth—'

'My birth is of the best!' The decided little chin rose higher. 'I am a de la Roche!'

'And I will ensure that you and your child lack for nothing, *madame*.'

The lady was not soothed. 'I won't accept charity.'

'It won't be charity, *madame*. I will not turn my back on a lady in distress who has clearly shown such bravery.'

Harriette added her persuasion. 'You must not go, Marie-Claude.'

The baby in Meggie's arms began to fuss and whimper. Now uncertain, Marie-Claude lifted him and held him close. The blanket fell away as the infant leaned and snatched towards Adam, grasping handfuls of empty air in his tiny hands. Automatically Adam held out his own hand to the little fingers. Then he laughed, startled, astonished.

'Luke…just look at this!'

Luke approached the child held high in his mother's arms, turned astonished eyes to his brother, then back to the child.

'Forgive me, *madame*.' His voice was suddenly full of emotion. 'For I see there is suddenly no doubt at all.'

Luke and Adam regarded the baby, beyond words. The similarity in so small an infant was remarkable. Dark hair with the same curl at the ends. The eye colour was wrong, the child inheriting the vivid blue of his mother. But the long nose, the indentation of the mouth. When on being the object of such scrutiny the baby grinned, displaying a shallow indentation in one cheek, Luke felt delight and grief rise in him, almost enough to unman him.

'What's wrong? Marie-Claude demanded, enfolding her son protectively.

'Nothing's wrong.' Adam chuckled as the child attempted to gnaw with toothless gums on his thumb.

'No. Nothing wrong at all. Oh, God, Marcus. If only you had lived to see him…' Luke murmured, touching his knuckle to the child's soft cheek.

'His name is Raoul,' Marie-Claude stated with tears in her voice.

'Welcome to the Hallaston family, Raoul.' Luke spoke softly as he smoothed the dark hair. Then Luke bowed gravely to Marie-Claude de la Roche. 'Forgive me, *madame*. I should never have doubted you. This is the best proof of all. You are a formidable lady—I can see why Marcus chose to wed you.'

'Thank you, my lord.' Marie Claude smiled at last. 'You are most gracious. Forgive me if my temper was not as sweet as—'

The library door opened. George Gadie hovered irresolutely on the threshold, cap twisted in his gnarled hands.

'George?' Harriette saw trouble in his face.

'The bastards! I'm right sorry, Cap'n Harry…'

'What is it?'

'The *Ghost*. The damned dragoons've fired *Lydyard's Ghost*.'

'The *Ghost*?' Harriette's face became as pale as death as blood drained. 'No! Oh, no!' Ruthlessly tearless, rigidly unmoving, yet beneath the control Luke saw the loss that wounded her far more painfully than the bullet. Rage, dark and relentless, surged within him. Even without proof he knew whose hand had fired the pistol. He knew who had alerted the Preventives. And Harriette had paid the price twice over. Luke's blood heated, demanding vengeance for her.

Without a word he strode to the door.

'Wait! Where are you going?' Harriette's cry stopped him, and he read knowledge in her face as she stretched out a hand. And Luke leaned close to feather his fingers, whisper-soft, over her cheek. Their bargain might be complete, but not quite. There was one more demand on him. He would strip bare the nasty little plot that had almost brought them all to ruin.

'You know where I'm going, Harriette,' he said, managing to keep the harsh temper from his voice. 'There's a debt to be paid here, and we both know who must pay it.'

'No, you mustn't. I'll come with you.'

His voice softened. 'No, my dear girl.' The gentle statement of intent was frightening. 'This is for me to finish.'

Chapter Thirteen

Still in the ruined coat and breeches of the previous night, Luke borrowed a horse from the stable and spurred towards Ellerdine Manor, mind set furiously on what he suspected. The rescue had been in jeopardy. Harriette had been shot. Harriette had lost her precious *Ghost*—and the blame lay at the feet of one man. Alexander Ellerdine, for some malicious reasoning of his own, had betrayed Harriett's trust and threatened her life. If it was the last thing he did for her, he would bring Ellerdine to retribution. Alexander Ellerdine would not walk away untouched from his treacherous night's work.

Habitual courtesy thrown to the winds, Luke leapt the steps of the Manor, flung back the door.

'Where is he?' he demanded of the startled manservant. Without waiting for a reply he made for the library where the door was ajar. He thrust it wide, strode in.

There sat Alexander Ellerdine at ease, boots propped on the edge of his desk, a tankard of ale in his hand. For a second Luke saw a dark uncertainty swim in his eyes, then it was gone and Alexander's mouth curled in a sharp smile.

'Venmore. I didn't expect to see you here. Thought you'd be on your way to London by now with the widow.'

Luke covered the distance between them. 'I want some answers.'

'And what would they be?' The smile widened. 'I can't imagine why you should think I can be of help.'

'No?' Luke advanced, anger balanced precariously. 'Get up, Ellerdine. It's even beneath me at this moment to strike a man sitting down.'

Alexander did not stir. 'What's this? A duel?'

'An affair between *gentlemen*? No, by God. You forfeited that title last night.'

'Insults, Venmore, will get you nowhere. Has Harriette sent you?' The smile became sly.

'No, she has not. At this moment she's mourning the loss of her precious cutter. All because of you! The Preventives fired the *Ghost*. I presume that little detail was never in your plan, Ellerdine!'

Alexander frowned. 'They fired it? No, by God…' He recovered quickly enough. 'What makes you think I had anything to do with last night's misfortunes?'

'You arrogant fool! Have you no sense?' Luke

growled. 'Are you not aware that one of your bullets—I expect it was meant for me—hit Harriette instead? She could have died on that beach.' And he saw the fingers tense around the tankard. That was what he had wanted to see. Luke's grip on his temper tightened further as he inhaled against the urge to pick the man up and shake the truth from him.

'You lie,' Alexander snarled. 'She is unharmed.'

'How would you know?' Luke taunted. 'A scar along her ribs tells it's own tale.'

'No…' Alexander struggled to his feet, eyes wild. 'I would never have meant for that to happen.'

It was all the proof he needed. Springing forwards with a speed and lethal accuracy belied by his disheveled state, Luke aimed a fast right to clip Alexander Ellerdine's jaw, another to his gut. There was no need for more. Taken by surprise, Alexander fell with a grunt to the worn threads of the carpet.

Luke stood over him. 'It's time we had a little talk, Ellerdine.' Luke dragged him to this feet and thrust him back into his chair.

'I've nothing to say to you.' Alexander dabbed at the blood with his cuff.

'I'm not beyond further violence, Ellerdine.' Luke drew a pistol from his pocket, hooked up a chair with his foot and sat across the desk, leaning his arms on the polished surface, the pistol placed before him. He fixed Alexander with a cold stare.

'I doubt you intend to kill me,' Alexander tried a sneer, but failed.

'Do you? I'm not so certain. At this moment there's nothing I would like more than to put a bullet through your black heart, Ellerdine.' The curve of Luke's mouth was lethal. 'But not yet. First I intend to take you to grovel at Harriette's feet. She trusted you. She saw you as a man of honour. I'll not have her deceived any longer.' Luke's eyes blazed with emerald fire. 'So, Mr Ellerdine—let us start with what you were doing last night. When you should have warned Harriette that the Preventives were on the cliff…'

'Your cousin has something to tell you, Harriette.'

Luke thrust Alexander bodily into the withdrawing room at Lydyard's Pride, too aware of what colour there was leaching from Harriette's face as she pushed herself to her feet. She had been sitting on the cushioned window seat, perhaps waiting for his return. All he wanted to do was to sweep her off her feet and carry her away from all this, but her self-possession held, and Luke curbed his impatience. There was no surprise in her face, only a sad regret. He feared he was about to make it worse for her, but she must know the truth.

'Perhaps you should sit.' His lips thinned. 'Ellerdine has decided to come clean.'

Harriette sank back to the cushions. Her cousin was worse for wear with a fast-developing bruise to his chin and a cut on his lip. His clothes and hair were disheveled, his manner uneasy, but then he looked little different from Luke, who still bore all the ravages of the previous night. Except that Luke's face was unmarked, but for the stamp of barely repressed temper in the lines at eyes and mouth.

'He said you were injured.' Alexander's first words, eyes wild, as he came across the room towards her, attempting to take her hands in his.

'Yes, I was hit by a bullet last night. Fortunately not fatally, as you see.' Harriette kept her voice level and held her hands up to bring him to a halt. Whatever Luke had discovered, she knew where the blame must lie. Now she must go through the pain of hearing it from her cousin's lips. 'Tell me about last night, Zan. Tell me what happened. Why it went so appallingly awry.'

'What do you want to know?' He shrugged. 'Everything worked out well in the end.'

'No, it did not, Zan! I lost the *Ghost*!'

'I regret that,' he admitted. 'It's a serious loss to us.'

'A serious loss? Alexander, I am not a fool. The signals were *wrong*. There was no help on the beach to get the cargo away, no protection for us. Shots were fired—deliberately at us, not as a warning. And you were absent through the whole débâcle.

How can you have left us with the dragoons almost on the beach and the lamp in the Tower signaling a clear run? Was it a mistake?'

'Tell her the truth, Ellerdine.' Luke spoke without inflection, but the threat was evident. He placed a loaded pistol on a dusty side table.

'Very well. Why not?' Self-assurance slid like a mask over Alexander's face and he fisted his hands on his hips. 'Did I make a mistake? Of course not! There was no mistake—only a little careful planning instead, for the future of smuggling from Old Wincomlee. For a closer and richer liaison with Monsieur Marcel and Port St Martin. Fame and fortune, Lydyard's Pride as our home, yours and mine, Harriette, restored to its former glory. Captain Harry and Alexander Ellerdine, hand in glove, with more gold in our hands than you could ever believe.' His smile was bright, confident.

'You informed on us,' Harriette accused. 'You lit the lamp and lured us in. Why would you do that? We could have all been killed.'

'No chance of that. Not from the Preventives. I made a deal with Captain Rodmell. Some timely interference from the Revenue and I promised to ensure a number of bales and barrels fell into his hands. He was more than willing with such a *coup* to parade before his superiors. And that might not be his only prize. I offered him the chance of one of even greater value…'

Harriette's face was pale in the morning sun, drawn from lack of sleep and sharp discomfort. Now Luke saw her muscles tense, the groove between her brows deepen, but she did not flinch. His gut churned, his hands clenched as if they were around Ellerdine's throat, but he would let it all play out. She deserved to hear what her cousin was capable of.

'But I don't understand why you would do something so irresponsible. Why would you ensure the failure of a run with certain capture? George and Gabriel and the rest to be hauled before the magistrates—'

'Not George and Gabriel so much as the Earl of Venmore! A perfect plan. To get rid of your entirely superfluous husband, of course.' Alexander grinned with irrepressible confidence, wincing at his hurt lip. 'His presence in your life harms the whole enterprise we had developed, and you know it. Since you wed him you've taken no part in the runs. He takes you away, keeps you in London, threatens to take you to The Venmore. He would force you to give up the Trade. I need your connections, Harriette, your facility with French.'

He took a step towards her again, his face full of appeal. 'I wasn't sure you'd part from him for good, but I need you. I need you here. I need the Pride, Harriette. Without you my schemes are put on hold.

So I needed to remove Venmore from the scene. A little humiliation for the noble Earl and his equally noble brother, their names smeared as common smugglers when they faced the local magistrate. The fisherman of Old Wincomlee would be released soon enough with a heavy bribe from me, but what a prize the Earl of Venmore and his brother would make. That would spur Venmore on his way to cut his connections with you. Think of the scandal.' Alexander laughed ruefully. 'How unfortunate my careful plotting failed. The Hallaston family would never hold up its head again.'

'So it was all to bring me back to Lydyard's Pride.'

'Of course. Venmore would be more than glad to be rid of you when his name was dragged through the gutters by the London gossip-mongers.'

Harriette looked storm-struck. Luke could see her fingers clench, white knuckled. Even knowing of the involvement of Alexander Ellerdine as he did, such a depth of scheming was terrifying.

'Tell her about the gunfire, Ellerdine,' Luke prompted.

'I think I already know.' Harriette stared at Alexander in horror. 'Was it you? They were pistol shots, and it was not Captain Rodmell. Who were the bullets meant for, Zan? Were they intended for Luke? You said you would rid yourself of my husband. Or were you aiming at me?'

'By God! I would never harm you, Harriette. I love you!'

'So it was Luke.' Harriette turned her face away. 'I can't believe you would do something so cruel just to bring me back here.'

'Enough of this. End it, Ellerdine,' Luke snapped, conscious of Harriette's distress.

'Yes, I fired the pistols,' Alexander snarled. 'Yes, I aimed them at Venmore. Just in the way of a friendly warning.' He snapped his fingers with callous unconcern. 'It's your own fault, Harry. If you'd let me use the Pride in your absence, I wouldn't have been driven to this. But you wouldn't, would you? You refused. And when you discovered my cache of contraband in your withdrawing room, you were quick to announce your displeasure. But I need the Pride, and I need it now.'

The muscles in Alexander's jaw tightened with implacable will, bitterness writ clear. 'My mother should never have left the Pride to you, Harriette. It should never have passed out of my hands. I'm as much a Lydyard as you, but she would have it that it should stay in the female line despite all my protestations. So she did as she wished.' He lifted his hands in what might have been charming self-deprecation if the naked ambition was not so clear. 'So there you are, Harriette. I need you. And I need the Pride. Its value is inestimable to me and my plans for the future.'

'I can't believe you would kill Luke to get your hands on the Pride.

'Venmore's death? No, I didn't seek that. I'm no murderer—but a well-placed bullet might encourage him to set you free!' Alexander laughed harshly. 'You don't love him. What would it matter to you if he took a bullet in the arm? Look, little cousin. You wanted the truth, so there it is. I threw last night's run to the dogs. Short-term failure, long-term gain. But we can still make it work together, you and I. With the Earl out of your life, we keep our heads down for a month or so to fool the Preventives, and then start up the operation again. Bigger and better than before.' He slid a malicious glance towards Luke before returning to Harriette. 'And when you are free of this travesty of a marriage—well, then you can wed me.'

'You say that you love me, yet you would cause me such pain.' The hurt in Harriette's voice, in her eyes, was too much. Luke fisted his hands, nails digging into palms. He could not allow this to go on much longer. 'I trusted you, Zan,' Harriette whispered, tears glimmering.

It spurred Luke into action. He took Harriette's arms and lifted her to her feet so that she could stand with him, sliding an arm around her to give her support, conscious of her frailty. 'Are you strong enough for this?' he asked.

'Yes. I'll not rest until it's finished.' Her reply was strong, despite the whiteness of her lips. 'Not until we've heard the rest of Alexander's plans for me and my home.'

Tense and watchful, Alexander glanced at Luke as he chose his words with care. 'Oh, I think I've said enough. And you've no proof that would sway a magistrate. It's your word against mine, Venmore.'

'True. But I think you did not confess all in your unburdening of your soul.' Luke faced him. 'Have you told my wife that it was *you* who informed me, man to man, of course, with no ill will intended, that she was a member of the despicable brotherhood of Wreckers? That you attempted to destroy our marriage from the very beginning?'

'I did no such thing…' His eyes cut to Harriette. 'Harriette—you would never believe that of me.'

But Luke's words were as smooth as polished steel and twice as deadly. 'Your word against mine, Ellerdine. And I think my wife might question any pronouncements you make, after what she has learned today.'

'You told him I was a Wrecker?' Harriette asked, eyes wide. 'How could you have implied that I was guilty of such an atrocity!'

'What if I did?' Alexander sneered. 'Your noble husband was quick enough to believe you guilty.'

'I did at first,' Luke admitted. 'To my eternal regret,

I did. Because you supplied me with a wealth of accurate information that could be checked and verified—the wreck of the *Lion d'Or*. But I know that Harriette was not involved. And if she was not…'

'So you'll brand me the Wrecker? If Harriette is innocent, then I must be the guilty party—is that what you want me to say?' Alexander's mouth set in uncompromising lines. 'You'll not lay the blame on my shoulders, Venmore.'

Luke tightened his arm around Harriette's shoulders as he felt her strength ebb against him and he addressed Alexander, grave as a hanging judge. 'I have spoken with Wiggins about this. The lamp was not lit by Harriette that night.'

'Then I suppose Wiggins did it. It would not be the first time.'

'Who gave the order? Wiggins does not light it without direction.'

Alexander lifted his brows. 'How would Wiggins remember? An old man too fond of the proceeds of our smuggling. He barely recalls his own name after a bottle of port!'

'Wiggins remembers very well. Your lad, Tom, came to order the lamp to be lit that night. So Wiggins lit the lamp and it brought the *Lion d'Or* into the bay, on to the rocks.'

Harriette's hands grasped Luke's arm hard. 'Is all this true? Zan?'

'By God, it is,' Luke swore. 'A heartlessly devious means of destroying any understanding between us. What man would wish to hear that his wife was capable of bringing innocent men to their deaths?'

'Yes, I told Venmore a lie.' A snarl of a grin gave Alexander's face a feral look. 'Anything to bring you to your senses and back to the Pride.' He held out his hand to her. 'It doesn't change anything, Harriette. You're back here and I wager his lordship will be on the road to London as soon as his horses can be put to. I still want you, Harriette. Don't throw away all we've worked for. I love you, Harriette.'

'Love? You've no idea what love means. And you certainly love Lydyard's Pride more than you love me.' Harriette turned her face against Luke's shoulder. 'I pity you, Zan. There's nothing in your life but ambition and greed. It will destroy you.'

'Get out,' Luke ordered quietly, aware that Harriette's strength was drawing to an end. 'Get out of this house before I boot you out of my sight.'

And when Ellerdine swung furiously from the room, Luke deposited Harriette back on the cushions and followed him to the steps where his horse waited.

With a hand on the bridle, a foot in the stirrup, Alexander Ellerdine looked back. 'You can't harm me, you know. We're all in this.'

'That's the only reason I don't hand you over to the authorities.'

'You dare not. I'd be quick to tell them how the Earl of Venmore sailed in the *Lydyard's Ghost* to bring a French woman and a cargo of contraband into England.'

'You'll get nowhere with that if you do. I've had enough of blackmail to last me a lifetime.' Luke reached one hand to grasp the bridle, the other Alexander's sleeve. 'I'll not touch you, for her sake. Not today. But beware. My control might not last.'

Alexander Ellerdine mounted and drove his horse close. 'One thing, Venmore. Whatever the evidence suggests—I am no Wrecker. That's beyond the pale even for me.' The set of his mouth held a bleak cynicism. 'Nor did I shoot to kill. Murder's not in my blood—but I don't expect you to believe me. God damn you!' He yanked on the reins. 'Let go of my horse!' And he spurred off, pushing his horse to leap the wall into the open parkland.

Harriette found herself unable to sit within the confines of the withdrawing room. Too restless, too disbelieving, too undermined. by the brutal truth. Since the sky had cleared and the sun shone with mild warmth she opened the door on to the stone-flagged terrace and escaped from all she had been subjected to. A rustic seat under the leafy overhang of a pergola offered her shelter out of the sharp breeze. If Luke wanted to find her there, he would do so.

How he must despise all Lydyards!

And there he was, striding along the terrace towards her, an easy, superbly co-ordinated stride. Dark hair lifting in the breeze, eyes narrowed against the brightness of the light reflected from the sea. Her heart beat faster and awareness shivered along her skin. This was it, the end, this was what Luke wanted. Their agreement was complete. She must finish it.

As he stood in the open window from the withdrawing room, Luke saw his love seated under a riot of late roses. There was no happiness in her. Only a strained stillness, as if waiting for an outcome she did not anticipate with pleasure.

What to do now? He had a promise to fulfil. He must keep it and arrange for her freedom from him. The knowledge that it was his duty to honour the agreement between them, to walk away from the woman he loved, slithered nastily. But what if…?

He watched as Harriette put up her hand to restrain her hair against the lively breeze. A pretty picture, but her eyes were sombre and chased with shadows. Of course she would not be happy, learning of her cousin's betrayal. And she had lost the *Ghost*.

He saw her lift her hands to her lips, as if her thoughts were elsewhere.

Did she have any feelings at all for him?

Would a woman who had no thought for him lie about her injury to ensure his safety? Would she risk her life to settle his debt of honour for a woman she did not know? Would she care so much for his safety that she would send him out of harm's way and face the Riding Officer and his dragoons on her own? Would she risk her beloved cutter for him?

Was this proof of love?

Perhaps the answer was no. Perhaps he was fooling himself. But suddenly Luke decided he would take the risk, gambling everything, all his future happiness, on the final turn of the card.

Chapter Fourteen

'Has Alexander gone?' Harriette asked, suddenly not caring.

'Yes.' Luke grimaced. 'With a final flourish of attempted blackmail. Don't worry. He'll get nowhere with that.'

'You know it all now.' Harriette breathed out slowly against the ugliness.

'Yes. It could only be Ellerdine. We both knew it. I don't think he cared what harm he caused, as long as he got his hands on this house.'

Luke was leaning back against the balustrade, arms folded, studying the irredeemable state of his boots. Keeping his distance, Harriette presumed. And who could blame him? Her family had not proved to be honourable. 'You must feel satisfied.'

He looked up sharply. 'Must I?'

'You achieved everything you hoped for. Noir's influence is at an end. Marie-Claude and the child are safe, you're convinced of Raoul's paternity.' She swallowed painfully, but continued. 'Now I claim my freedom, and give you yours in return, as we agreed.'

'We did agree that, didn't we?' Once more Luke considered his dull, scuffed boots. 'But I've changed my mind.' His eyes, lifted to hers, were formidably direct. 'I won't give you your freedom.'

'But…' Harriette sought for some logic that had apparently eluded her in her confused state. 'You don't want me as your wife. You never did. And don't tell me that you have a duty towards me because I saved your life.' She controlled her words carefully as they snatched at her breath. 'That's just gratitude and no reason to change your decision.'

'Then I shall, of course, tell you no such thing.' Moving with startling speed, before she could blink, Luke had closed the distance between them, lifting her by her forearms, careful of her hurts, until she was standing closer to him than she cared to be. '*You* might want to close the bargain, but *I* will not.'

'Why not?'

'I love you.'

'*No…*' The word shattered. She could not bear his kindness, his instinct to protect.

Luke placed his fingers against her lips to silence her. 'It's not gratitude. I have discovered that I *don't* have all I want. I want *you*. So I won't keep the promise I made you. For the first time in my life I'll break my word as a gentleman, so you can damn me for dishonour if you so wish. But I want you, Harriette. I love you. And I'm damned if I'm going to live without you for the sake of a pledge made under duress.' Unsmiling, he kissed her with unnerving severity, robbing Harriette of any breath she had left. 'There's only one way I'll give you your freedom. And that's if you tell me that you do not—cannot—return my love.'

'No…' Harriette struggled to take it in. 'I don't believe you.'

'Do you love me?'

Luke's hands on hers were strong, as if he would never release her, his eyes, more grey than green with swirling emotions, demanded that she reply with truth, whilst the lines of tension beside his mouth told their own tale. Beneath the habitual mask of reserve she saw an aching loneliness that wounded her heart. He had shouldered the burden alone because he had seen no other way to protect those involved, including herself. But now he had had the courage to confess his love for her, and his stern resolve that Harriette, too, should open her heart poured over her, destroying all her defences.

'Tell me the truth,' he demanded. 'You're under orders here, Captain Harry. Do you love me? I'll allow no dissembling—we're past the time for that.'

'Ah…Luke!'

'Well, do you?'

'Yes,' she said simply at last. 'I have loved you since I first saw you, without sense, without reason. When you seemed to be nothing but a man without honour and a traitor.'

Harriette watched as the smile of relief lit his eyes, transforming them into brilliant emerald again, but still the tension remained in every muscle of his body. He looked down to their clasped hands, brushing his fingers over the ring he had placed there so few weeks ago.

'Can you forgive me for not trusting you, for not taking you into my confidence?' he asked softly.

'Yes. For did I not believe you capable of vile treason?'

'It's no excuse for my damnable pride.'

Harriette leaned forwards to rub her cheek against their linked fingers. 'I can't believe that you still want me.'

'I do and I'll prove it.' And he swept her up into his arms, holding her close when she insisted, breathlessly, hopelessly, on her ability to walk unaided, and carried her back to her room.

'I should leave you here to sleep.' And would, whatever it cost him if that is what she would ask of him.

'No. Don't go.' Harriette held out her arms, an irresistible invitation.

'I might hurt you.' His heart beat hard. He knew the limitations of his control.

Now her hands were tightly clasped on his shoulders. 'You will hurt me more if you leave me alone. I love you, Luke, I adore you. I want to lie in your arms and know that your love is not some make-believe of my own imagination that will fall around my feet, an insubstantial dream, when I wake.'

Luke locked the door.

He was very gentle with her, holding her as if she were a fragile bloom, its newly opened petals threatened by a freakish gale. Naked, skin warm against silken skin, her head cushioned on his shoulder, they lay for a long time not speaking—there was no need. Motionless except for the rise and fall of heightened breathing, savouring the pressure of soft curve against hard muscle, the mingling of warm breath.

Until for Luke her nearness became too much, his erection hard, insistently demanding release. On an indrawn breath he moved from her, the few inches between them yawning as so many miles as he regretted immediately the cooling of flesh.

'Luke…?' Still uncertain of this new, bright love. Harriette's eyes were wide with apprehension.

'My love.' He reached across the divide, his lips completely reassuring against her brow. 'I want you, but I can't.'

'Why not?'

'To inflict more pain on you than I have already done?'

All she could see was his love for her shining in his eyes. Harriette placed her fingertips on his chest, allowing them to stroke softly down, resting lightly on his hips before skimming across the muscled contours of his flat belly to enclose him in her palm. She pressed her lips to the pulse that hammered at the base of his throat. 'Why can you not?' she repeated.

It was Luke's undoing.

Hands at her waist, in one powerful tensing of muscle, Luke raised her above him as he rolled, lowered her slowly, gently, straining to take her weight on his arms until she covered him, surrounded him. Until, sinking down, she took him in, a dark satin that robbed him of all thought. She was all heat and slick demand to be filled, possessed by him as she set her own rhythm and he could do nothing but allow it. And Harriette leaned to kiss his mouth, her hair falling to envelop him in a shining curtain of living silk.

'See? I am not so broken that you cannot touch me.' Her lips teased, her smile was joyous.

'No, but you are hurt and I would have a care.'

'You have healed me.' Her eyes were glorious.

Luke moved with her, protective of her, conscious of the linen bandaging. How compelling she was, how alluring, how impossible to resist. He could not have refused her even if he had wished it. As heat and power built and built, Luke exerted every grain of control, hovering on a knife edge of relentless need. Without mercy Harriette drove him on and, hands holding her hips strongly against him, he responded thrust for thrust, until he felt the rippling clench of her muscles around him. Harriette shuddered, cried out, and he could cling to that edge no more.

Luke fell into the darkest of pleasure, aware at the last that her breathing was as challenged as his. And that Harriette's gasp, her cry, was one of satisfaction, not of pain, as he pulled her to his chest and buried his face in her hair.

By tacit agreement they rose, robed, linked hands, and, Luke carrying a branch of candles, made their leisurely way to the Tower Room, his arm lightly on her shoulders, stopping when the urge took them to exchange kisses, to whisper in inviting corners. Once there, oblivious to dust and cobwebs, they crossed the room to stand at the unshuttered window from where they could watch the dusk fall, encroaching across the sea, the cliff top, shrouding everything in anonymity.

Studying their reflections in the darkened glass, so close, so intimate, Luke's surrounding and protecting hers, Harriette knew what she must say, and spoke to their mirror-images. 'I have made my last run. On my honour. No more smuggling, Luke. No more Captain Harry.'

Luke watched her face in the reflection. This was the decision he had wanted from her, but would not have forced her to make. No smuggling, no dance with death or arrest. No risk of a hostile sea and a dangerous shore in the dark of the night. It was none of his doing, she had come to it in her own time, yet still he held on to the victory that burned through his blood.

'Will you miss it? The excitement of it? The wild thrill of outsmarting the Prenventives?'

'No.' Harriette affirmed without demur. 'Once I did. Now that is past.'

Stepping from his embrace, Harriette lifted the lamp from the table and set it on the floor in the corner of the room. Closed and fixed the shutters so that no light would shine from the Tower. Such a simple action, yet a symbol of their new life together. She returned again to stand with him and they joined hands.

'Any regrets?' he asked.

'That I rescued a waterlogged, bloodied spy? No, I have none.'

Luke pressed his lips like a whisper of love to her cheeks, the line of her jaw, the elegant curve of her neck, her closed eyes…where he tasted the salt of tears.

'Ah, Harriette… Do my kisses make you weep?'

'No.' But her eyes shone silver in the light. 'Oh, Luke—I've lost the *Ghost* and I loved her dearly. How shall I teach our children to sail?'

Luke kissed away the tears, inordinately touched. 'You shall have another.' His smile was a little wry. 'Who would believe I would take a bride who'd rather I give her planks of wood than a diamond necklace? But on one condition…' lifting her chin with his hand so that he could see her face '…a new vessel, a new name for her.'

'What would you call her?'

'*Venmore's Prize*. For that's what you are to me, my dear love. A prize I shall treasure for the rest of my days on this earth, and beyond.'

How fitting. Enclosed within Luke's strong arms, Harriette felt as if she had at last come safe home to harbour.

HISTORICAL

Large Print

TALL, DARK AND DISREPUTABLE
Deb Marlowe

Mateo Cardea's dark good-looks filled Portia Tofton's girlish dreams – dreams that were shattered when Mateo rejected her hand in marriage. Now Portia's home has been gambled away, and Mateo is the only man who can help. However, she has in her possession something he wants – so she strikes a deal with the devil himself!

THE MISTRESS OF HANOVER SQUARE
Anne Herries

Forever generous, matchmaker Amelia Royston will do any-thing to help others' dreams come true – yet will her own feet ever be swept off the ground? Then the charismatic Earl of Ravenshead returns to tip her world upside down! He finally declares his intention to marry her – but is he only wanting a convenient bride…?

THE ACCIDENTAL COUNTESS
Michelle Willingham

When Stephen Chesterfield, the Earl of Whitmore, awakes to find a beautiful woman berating him, he knows he is in trouble! He cannot recall the last three months of his life, never mind having a wife! What's more, someone is trying to silence him before his memory returns… Can he find trust and love before it is too late?

 MILLS & BOON

HISTORICAL

Large Print

THE ROGUE'S DISGRACED LADY
Carole Mortimer

Lady Juliet Boyd has kept out of the public eye since the suspicious death of her husband, until she meets the scandalous Sebastian St Claire, who makes her feel things, *need* things she's never experienced before. Juliet finds his lovemaking irresistible. But does he really want her – or just the truth behind her disgrace?

A MARRIAGEABLE MISS
Dorothy Elbury

When Miss Helena Wheatley's father falls ill, she is forced to turn to one of her suitors to avoid an unwelcome marriage! The Earl of Markfield honourably agrees to squire her around Town until her father recovers. Then they are caught alone together, and their temporary agreement suddenly looks set to become a lot more permanent…

WICKED RAKE,
DEFIANT MISTRESS
Ann Lethbridge

When a mysterious woman holds him at gunpoint, Garrick Le Clere, Marquess of Beauworth, knows he's finally met his match! Alone, Lady Eleanor Hadley is without hope, until the notorious rake offers a way out of her predicament… Now Garrick has a new mistress, and she's not only a virgin, but a Lady – with a dangerous secret!

MILLS & BOON